White Horse, Red Horse
Black Horse, Dead Horse

# White Horse, Red Horse
# Black Horse, Dead Horse

**KISA Burnett**

First Printing: 2014

ISBN 978-0-9903878-2-4

kisawrites.blogspot.com

# Chapter 1

The thing about endings is that people all too often never even realize there was a beginning. Everyone always notices the beginnings when it's something obvious like a creation or an invention. But the quieter, subtler beginnings which set an ending in motion are almost always missed or even ignored. When the end of Earth itself finally arrives, the living won't even think to wonder where the Apocalypse began until it's all over. And once it's over, the majority of those formerly living will most likely spend eternity contemplating more obvious things, such as the nature of eternity.

Not everyone will be unaware of the beginning of the end. Plenty of beings have been extremely well-informed about impending events, both seen and unseen. But unfortunately, humans tend to only realize and understand things when they have their hands in them.

Elijah Blanco was no different. He only knew, and still knows, how the biggest ending began because after he died, he was pulled into a race to the finish line; the very last finish line for Earth's current run.

Elijah's life hadn't been a terribly long one, and it certainly hadn't been a very pleasant one. In fact, Elijah was actually relieved when he was informed he was to be executed for his crimes. One could assume this was because he was a godly man and believed something better awaited him after death. But one would be very mistaken.

The truth was Elijah was sick of the whole business of life in general. People told him he was supposed to enjoy his time on Earth, but every time he tried, he found out people really, really didn't like his methods. So after thirty-three years of being shot at, chased, cursed, and other unpleasant things which finally culminated in a hanging sentence, he was simply glad it was all coming to an end.

Of course, the people who were hanging him couldn't even let him have a quick and easy death. Apparently, the end of a wanted criminal had to be a grand ceremonial event, complete with being marched to a poorly-made gallows in the center of town. Elijah wasn't convinced the execution site could do what it was built for, but his

1

judge-and-jury crowd of escorts assured him it hadn't let them down yet.

"Your rope ain't even thick enough to hang cats with," Elijah insisted with a disappointed frown as he surveyed the gallows. "You're gonna have a hell of a problem when I drop to the ground and get back up, 'cause when that happens, I'll be comin' for all'a ya."

Elijah's wish that his snide comments would piss people off and get things moving faster was fulfilled pretty quickly. He was promptly dragged to the platform, silently thankful he wouldn't have to put up with anything at all for much longer. He was more than ready to embrace oblivion.

Unfortunately for Elijah, after his neck snapped and his brain waves stopped, he didn't find oblivion. He didn't find Heaven, he didn't find Hell, and he didn't find himself suddenly a worm, as someone had once warned him would be his fate.

No, instead Elijah found himself sitting on his horse in a very large, empty, black space. He stared around for a while, baffled, then finally looked down at his dapple grey mare, who looked back towards him and seemed just as confused.

"Wait, did they kill you too?" Elijah demanded of the horse angrily. "That's their idea of justice? I don't recall you shootin' a man in cold blood! Filthy bastards!"

The horse didn't seem terribly bothered by it, but Elijah was still livid. Delilah was a wonderful and loyal little mustang, and she deserved better than being slaughtered by a mob of angry idiots. Elijah was so insulted on Delilah's behalf that he honestly would've sat and fumed for a good while longer, but then Delilah's ears pricked up, and she looked out intently at something. Elijah looked out in the same direction to see what she found so interesting, and he saw a twinkle, like a distant star.

Elijah watched in silence for a moment, then looked down at Delilah again. She swiveled one ear back in his direction, but kept looking ahead. With a shrug, Elijah had Delilah walk on towards the starlight. He wasn't certain how being dead worked yet, but he imagined sitting and staring at lights in the distance didn't get a person very far.

The starlight turned out to be a petite woman on a strange, white horse. She wore a figure-fitted body suit made of white fabric embedded with crystals and tiny bulbs of light. How it worked, and why she would wear something like that, was far beyond Elijah. A matching wide-brimmed hat rested on the woman's head and kept Elijah from seeing any of her face at first, but then the woman tilted her head back and peered at him with hazel eyes. Despite her strange outfit, she looked like she could have been from one of the Italian-American families from back home.

Lips painted a deep red pursed, and then opened so the woman could say, "Didn't think I'd see a cowboy first thing in Hell."

"Didn't think demons wore lights in their clothes," Elijah shot back. He was hardly a cowboy, but he *had* lived in western America in the late Eighteen-Hundreds, and he had a thing for the color black. He thought it was dramatic. Little did he realize all it did was remind the woman of the villains in Ancient American Old West films she'd seen on archival internet sites.

Although the woman's get-up was strange to Elijah, the sparkling lights and ridiculous hat were nothing compared to the horse the woman was sitting on. At first glance, Elijah thought it was wearing armor, but that wasn't it at all. The horse itself was made out of some sort of jointed metal which was painted white. Its mane and tail were comprised of metallic threads which were pliable enough to move when the horse did. As if all of that wasn't enough, the horse's eyes glowed a deep blue, and when the horse snorted, wisps of steam curled from its nostrils.

While Elijah tried to wrap his head around the mechanical horse, the woman smiled slightly and asked him, "What's your name?"

"Elijah Blanco," Elijah replied, looking back up to the stranger's face. The fact she looked and sounded American somehow only added to her weirdness. How could someone from his home have a horse like that? Had he missed some amazing breakthrough invention during his time on the run? "What about you?"

"Caprice DeGaglia," the woman said. "Are you dead?"

"That's a hell of a question to ask someone you just met," Elijah pointed out with a raised eyebrow.

"It's a fair question to ask if the person asking it has just died," Caprice countered. She shifted on her horse to take a more relaxed

3

position and rested one hand on her hip. "How about I rephrase it?" she offered evenly. "Hello, my name is Caprice DeGaglia and I believe I'm dead. Are you dead as well?"

"Yeah, I'm dead," Elijah admitted. He crossed his arms over the horn of his saddle and rested on them to give Caprice the same air of carelessness she was giving him. "No idea where this place is supposed to be, though, so don't bother askin'."

"Noted," Caprice said with a smirk. She looked around, patting her horse's neck idly. The metal steed shook its head and shifted its weight restlessly, but stayed where it was, watching Elijah and Delilah.

"So what the hell's that thing?" Elijah decided to come out and ask. "Weirdest damn horse I've ever seen."

"Exactly what it looks like," Caprice replied easily. "An artificial horse."

"What the hell for?" Elijah pressed. "How'd you even get it?"

"I bought him," Caprice said airily. It was pretty clear she wouldn't be terribly helpful if it didn't suit her. "He's run by an artificial intelligence."

Elijah stared at her blankly. The nice thing about death, Elijah would learn, was it lifted the barrier of language and dialects. Not just those established by region and culture, but by time as well. Communication became universal, as it always should have been. Unfortunately, it didn't give a person an instant upload of knowledge concerning everything in their world's history and future. So even though Caprice could speak Greek and be understood by the man in black, talking about things not of Elijah's time was like speaking Greek he still couldn't understand.

"His name is Shu," Caprice went on. She was apparently going to pretend Elijah wasn't staring at her like she had snakes coming out of her ears. "After the Ancient Egyptian god who held up the sky goddess Nut."

"So you're a goddess?" Elijah asked dryly.

"To some," Caprice replied with another smirk. She seemed to be great at that. "What's your horse's name?"

"Delilah," Elijah said, though he was seriously considering riding away. This woman seemed like she could possibly be bad news.

4

Sirens generally were, in his experience. And women as beautiful and well-spoken as Caprice were generally sirens. Though that was again in his experience.

"Delilah?" Caprice repeated with a tilt of her head. "Are you worried she'll betray you?"

"Hasn't yet," Elijah said flatly. "Can't say the same about human women." Caprice laughed and Elijah looked around. Was this all there was to death? Being in a black expanse with nothing but a horse and random strangers? He knew a few preachers who were in for a big shock.

A soft, hazy glow in the distance caught Elijah's attention. It seemed to be coming from a horizon he hadn't been able to see before. He frowned and squinted at the light, trying to see if it was another person. "What's that?" he muttered. Caprice followed his gaze to the glow and lifted the brim of her hat a little so she could see more clearly.

"I can't tell," she said. She looked at Elijah and jerked her head in that direction. "Let's go see."

Caprice signaled to her horse to get moving, and the robotic beast took off with thundering hoof beats. He certainly went a lot faster than Elijah would have expected. Delilah apparently didn't mind a little race one bit, because she sprang after Shu energetically and didn't waste any time catching up.

The two horses and their riders raced on for the glow in the distance, which grew as they got closer, but still didn't reveal exactly what it was coming from. It wasn't until the four of them were completely immersed in the light that everything cleared and they found themselves in a massive, ivory chamber. And not on their own.

An impressive crowd of riders had gathered there, though not all of them sat on horses, whether artificial or otherwise. There were people on camels, donkeys, mules, elephants, and even bicycles and machines Elijah had never seen before.

As Elijah looked around, he spotted multiple people who looked as though they had ridden straight out of history books. That was when it suddenly hit him why Caprice and so many others wore such strange outfits, and rode creatures and things he'd never even dreamed of. They all came from different times. The people there had been collected from every point in Earth's history, ranging over what looked like thousands and thousands of years.

The entire group stood there in confusion for a while, looking at one another and wondering exactly what it was they were supposed to be doing.

Then there was a deafening crack, and a hole opened in the fabric of space itself in front of the crowd. At first there wasn't anything to see through the hole except empty darkness, but then a towering male figure stepped out. He was extremely tall, and covered in armor of metal which glowed gold and made him look rather alien. Elijah found he somehow knew the figure was an angel, though he didn't know what made him so sure. The man certainly didn't look like any angel Elijah had ever imagined.

As the Angel entered the chamber, those closest to him warily backed away. A tense silence followed, and then the Angel lifted his hand and slammed it into the darkness behind him, causing a loud thunderclap. Elijah figured it was probably a good thing everyone there was no longer living, because it looked like some of them would've dropped dead out of terror right then and there.

"You have been brought here," the Angel said in a powerful voice, "to make a choice."

Elijah wondered if he was the only one under the impression this Angel had been excited about the destruction of sinners for quite some time. The way he loomed over the riders and watched them through the glowing slits in his helmet didn't exactly make for a comforting presence. Weren't angels supposed to be reassuring?

"You have also been brought here," the Angel went on, "to compete for a chance to win back God's favor."

Elijah lifted an eyebrow and glanced at Caprice. The way she looked back at him told Elijah he wasn't alone in wondering why he should care about God's opinion when God never cared about his.

"You have all lived your lives in sin, chasing after worldly pursuits with no regard for your soul's final destination," the Angel said gravely. "You ignored the warnings of Hellfire and eternal separation from your Creator, and chose to indulge in the makings of your own self-destruction."

The Angel paused there and stared at the humans who were all watching him intently. Finally the Angel concluded, "And that is why you will be perfect."

"Perfect for what?" asked a tall and proud man with leathery skin and sharp eyes. His large, sorrel horse bobbed her head gently as if seconding the question. Elijah wondered if the man was a Roman soldier. He was certainly dressed like one.

"The time has come to elect the Four Horsemen of the Apocalypse," the Angel explained. "This is how those positions will be assigned."

"I don't remember that part in the book of Revelations, do you?" Caprice asked Elijah.

"Didn't really make a habit of readin' any of the Bible," Elijah replied flatly. Though, that being said, he couldn't deny the Angel had him interested. Not in the chance of winning God over, but in becoming a Horseman of the Apocalypse. What the hell did that even mean?

"You must all prove your worthiness by hunting and capturing one target for every sin you committed over the course of your lives," the Angel continued, ignoring the quiet commentaries. "The four horsemen who first achieve this goal—"

"Excuse me, shouldn't that be horsepeople?" Caprice interjected. The Angel stopped and looked at her, and so did the rest of the crowd. Elijah just hoped to Hell he wasn't close enough to get singed by any fire and brimstone about to get shot her way.

"It isn't gender-specific," said a lean male rider with dark skin, perched on what Elijah would later learn to be a motorcycle. He sounded English to Elijah, though Elijah had never seen an Englishman all dressed up in black leather and denim. "They say it like that all the time in the Bible, don't they?" the rider went on. His dark brown eyes were scrunched up in subdued amusement at Caprice's little protest. At least someone found her funny, Elijah thought.

"If that's the case, it seems lazy to me to not just fix the wording," Caprice said with a shrug. "Assuming it's not actually thinly-veiled sexism. But try telling any of that to the church."

"Outta curiosity, have you ever actually been in one?" Elijah asked her. "Is that how you died? You stepped into one and burst into

7

flames?" The look he got from Caprice in reply was almost impressively nasty.

"Are we honestly having a debate about political correctness in the afterlife, in front of an angel?" a woman asked incredulously from her steam-powered camel. She was richly dressed in fine silks and jewels, but her grand appearance and sour expression didn't put Caprice off one bit.

"He's got all of eternity to finish his explanation," Caprice pointed out. "He's got time to address an equal rights issue."

Elijah pinched the bridge of his nose. Honestly, the neck-snapping had been far more pleasant than what he was being subjected to right then.

"Fine," the Angel said. Nearly everyone was rather surprised to note that he didn't sound terribly irritated or even inconvenienced. "The four horse*people* who first achieve the stated goal will be given the opportunity to capture one of the Four Ends, which will in turn determine the horse*person's* eternal designation."

Caprice gave an approving nod. There was quite a bit of eye-rolling from the group, but no one said anything. Elijah had to assume it was out of fear that Caprice would talk some more if they did.

"Those who do not wish to participate may depart now," the Angel announced.

After a pause, the crowd looked at one another briefly before looking back to the Angel.

"No offense," said a pale man riding an Appaloosa, "but that's not a tough choice."

The rest of the group nodded, staying right where they were. The Angel nodded slowly and said, "In that case..."

He trailed off and lifted his left hand. A panel of light appeared in the air below the Angel's hand, and he began gently sweeping his fingers over the surface of the panel. Elijah had no idea what the hell he was witnessing, but when he glanced over at Caprice, he could tell it was no great mystery to her. Several other riders apparently recognized the Angel's action as well, but Elijah took comfort in noticing there were plenty of people who looked just as confused as he felt.

The Angel tapped the panel then, and a moving picture made of light sprang to life above the gathered crowd. It was a herd of wild ponies who reared, bucked, and shrieked like possessed things. Their eyes flashed like lightning, and they snorted fire as they bared their teeth fiercely at one another.

"Are they what we're supposed to catch?" a dubious voice asked.

"Yes," the Angel replied. "This herd is about to be released onto the Earth and the planes beyond. You will pursue and capture them as you are able. We will keep the score."

"Now that ain't fair," Elijah snapped. "What do you mean, you'll keep the score? How do we know you won't be pullin' for your favorite and doin' them favors behind our backs?"

"We have nothing to gain or lose by the success of any one of you," the Angel said evenly. "You have lived your lives being ranked and classed by one another, but to us, you are all simply humans."

"Well, that's nice," someone muttered. The Angel either didn't hear it or didn't care.

"You will each be provided with a length of Heaven's rope," the Angel said. "Subdue your intended pony, and it will be transported to your Keep."

"What, you mean a corral?" a cowboy with a white hat asked with a puzzled frown.

"Yes," the Angel replied, still not appearing bothered by any of the interruptions. "You may inquire of this Keep—or corral—in your mind and hear your quarry's total at any time."

"This is sounding more and more like a video game," Caprice remarked to Elijah. He gave her a blank stare in response. Sounded like a what?

"There are things you must learn on your own," the Angel informed the riders somberly. "You have passed beyond Time's realm, but do not think you are beyond peril." He took a step back, obviously preparing to leave. "Go with blessings."

"So, wait, you're just chucking us out like this?" a short man on a pony said in surprise. "That hardly seems fair!"

"To borrow the words of another place in a time beyond yours," the Angel replied directly to the man, "*deal with it.*"

With that, the Angel vanished in a flash of fiery orange light, leaving the dead riders blinking in stunned silence.

# Chapter 2

"Well, that's just freakin' perfect!" snapped a woman in leather on a red, white, and blue motorcycle.

"What's wrong?" Elijah asked as he looked at the chamber surrounding them. "Never had to figure stuff out on your own before?"

"You think this is a joke?" the woman asked irritably.

"Nah," Elijah replied. He signaled Delilah to start walking and gave a flippant wave to the others. "I think it's like livin'. Nobody gives you any starter lessons for that, neither."

"They certainly didn't give you any for proper grammar," Caprice remarked. Elijah turned in the saddle to tell her to can it, but then there was a flash of light. The riders looked around in confusion, and found the chamber had suddenly expanded into an impossibly long corridor with a series of large doorways set in the ivory walls. The doorways opened into swirling vortexes of light in various colors, and there were neat ramps leading up into the entries.

"What the hell are those?" Elijah blurted out, staring at the doorways.

"They look like portals," Caprice remarked. She looked at Elijah and then explained, "Portals are like shortcuts through space, and sometimes even time."

Before Elijah could ask how she even thought to guess that, he noticed that a length of rope constructed of light had materialized at Caprice's waist. Upon looking down, Elijah found he had one as well, hanging on his belt by a hook which hadn't been there before. Elijah looked around to see the other riders had acquired the same thing. Most likely in the same manner, going by the surprised and puzzled looks on their faces.

"What the hell is this?" someone near the other side of the crowd wondered out loud.

"This is only a guess, but this *might* be that Heaven's rope our host was talking about," a man said. Elijah turned to look at whoever was speaking and saw the Englishman in denim and leather who had bantered with Caprice earlier. "But there might be another reason it appeared out of nowhere and is now glowing," the man on the motorcycle added.

"Maybe it's magic," Elijah said dryly. The man chuckled, and Caprice tilted her head in curiosity as she watched the stranger.

"What's your name?" she asked.

"Stephen," the man replied. "Stephen Pritchett."

"It's a pleasure," Caprice said politely. "My name's Caprice DeGaglia, and this is Elijah Blanco." Elijah did a double-take.

"You mind not speakin' for me?" Elijah asked with slanted eyes. "Last I checked, I ain't your husband."

"Of course you're not," Caprice said with a flippant wave of her hand. "My husband is far more charming than you are." Elijah rolled his eyes and Stephen grinned at the two of them.

"Pleasure," Stephen said. He pointed to the doorways and asked, "Any idea where you'll go first?"

"Don't think it really matters which one you pick right now," Elijah replied, eyeing the strange exits. "Not like you can see any real difference."

"So just pick one and let's see what we find," Caprice urged. Elijah looked at her again, rather fed up at that point.

"Since when is this a group activity?" he demanded. "I don't recall partnerin' up with anybody. Pick your own portal or whatever you called it."

Caprice held up her hands in surrender and said, "Well, fine then. Run along." Elijah glowered at her for a moment and then signaled Delilah forward for one of the doorways. He got up to the ramp leading up into the passage and glanced back to find Caprice and Stephen watching him closely.

"The hell is this?" Elijah asked, a bit confused.

"We're hoping that we'll be able to tell from here if you end up in Hell, or land in a pit of lava, or something along those lines," Stephen said, completely serious. Caprice nodded in agreement.

Elijah's eyes narrowed again and he turned back to the portal as he kicked Delilah on. The horse leaped through the doorway, and for a moment Elijah saw nothing but stars rushing past him. It only lasted a second, however, and then Delilah was landing in the middle of a strange landscape.

It was difficult to tell exactly what the place was supposed to be. Blurred colors formed the vague shapes of towering buildings and objects Elijah couldn't make out. It was like a painting of a city someone had poured water over, letting the colors bleed and blend into one another. Elijah was puzzled at first, but then he realized it was probably because he was dead. After all, when people talked about seeing ghosts and specters, they always said they looked blurry or unclear. It made sense it would go both ways.

Of course, that was what people said in ghost stories told around campfires. Elijah admittedly had a talent for remembering fictional stories as first-eye-witness accounts. Even he occasionally lost track of why he accepted some "truths" in the first place.

Elijah looked back over his shoulder to find out if he could see the portal he'd used to get there. Thankfully he could, but it looked different on that side. Colors swirled and rippled in a semi-circular shape about eleven feet high and seven feet wide, simply hanging a few inches off the ground. The passages looked strange enough in the big ivory room, but seeing one without even a door frame around it was somehow even stranger.

Curious, Elijah dismounted Delilah and took hold of her reins to lead her back over to the portal. Once there, he leaned through to poke his head back out the other side. He found Caprice and Stephen still there, watching the doorway expectantly.

"No hellfire yet," Elijah told them. Caprice lifted an eyebrow and Stephen grinned in amusement. Elijah pulled back, but then after a brief contemplation, peered into the ivory chamber again. "Any idea if there's any way back here besides this thing?" he asked.

"Not a clue," Caprice said, examining her elaborately decorated nails. "You might want to try not getting lost."

"Any suggestions?" Elijah asked impatiently. Caprice looked at him and then at Stephen, who shrugged and then looked at Elijah.

"Breadcrumbs?" Stephen offered as his advice.

There was a pause.

"Great, thanks a lot," Elijah said as he pulled back once again. He turned to examine the other world and pursed his lips slightly as he considered his options. Part of him didn't know why he was so concerned. After all, it wasn't as though he had a home or anything, so there was no danger of losing his way back to it. And he didn't have friends, so there wasn't a risk of getting separated from his loved ones.

So why was he thinking twice about taking actions which could end in his not being able to get back to those two morons?

Asking himself that question immediately had Elijah wondering when exactly he became so soft. He decided to correct that by getting back on Delilah and setting off. After all, potential emotional attachments were nothing but problems.

Elijah and Delilah went off into the world of bleeding colors, watching the world around them as they went. Elijah was finding if he focused enough on a certain spot, the colors would sharpen and begin to form recognizable shapes. Well, somewhat recognizable, since he was riding through a city which wouldn't exist in that form until decades after his death.

Elijah was also beginning to notice dim outlines of figures blinking in and out of view around him. What he didn't realize was he was actually seeing momentary glimpses of living people. As a person no longer affected by Time, Elijah had no way of perceiving events as he would have while he was alive.

Since he didn't even think to consider all that, Elijah continued observing passively as Delilah carried him over the city streets. They went on in watchful silence for a while before something caught Elijah's eye. Down what he could see to be an alley if he squinted enough, there was a shimmering pony. Thankfully, unlike the world around it, the pony was actually clear and vivid. It glowed and flickered like candlelight, and its eyes were wild and alert. It looked just like the ponies Elijah and the other riders had seen in the Angel's projection earlier.

The pony hadn't noticed Elijah yet, and it stood sniffing the air for something. Elijah looked down at the Heaven's Rope still hanging from his belt. With his luck, it would burn through his hand when he tried to grab hold of it. Honestly, he was a little surprised anything from Heaven had gotten near him and not made him instantly burst into flames.

Elijah took hold of the rope—noted that he wasn't struck by lightning for doing so—and pulled it off his belt as he signaled Delilah to ease closer to the otherworldly pony creature. Delilah seemed to sense how delicate her little mission was, and she set a quiet, cautious pace. Unfortunately, it wasn't enough to keep the pony from detecting its hunters. It looked directly at Elijah and reared with a shriek which sounded more like a train whistle from Hell than any sound a pony might make. As it screamed, the creature's entire body burst into holographic flames. Elijah's eyes went wide, and he pulled away in spite of himself. Delilah shied away as well, but then pinned her ears flat against her head and lunged for the pony.

Elijah had ridden Delilah for over fifteen years before the two of them met their untimely end, and Elijah couldn't think of any horse he'd rather ride into eternity. Really, at the end of the day, Delilah was the only partner Elijah cared to have. But like in any partnership, there were definite highs and lows.

Although Elijah and Delilah were the only friends each of them had, Elijah firmly maintained that the mustang was occasionally a shocking pain in the ass. He had more than once fallen victim to Delilah's snap navigational decisions which resulted in Elijah's hitting the ground.

For the most part, Elijah was glad he'd never acted on the impulse to sell Delilah for slaughter, but there were times he had to think real hard to remember why he hadn't. Desperately trying to keep seated while Delilah bolted for a fiery phantom pony was turning out to be one of those times.

Delilah raced through the blurred cityscape after the pony, with Elijah clinging onto her neck for dear life. Once Elijah was settled on Delilah's back again, he released his grip on the horse's neck and mane, and brought up the Heaven's rope. Delilah was hell-bent on nothing but the pony ahead of them, so while Elijah still held the reins in one hand, there was no need to direct her.

"You throw me off, and we're findin' Hell's glue factory so you can spend eternity there!" Elijah threatened over the thunder of hooves. Delilah snorted, and Elijah tied one end of the Heaven's rope to the horn of Delilah's saddle. He was dead, but he didn't want to find out what having his arms pulled off would feel like, even in the afterlife.

Once the rope was tied off, Elijah tied a quick lasso into its free end and looked up for his target. Delilah had done an impressive job of closing the distance, and she was held steady a few feet behind and to the left of the pony. After a few swings of the lasso over his head, Elijah threw the looped end of the rope, and cast it over the pony's head. As the rope made contact with the pony's neck, the rope flashed even brighter, and the pony halted with a deafening scream. Delilah slid to a stop and started backing up to take up the slack. Elijah kept his hand on the rope and stared as the pony reared and shrieked like it was being burned.

"They're supposed to take it from here, right?" Elijah asked Delilah, even though he knew she wouldn't give him an answer. Not because she was a horse, but because she generally forced him to remember things on his own. Elijah was trying to figure out exactly what he was going to do at that point when he heard a woman speak inside his head.

"Sin-Bearer subdued," the woman said. Her voice was deep, and her tone was clipped and professional. And Elijah had no idea who she was or from where she was speaking.

"What the hell?" Elijah said, looking around. "Who the hell is that?"

There was a flash, and suddenly the pony was gone, leaving the rope to drop to the ground. Elijah and Delilah stared at the newly vacant space and tried to wrap their minds around what they had just seen. They weren't doing a fantastic job of it, so Elijah gave up on thinking and started coiling up the rope, which magically shortened in length as he did.

"All right," he said as he got the rope untied from the saddle and hooked on his belt. "Let's get back to those two morons." He started to guide Delilah back the way they came, but then he brought her to a halt as something caught his eye.

While Elijah had noticed the dim shapes of figures amidst the smeared colors of the city, he hadn't thought much of them. After all, everything looked so abstract that it would be hideously time-consuming to ponder every single thing he saw. But there on the sidewalk across the street from him, Elijah could see a boy standing and staring at him. Not just a figure or a shape that only looked something like a boy. A clearly-defined, living, breathing little boy. Blobs of color and shadows kept obstructing Elijah's view of the boy now and again, but the kid was definitely there, and he could definitely see Elijah and Delilah, judging by the way he stared.

"Hey," Elijah called. "How come you're easy to see but the rest of this place is a mess?"

The boy blinked and seemed to be trying to decide if Elijah was actually there. Elijah figured that was fair, since he was trying to decide the same thing about the boy.

"You hear me?" Elijah asked. The boy nodded slowly, but then something that Elijah couldn't quite make out took hold of the kid's hand and started pulling him along. As the boy was pulled, he faded into just another shape bleeding into the background. Elijah frowned, but since there wasn't much he could do, he signaled Delilah to move along.

It was quite a walk back to the portal, so Elijah used the journey to better take in his surroundings. Now that he was looking out for them, he noticed more of the figure-like shapes wandering the city. There were also much larger moving shapes which traveled down the street with surprising speed. Elijah assumed those were wagons or something like them. No matter how big or small any shape or figure was, though, Elijah found he and Delilah could pass right through them. It was odd, but he supposed since people could walk right through ghosts (he had heard), ghosts could walk right through people too.

Elijah and Delilah finally made it back to the portal, and they went through to find Caprice and Stephen still waiting for them on the other side. The rest of the group had dispersed to begin their own hunts, which made the fact that Caprice and Stephen hadn't moved even stranger to Elijah.

"Still here, huh?" Elijah said, trying to mask his surprise.

"It seemed rude to simply leave while you were off doing whatever it was you were doing in there," Caprice replied casually. That was a ridiculous response, Elijah thought. Who cared about manners during a competition?

"I'm assuming you caught something," Stephen said, relaxing against the handlebars of his motorcycle. "People have been popping in and out of these portal things, saying those ponies are everywhere."

"So you two just stood here and waited while everybody else got a head start on you," Elijah said, trying to make sure he was understanding the situation correctly.

"Oh, they can have all the head start they need," Caprice replied with a cool smile. "They still won't beat me."

"Or me," Stephen agreed. Elijah stared at them. So arrogance kept them there waiting for him? That didn't make any sense either.

"Anyway," Caprice lilted, "now that we know for certain we won't be annihilated by going through those portals, and that it's even possible to make your way back after running around in there, I'm more than happy to get started." She nudged Shu to head for another one of the portals, and Elijah watched her go, stunned.

"You waited this whole time just to up and leave?" Elijah asked incredulously. Stephen shrugged and fired up the engine of his motorcycle, startling the hell out of Elijah.

"Doesn't seem like you need any help," Stephen pointed out. He and Caprice rode off for separate portals, and Elijah watched them go for a moment before shaking his head and looking down at Delilah.

"Bunch of damn lunatics even here," he declared. Delilah snorted.

# Chapter 3

It wasn't long before Elijah earned quite the reputation in the race to be a Horseperson of the Apocalypse. He found it odd so many people who had led their lives in ways that branded them "Hell-bound" would throw such extreme tantrums over the fact he did whatever it took to win.

All right, so he had to admit it was *probably* rather infuriating to others when someone swooped in and roped their target pony at the last possible second. Still, they didn't have to be so goddamn whiny about it.

It turned out there was a lot more to the afterlife than Elijah had ever fathomed. In fact, he was pretty certain *no one alive* had ever fathomed exactly how much was involved in the planes beyond. The portals in the ivory chamber the riders had begun calling "the Hub" didn't only lead to Earth in different points in time. Some led to completely different worlds with completely different sorts of people inhabiting them. With practice, Elijah gained the ability to see more than smeared colors in the worlds of the living, so he took to exploring places where beings other than humans could be found

Fortunately, it didn't hurt his chances in the competition when he went exploring. Even in other worlds, Elijah never had a lack of ponies to capture. It seemed sin was everywhere, regardless of species. While a lot of people would find it a compelling commentary on the state of sentient existence, Elijah simply thought it was convenient. He got to see places besides Earth and continued to be an active player in the ongoing game.

One of his favorite places to visit was a very small world with a capital city made of glass. Water streamed up from the ground within the crystal-like structures and trickled up past Elijah's range of vision. For all his practice, he wasn't able to see any further than the top of buildings in any given place.

The people there were equally interesting. They were tall and lean, and many of them wore clothes which were as sheer and revealing as the walls of their buildings. All of them looked human, but they had eyes which glowed brightly in an apparently unending night. Elijah had never seen the place in daylight, despite how many times he'd visited. For all he knew, the world didn't even have a sun. It made the light of the inhabitants' eyes stand out even more. The glow wisped out into the air like a lighted mist, and it gave even the friendliest-looking individual a sort of eerie appearance.

Elijah spent enough time there to notice certain recurring patterns in the colors of people's eyes and their overall appearance. Eyes that glowed green were always accompanied by red hair and a pinker shade of skin. Individuals with rose red eyes had black hair, and skin with lovely brown undertones. Sky blue eyes went with flaxen hair, pale ivory skin, and sharper facial features. Violet eyes always graced those with heart-shaped faces, and hair the color of chocolate. The list went on, with the eye colors ranging from fiery orange, to a muted blush pink, to colors that shifted ever so slightly in hue.

But the best part about the lovely world of night was the fact that not too many dead riders went there. It was a very small world, so the list of places the ponies could hide was short. Most riders preferred to stay in dimensions with a promise of higher payoff, so whenever Elijah wanted a break from the competition, the city of glass was always a safe bet.

That is, until Elijah returned and found Caprice astride Shu. If Caprice noticed Elijah, she certainly didn't show it. She was too busy searching the crowd around her with interested eyes.

"Oh, for— What are you doing here?" Elijah demanded of the woman. Caprice looked over at him and tilted her head back so he could see her eyes beneath her hat. When she realized who he was, she pursed her lips.

"Do you own Ervonia now?" she asked dryly. "Relax. I'm not here to cramp your style."

"What the hell's Ervonia?" Elijah asked irritably. He realized it was a stupid question after it came out of his mouth, but it was a little late. Caprice stared at him, and Elijah did his best not to show he was mentally kicking himself for sounding like an idiot.

"You're lucky we're dead," Caprice informed Elijah. "I would have suffered even more second-hand embarrassment if people around us had heard that." Elijah gave Caprice a rather rude gesture and Caprice smirked. "This place is Ervonia," she said in reply to his question. "It's a moon which orbits Platana in a solar system a very long way from our Earth."

"How do you know all that?" Elijah asked suspiciously.

"I used to come here when I was alive," Caprice replied with a small shrug. Elijah's eyebrows shot up.

"What?" He sat there on Delilah for a moment, blinking and trying to wrap his head around what Caprice just said. "How?"

"Oh, that's right, you wouldn't know about all that," Caprice said apologetically. "In my time, hundreds and hundreds of years after you were alive, we had giant metal ships which floated through the stars. We could go just about anywhere in the galaxy and beyond."

Elijah had to take a second to imagine that. It sounded incredibly unlikely, but he had found since his death, he'd been obliged to be far more open-minded about a lot of things in life. As a result, he decided to simply accept Caprice most likely wasn't lying and move on.

"So, what, you came back for nostalgia?" Elijah asked. Caprice smiled and nodded as she looked around.

"It was always one of my favorite places to visit," she said somewhat wistfully. She looked back to Elijah and asked, "What do you know about this place? Anything?"

"I know it's called Ervonia," Elijah replied. Caprice laughed and Elijah wondered why she didn't do that more often. It was nicer than her ice queen act she'd been playing with him so far. "And I know people's eyes glow here," he added.

"Very observant," Caprice remarked, sounding only a little patronizing. She signaled Shu to walk on, and Elijah went ahead and let Delilah go right along. Caprice clearly had more to say, and he was actually interested.

"Their eye color designates their class," Caprice explained as they rode. "Ervonians believe everyone in life has a role to fill, and their classes all perfectly balance one another. The classes were established because each particular group has a different vision-based ability. All Ervonians are able to see the unseen in some way, whether it's love, intentions, morals, or even fairies or angels."

"What about the dead?" Elijah asked. Caprice looked over at him.

"One class can see the dead," she replied with a nod. "But you won't see them out and about with everyone else." She turned back to face the path ahead and quietly added, "Except for one. If he's here."

Elijah was about to ask whom she meant, but suddenly Caprice's horse Shu stopped in his tracks and lifted his head. Shu's metal ears pricked forward as he stared intently at something in the distance. Caprice looked out in the same direction and stood up in her stirrups. Confused, Elijah brought Delilah to a halt and asked, "What is it?"

"Shh," Caprice said, slowly waving a hand at him. There was a heavy pause, and then Caprice sat back down in the saddle just as Shu took off at a run. Elijah saw Caprice reach for her Heaven's rope, and he urged Delilah to go after the other horse and rider. After all, if Elijah had a chance to take the capture away from Caprice, he would.

When Caprice pulled her rope free, Elijah noticed she didn't have a lasso tied into the end of it. He could tell it was intentional too, because she swung it like someone experienced with a whip. Part of Elijah wondered where Caprice had learned that sort of skill. The rest of him really didn't want to know.

It wasn't a terribly long chase. Caprice herded the kicking and shrieking pony down the streets with obvious knowledge of where she was going. With the help of an angled passage between buildings, it was a simple task to head the pony off. As soon as Shu had the opportunity, the metal horse charged in front of his target, and Caprice whipped her rope at the pony, meaning to lash the rope around its neck.

Unfortunately for Caprice, Elijah managed to land his rope on the beast first, and when the pony disappeared, Elijah was the one to receive the success notification from the disembodied voice. Caprice heard the voice inside her head as well, but to her it said, "Target lost. Point to Elijah Blanco."

"Sorry," Elijah said without any sincerity in his tone. Caprice stared at him, shocked.

"You stole that pony from me," she said. Elijah put his rope back on his belt and shrugged.

"Part of the game, right?" he said. Caprice continued staring at him, but her expression shifted into something dark and angry.

"You owe me a pony," she said coldly.

"Listen, lady," Elijah began, but he never got to finish that thought. Caprice whipped her rope at Elijah and caught him by the neck, then viciously ripped him off of Delilah. Both Elijah and Delilah were rather shocked by that move. Elijah just thanked his lucky stars he was dead, because while it certainly didn't feel good, he didn't have to worry about being choked.

Elijah moved to get up and found Caprice had already dropped off of Shu and was storming over to him. "What the hell was that for?" he snapped.

"'What the hell was that for'?" Caprice echoed wrathfully. She stopped mere inches from Elijah's face and snarled at him from beneath her hat. "You might think this is just a game or some convenient way to pass the time now that you're dead, but some of us are actually hoping to earn something!"

"Yeah? Like what?" Elijah demanded. "A special place at the table with a God you never gave a shit about? Or are you scared of hellfire? I imagine it'd ruin those pretty clothes of yours!"

"What I'm scared of is never seeing my husband again!" Caprice shouted. Elijah drew back a little in surprise. He hadn't really expected a heartfelt response. Caprice looked away with her jaw clenched and Elijah found himself unable to even shoot back with some harsh reply. When Caprice spoke again, her voice was low, cold and hard. "Not all of us are only in this for ourselves." She turned her eyes on Elijah again. "If you ever do that again, I'll make you wish you had gone straight to Hell."

Elijah knew it was sometimes better to back down, so he raised his hands and took a step back. Caprice simply glared at him in hateful silence, so he said, "All right, I get it. Relax. It's just one pony."

"Don't tell me to relax," Caprice warned. "It's condescending. I've got every reason to not 'relax' with you anywhere near me right now. So you don't get to tell me to relax."

Elijah opened his mouth to reply, but then a deep male voice could be heard from behind the very angry woman.

"Caprice?"

Caprice's face fell, and she turned in surprise to look at a tall, pale man in a long, deep grey coat. He was well-dressed and stood with an air of sophistication, but his dark hair was a bit of a mess. It was a strange combination, but the man himself looked a bit strange, so it was oddly fitting. He seemed equally surprised to see Caprice, and he stared at her with eyes glowing a brilliant turquoise. He was definitely Ervonian as far as Elijah could tell, but Elijah had never seen an Ervonian with eyes that color. And he'd certainly never seen an Ervonian interact with a dead rider.

"Nigel," Caprice said in a tight voice. Elijah suddenly recalled her mentioning an Ervonian who could see the dead. So this was a friend of hers?

The Ervonian called Nigel continued staring at the woman in disbelief for a moment. He seemed to be trying to fully process what he was seeing, and once he had, his expression became incredibly sad.

"Oh, love," Nigel murmured quietly. "I am so sorry."

Caprice smiled sadly and shrugged. "Everybody dies, remember?" she said. She glanced back at Elijah, who honestly wasn't sure what to say. Hell, he wasn't even sure he should be standing there, but before he could slip away, Caprice said, "Elijah Blanco, this is Nigel Cairnahm. An old friend."

Elijah nodded to the Ervonian, who responded in kind. He clearly wasn't a man of many words, and Elijah was fine with that. "What of your husband?" Nigel asked, looking back to Caprice. She hesitated for a moment and then shook her head.

"I don't know," she replied. Nigel frowned and looked off to the side. He seemed to be watching something or someone pass by, but when Elijah followed the man's gaze, he couldn't see anything there.

It made sense that Caprice would have weird friends.

Nigel again focused on Caprice after a moment and asked, "What are you doing here? Did you need my help?"

"No," Caprice said with a sad smile. She reached out hesitantly for Nigel's hands, marking the first time Elijah had seen her act unsure of herself.

"It won't work," Nigel told her quietly. "You and I are on completely different planes now, love. Just because we can see and hear one another doesn't mean we're actually together."

Caprice stopped and slowly lowered her hands again with a sad nod. She kept her eyes down for a moment and then put on a smile and looked back up to Nigel's face. "I'm competing," she said in reply to his question. "Both Mr. Blanco and I are competing, actually."

Nigel glanced over at Elijah momentarily, and Elijah wondered why he found Nigel so vaguely unnerving. Maybe it was the voice. Even though the man was behaving in such a docile way at the moment, Nigel had a voice that was deep and potentially commanding.

"Tell me nothing of it," Nigel advised, looking back to Caprice. "There are some things the living are not meant to know."

"You ain't even curious?" Elijah asked. If it were him, he'd want to know everything.

"Of course I am," Nigel replied calmly. He looked Elijah in the eye and tilted his head. "But there are times curiosity is not meant to be satisfied."

"Guess the cat would probably agree with you," Elijah remarked, getting a blank stare in reply.

"The cat?" Nigel repeated in confusion. "What cat?"

"He means the human turn of phrase, Nigel," Caprice explained. "Curiosity killed the cat; satisfaction brought him back?"

"Oh," Nigel said with a blink. He still seemed as though he didn't completely get it, but he said, "I suppose." Caprice chuckled and shook her head, and Elijah just stared. Seriously? And he was the one who got treated like a moron?

"We really shouldn't stay," Caprice told Nigel gently. "I just..." She trailed off and looked down.

"You wanted to see a familiar face," Nigel guessed patiently. "Don't we all?" Caprice looked up and gave him a sad smile. Elijah finally turned and went back to the waiting Delilah to get on her back, but he didn't leave yet. He figured it wouldn't hurt to wait for the woman. Not that he cared or anything. He simply owed her a pony and didn't want her running him down and screaming at him some more.

"I'll be back," Caprice told Nigel, who nodded. Caprice gave Nigel one last smile and turned away to walk back to Shu.

Elijah would be the first to tell anyone he wasn't the best when it came to dealing with people directly. He understood how they worked on a strictly academic level, but he wasn't a particularly sympathetic or empathetic person. As far as Elijah was concerned, everyone was given their problems in life and they were all supposed to learn to handle them.

Despite all that, he was still fairly good at *reading* people, and right then he could tell Caprice was feeling the effects of being dead. He couldn't blame her. It was becoming more and more apparent she'd actually had things to live for. Watching someone like that deal with an early death was a bit sobering.

Without a word, Caprice mounted Shu and started away from Nigel. Elijah looked to Nigel and gave him a nod, and then signaled for Delilah to go after the departing horsewoman.

"Peace find you both," Nigel said in farewell.

"Uh, you too," Elijah called back over his shoulder, hoping it would be the proper thing to say. It probably would've been a lot more proper if he'd said something nicer than that, but he was hardly the epitome of proper. If he was honest with himself, he wouldn't even say he was a loose definition of it.

Elijah caught up with Caprice and said, "So that's the guy you were talkin' about before?"

"Yes," Caprice replied without taking her eyes off of the path ahead. "He's one of the Gorvon. They're a warrior class of Ervonian."

"Looks kinda skinny for a warrior," Elijah commented, looking back to see if Nigel was still there. He wasn't.

"Looks can be deceiving," Caprice pointed out. Elijah supposed she had a point. He'd once shot a man in the leg who looked as though he could take down an entire army, only to discover the man had a surprisingly low pain tolerance.

They rode on in silence for a while before Elijah said, "All right, I'll help you catch two ponies, then I'm out. Got it?"

"I don't need your help doing anything," Caprice said firmly. "I just need you not to steal things out from under my nose."

"Yeah, well, it's easier with help, right?" Elijah said. "But fine, if you don't want my help, go on by yourself."

Caprice looked Elijah over critically. She was obviously trying to determine if he was just hoping for another opportunity to take advantage of her. Finally she said, "Fine. Two ponies, and then I don't want to see you again anytime soon."

"I'm fine with that," Elijah assured her. The experience so far had reminded him exactly why he preferred being on his own. The two riders fell silent again, and Elijah took the time to try and figure out exactly when he became such a sucker. Why was he even helping her? Was it guilt? That didn't seem likely since he'd done a lot worse than snatch a pony out from under someone's nose, but the question stood.

"So how close are you?" Caprice asked after a lengthy pause. "To catching all your sins, I mean."

Damn it, now they had to make conversation too? "Barely scratched the surface," Elijah replied, hoping that if he looked around and seemed distracted, she would go back to not speaking.

Of course, she didn't. "It's funny, isn't it?"

"What is?" Elijah asked.

"Well," Caprice said as she tapped her chin, "I'd never thought about how many sins I could have committed over the course of my entire lifetime. I noticed the obvious ones, of course, but it's a bit strange to think about someone keeping score of every little thing."

"I guess," Elijah replied dismissively, even though he completely agreed with her. He didn't really understand it, to be honest. What was the point of it all? Why even create humans and give them a will of their own if you were just going to judge their every waking minute? He looked around a bit more and then said, "Hey, let me ask you somethin'."

"What is it?" Caprice asked. At least she sounded a lot less pissed than she had a few minutes ago.

"Have you seen any dead people who ain't part of our group?" Elijah asked. Caprice pursed her lips and thought about it. Finally, she shook her head.

"Actually, now that you mention it, no," she said with a hint of surprise in her voice. "That's strange, isn't it?"

"That's what I thought," Elijah said, rubbing his chin with a frown. "Can't say I'm some kinda expert, but I seriously doubt we're the only dead people out there. After all, not every sinner's a rider, right? And where are all the righteous folk that apparently did everything right?"

"I don't know," Caprice admitted. "Maybe all the saved are already in Heaven."

"Doubt it," Elijah muttered. Caprice looked at him curiously.

"Why's that?" she asked.

"Think about it," Elijah urged. "According to all the folks who knew anything about the Bible when I was alive, once you died, you either went to Heaven or you went to Hell. So we die and don't end up in Heaven, but we don't get thrown into Hell just yet. Instead we've got that Angel makin' deals with us, and we're off herdin' ponies. If it's this weird for us, who's to say it's not just as weird for people on the right side of things?"

Caprice went quiet and was obviously thinking it over. After a moment, she conceded, "I hadn't really considered that."

"I'm just sayin' I think we're far from done seein' weird shit," Elijah said with a shrug. "It's not all that bad, though. Hell of a lot more to do here than there was when I was alive."

Caprice smirked, but before the conversation could go any further, both she and Shu were looking off to their left at the sound of a whinny.

"Bingo," Caprice said as her eyes lit up.

"Hurry up before I change my mind about helpin' you," Elijah said, kicking Delilah on. Both he and Caprice went racing after the sound and found the pony a couple of streets away, near what looked like a massive greenhouse. It was difficult to tell exactly what the structure was since Elijah still had to stop and focus to make things look completely clear in worlds of the living. Since it didn't matter enough at the moment to do so, Elijah decided it would have to remain a mystery.

As Caprice and Shu continued after the pony, Elijah and Delilah veered off to the right to try and pass the pony on the outside. Elijah was hoping if they could overtake the pony, they could head it off and at least slow it down so Caprice could get a better shot at it. Caprice glanced over at him and reined Shu in just a little. She would give Elijah and Delilah a bit of room.

Delilah saw her chance and sprang after the pony with even more enthusiasm. The sudden burst of energy grabbed the pony's attention, and it pinned its ears and bared its teeth fiercely at Delilah, kicking out at her. Undeterred, Delilah charged on, hemming the pony in against a building. The ruse worked, because while the pony was occupied with trying to get Delilah to back off, Shu and Caprice slipped in closer.

Quick as lightning, Caprice's rope whipped out and around the pony's neck. The beast slammed to a halt and reared with a scream, but Caprice didn't seem bothered in the least. In fact, she looked quite calm as she held onto the rope. It was clear that she had roped quite a few ponies on her own before running into Elijah again. After a brief moment, the pony vanished, and a smile crept over Caprice's lips as she was informed of her successful catch.

"That's one," Elijah told her, holding up his index finger. Caprice chuckled and nodded her head as she signaled Shu forward.

"And one to go," she reminded Elijah, coiling up her rope.

# Chapter 4

Traveling with Caprice turned out to be a lot less awful than Elijah first assumed it would be. She was a smartass, a showoff, and she exuded confidence that could be pretty irritating. Mostly because she was right about everything a large percentage of the time. But she was also intelligent, funny, charming, and fairly interesting when it fancied her. Elijah supposed that he could've done a lot worse.

Elijah hadn't exactly planned on sticking with Caprice after he helped her rope her second pony, but it ended up happening anyway. By the time the two riders settled the score and called things square, it felt almost natural to be riding together. That was sort of an odd thing to feel on Elijah's part since he'd spent the majority of his days as a living man on his own. Partnerships had never ended well while he was alive. But since this wasn't a partnership, Elijah was fairly confident that there was no real risk in going around with Caprice for a while.

They actually made a good team. Not that they were a team, Elijah kept telling himself. They just *happened* to work together sometimes since they *happened* to be heading in the same direction. And anyway, Caprice knew her way around on a horse, even if it was an artificial one, and she and Shu had no problem keeping up with Elijah and Delilah. Caprice was also intuitive and could usually tell what Elijah was trying to accomplish. Most of the time that meant she did her best to accommodate Elijah's intentions, but there were times she found it more amusing to be a deliberate pain in the ass.

A case in point arose when Elijah attempted to line up with Caprice to cut off a fleeing pony. Caprice's response was to rein Shu in and give the pony an opening between her and Elijah, which was promptly utilized. Since it was a bit of a squeeze between Shu and Delilah, the pony slammed into Delilah rather aggressively, and Elijah ended up toppling off the saddle and to the ground.

"Real nice!" Elijah snapped at Caprice as he clumsily got to his feet and climbed back onto Delilah. "I'll remember that!" It wasn't his best comeback, and all it did was make Caprice laugh at him as she roped the pony.

"I'm quaking in my boots," Caprice assured Elijah, still giggling. She put on a concerned expression then, and asked, "You aren't hurt, are you?"

"Go to hell," Elijah said irritably. Asking a dead man if he was hurt? Really? Caprice laughed even more, and Elijah took to sulking. God, she could be irritating.

"Oh, Elijah, lighten up," Caprice said. "If you can't laugh at yourself and your own circumstances, you're going to have a very miserable life. I mean, afterlife."

"I laugh plenty," Elijah said obstinately. "Just not at people gettin' me knocked off my damn horse."

"But that's exactly the sort of thing you *should* laugh at," Caprice insisted. She tilted her head and added, "Pardon my grammar there." Elijah looked confused, but Caprice waved a hand dismissively. "You know, you remind me of someone," she said.

"Yeah, I bet," Elijah muttered, signaling Delilah to start walking in another direction. Caprice wasn't deterred and guided Shu right along with them.

"I never asked before, so I'll ask now," Caprice said casually, clearly determined to make small talk. "What did you do while you were alive? As a job, I mean."

"I robbed people," Elijah replied flatly.

"What sort of people?"

"People who had stuff to steal!" Elijah turned and gave Caprice an exasperated look. "Are we seriously havin' this conversation, or is this a nightmare I'm havin' right now?"

"There's no need to get irritable," Caprice said airily. She looked away and patted at her hair that was firmly knotted beneath her hat somewhere or another. "You really should work on that attitude of yours."

Elijah was proud of the fact that no matter how horrible he'd been as a living person, he had never laid a hand on a woman. As far as he was concerned, striking females was barbaric and inexcusable. One didn't hurt women, and one didn't hurt children, full stop.

But he was having a hell of a time refraining from knocking Caprice right off her horse at that moment.

"Did you die robbing people?" Caprice asked. It might have seemed like a rather personal and insulting question to someone who was still alive, but for some reason Elijah found it didn't bother him as much as he would have guessed it would. Being dead was just a fact of life at that point.

"No, but I died *for* robbin' people," Elijah replied carelessly. "Why do you care so much, anyway? Worried I'll tarnish your reputation?"

"I've always done a fine job of tarnishing my own reputation," Caprice assured Elijah with a twisted grin. It was starting to get to him that he rarely ever got a clear view of her eyes. It was usually nothing more than a hat and a chin with a pair of lips talking to him. How the hell could she even see?

"So what did *you* do while you were alive?" Elijah asked in a tone that made it sound like he was arguing with her somehow. "Irritate the hell outta everybody?"

"Yes, and I was also a singer, a songwriter, a pianist, a cellist, and occasionally a D.J.," Caprice replied. "You don't know what a D.J. is, so I'll go ahead and tell you: it's someone who makes music out of magical sound boxes." She grinned at the confused stare Elijah gave her and added, "If you really want to see for yourself, we could always track down a portal that leads to the Earth of my time."

"I'm good," Elijah said a little warily. Magical sound boxes? What the hell? "Is that all you did?"

"Ah, ah," Caprice chastised with a wave of her finger. "All you told me about yourself is that you 'robbed people', so I'm not obligated to give you anything else about me."

Elijah couldn't keep from smirking a bit at that response. One of the things he did like about Caprice was she could give as good as she got. She made things a bit of a challenge, and Elijah liked challenges that weren't annoying or stupid.

The distant roar of what Elijah had learned to be a vehicle's engine abruptly cut the conversation there, and the horses and riders came to a halt and looked off to their right. A man on a motorcycle was heading straight for them at a pretty impressive speed.

"Oh, it's Mr. Pritchett," Caprice commented, making Elijah wonder how she could tell from that far away. Of course, he was still pondering over the mystery that was how she managed to see anything with that damn hat. Regardless, Caprice was giving Stephen a wave as he approached, which was returned casually. Stephen slowed to a stop next to the horses, and tilted his head so he could peer over his sunglasses at Caprice and Elijah.

"All right, Caprice?" he greeted. "And...Elijah, right?" Elijah nodded and gave him a short wave, and Caprice smiled.

"Good to see you, Mr. Pritchett," she said warmly. She certainly seemed familiar with Stephen. Elijah wondered if the two of them had been riding together for a while between when he parted ways with them in the Hub and when he ran into Caprice again in Ervonia. "Been keeping busy?"

"A bit," Stephen replied as he sat back in the motorcycle's saddle. He took off his sunglasses and put them in his jacket pocket. "Surprised to see you two together. Didn't believe the stories, myself."

"Stories?" Elijah said sharply. "What stories?"

"Just that the two of you teamed up," Stephen said with a shrug of one shoulder. "That worry you?"

"It worries me that anyone thinks this is their business," was Elijah's irritable response. To be perfectly honest, he didn't mind being talked about too much when it came to just him. It was even flattering at times to have a reputation. But he didn't care to imagine what people were saying about his hanging around with Caprice.

"You act like you've got a wife and you've been spotted with your mistress," Caprice remarked in a tone of voice suggesting she had an eyebrow lifted. "What does it matter what people say?"

"I wouldn't expect you to understand," Elijah snapped, gesturing at Caprice with a wave of his hand. "Look at you. You'd probably ride down the street buck naked like Lady Godiva to get people talkin'."

"I've actually done that," Caprice informed Stephen, who looked surprised for some reason. Elijah wasn't sure why. Caprice was obviously starved for attention.

"Well, now I'm Lady Godiva's damn babysitter," Elijah went on complaining.

"Being known as Lady Godiva's babysitter is an improvement from what people were saying about you before," Stephen pointed out, and Elijah did a double-take.

"What were they saying before?" he asked with a puzzled expression.

"You were a cheating arse," was Stephen's complacent reply.

"Well, they aren't wrong," Caprice pointed out. Elijah considered that and then shrugged and nodded. They really weren't.

"So where are you two off to now?" Stephen asked. Elijah wasn't sure whether or not it was a deliberate attempt to change the subject, but decided to go with it regardless.

"Didn't really make plans," Elijah said dryly. "Don't know about you, but I've been playin' this whole death thing by ear."

"Have for the most part, but I've also been taking into consideration where I'd like to see next," Stephen replied, apparently unaffected by Elijah's sarcasm. For all his leather, denim, and metal studs, Stephen seemed to be the sort of man who was difficult to anger. Elijah had a feeling he could have physically thrown something at Stephen without any real consequences. "Have either of you been keeping track of the places we have access to?" Stephen asked.

"Somewhat," Caprice replied. She tilted her head and asked, "Why? Something in particular you're wanting to find?"

Stephen grinned a little and revved the engine of his motorcycle, then started off, turning to go back the way he came. Elijah and Caprice looked at one another, and then Elijah shrugged and urged Delilah on after Stephen. Caprice was right behind him, and Elijah knew she was as intrigued as he was. Stephen obviously had something to share or show off, and Elijah was curious enough to see what it was.

The trio rode back through the portal to the Hub, and Stephen led the others down the seemingly endless corridor. It turned out the corridor wasn't actually endless after all, because after riding for quite some time, the riders came to a wall which blocked them from going any further. Set in that wall was a doorway with a frame carved out of what looked like black obsidian rather than the ivory material that made up everything else in the Hub. The wall and black doorway stood quite some distance away from the other portals the dead had been using, as though it had been tucked away for later.

The doorway's material wasn't the only thing that was different. The vortex within the black frame looked less like the simple contortion of light the riders usually passed through, and more like a vertical pool of rippling liquid.

"Where does this one go?" Caprice asked as she stared at the strange portal. "I don't think I've ever even seen it before."

"Haven't gone through yet, but I've been asking around," Stephen replied. He leaned forward to rest his elbows on the handlebars of his motorcycle and nodded to the portal. "I've been told this leads to a world that's neither for the living nor the dead. It's something else. "

"Who told you that?" Elijah asked, looking at Stephen.

"Some of the other riders were talking about it," Stephen explained. "According to them, someone went through and came back completely mad. They think he met the Embodied in there."

"I didn't realize you could go insane after death," Caprice remarked as she looked the doorway over. "I suppose it makes sense, though. We're still our minds, after all."

"At any rate, a lot of stories have been going around about what's beyond that gate," Stephen said, nodding his head to the strange, upright pool. "Couldn't tell you which are true."

"You said somethin' about the Embodied," Elijah remarked, tearing his gaze off of the black fluid to look at Stephen. "What's that?"

"Christ, man, how long have we been here now?" Stephen said with a lifted eyebrow. "Haven't you paid any attention at all?"

"He's been too busy running around and cheating," Caprice muttered.

"You know," Stephen said to Elijah pointedly, "I'm fairly certain cheating's what gets you into Hell in the first place."

"You gonna answer the damn question or not?" Elijah asked irritably. Stephen was turning out to be just as bad as Caprice, and he was confident he didn't have the patience to hang around with both of them for terribly long.

"The Embodied are beings who were created to handle different parts of life," Stephen explained finally. "There are four we know of so far: Time, Fate, Birth, and Death. I'd never heard of them when I was alive, but apparently it's a common story for some people, and it only gets more common here."

"You ever heard of this?" Elijah asked Caprice. She nodded and was ready to leave it at that, but then Elijah stared at her and silently demanded she elaborate, so she rolled her eyes and responded verbally.

"The Ervonians worship the Embodied," she explained. "Anyone who spends any significant time with them ends up hearing a few stories eventually. They even have a Mother Priestess called Maral who communicates directly with Time and Fate. I don't know much beyond that, though. Ervonians keep some aspects of their culture completely hidden from outsiders, even if you're very close with them."

Elijah looked back to the portal thoughtfully and said, "Well. Might as well go meet these Embodied for ourselves, then."

Stephen and Caprice both looked at him in surprise, but Elijah ignored them and simply signaled Delilah forward, goading her to trot right into the portal. He heard Caprice call "Wait!" but it was far too late. Elijah had already made up his mind, and within seconds he and Delilah had already gone through the gate.

# Chapter 5

It turned out there was a pointed difference between crossing dimensions meant for mortals—whether living or deceased—and dimensions meant for those who were definitely not. As soon as Elijah and Delilah passed through the portal into the realm of the Embodied, Elijah could feel they had just done something that held a lot more significance than he could have predicted.

Once on the other side of the strange liquid in the black doorway, Delilah landed on a flat, black surface like slick glass. The surface rested beneath a vast expanse of black sky pricked with millions of twinkling white stars. When Elijah took a moment and watched the stars, he saw that some of them were slowly shifting their position and rearranging themselves. There was a cool and pleasant breeze in the air, and it carried a scent that was somehow familiar, though Elijah couldn't pin down what it was. He supposed it was probably some sort of flower. He rarely had the chance to smell flowers when he was alive, but it had happened a handful of times.

Besides the wind and the swirling stars, nothing moved, there was no sound, and the only light came from the soft glow of the stars above, along with their reflection off of the ground below.

Delilah was understandably spooked by the surroundings, and it showed in the way she anxiously shifted and looked around with wide eyes and pricked ears. Elijah reached down to pat her neck, though a very small part of him had to very secretly admit he was spooked as well.

"Embodied, huh?" he muttered to Delilah. "Don't see any embodied anything, do you?"

Delilah snorted quietly and Elijah said, "That's what I thought."

What Elijah *did* see was a strange building off in the distance that looked like it had been made of black marble and gold. If he had to guess, he would say it was some sort of temple or church. He had just made up his mind to go and investigate when he heard the clatter of hooves behind him, closely followed by the roar of a motorcycle engine. Elijah looked over his shoulder and found Caprice, Shu, and

36

Stephen there and staring around much like Elijah had been only a moment ago.

"What took you so long?" Elijah asked.

"We were waiting for any sort of horrible screams or body parts to come flying through," Stephen replied a bit distractedly as he continued looking around. Caprice ignored the question entirely and looked over at the structure Elijah had been studying.

"Well, the Embodied certainly have good taste," Caprice remarked in a tone of admiration. Elijah rolled his eyes and turned to look at the building again.

"Yeah, about them," Elijah said, keeping his tone casual. "They supposed to be benevolent, or the sort to strike you with lightning or somethin' if you piss 'em off?"

"Well, think about it," Caprice prompted. She turned to face Elijah and then tipped her head back so she could peer at him from beneath the brim of her hat. "Each of them is the literal incarnation of the aspect of life they're named for. Would you consider Time cruel or simply firm and relentless? Is Death hateful or just a natural partner of Birth?"

"Interesting way to think about it," Stephen remarked. "Funny what so many of us miss whilst alive."

"Yeah, hilarious," Elijah said, nudging Delilah to head towards the building. The horse wasn't crazy about that idea, but she obeyed, looking around with worry. Caprice and Stephen were right behind them, and Elijah looked over at Shu curiously to see if he was showing the same nervousness Delilah was. Could fake horses feel fear? The way the massive, white, steel equine glanced around and snorted steam restlessly told Elijah yes, they could. Of course, Elijah couldn't be sure. It wasn't like he was used to reading behaviors of mechanical horses.

The ride over to the black and gold temple was longer than Elijah had anticipated. The wide-open space made judging distances a bit tricky. All three riders kept their thoughts to themselves during the journey; mostly thanks to a creeping feeling of intimidation slowly making its way up their spines and into their brains. None of them really had any idea of what they were in for, and that was a terribly unsettling thing for any mind.

The closer they came to the temple, the more clearly the riders could see just how ornate the building actually was. It was designed with sharp, symmetrical lines and corners, giving the impression of a giant cut and polished gemstone. Giant arches, made of what looked like solid gold, were set into the black walls where openings like doorways stood. There were no doors beneath the arches, and no glass panes. Instead there were drapes of black velvet and golden silk, billowing out gently in the breeze.

"Bit strange that they would just leave it open like this," Stephen remarked in a hushed tone as the three cautiously continued their approach. "No guards or anything, either."

"I don't think they need them," Caprice said in an equally quiet voice. "They probably know the second any visitors arrive in this world."

"You think?" Elijah asked, not taking his eyes off the temple. He saw Caprice nod out of the corner of his eye, and he frowned slightly. Elijah hadn't had a whole lot of time to sit and reflect on his feelings about the fact God and angels and all those sorts of beings actually existed. Of course, philosophical ponderings had never been Elijah's strong suit in the first place, so there really wasn't a very high chance of his contemplating all of that when he finally did get the time.

When they reached the threshold of the temple, Delilah and Shu abruptly stopped and planted their feet in the ground, stoutly refusing to go any further.

"Oh, come on," Elijah said irritably, mostly because he was already anxious, and the horses' acting frightened didn't help. Delilah tossed her head and Shu stomped the ground once with his front hoof.

"Let's try this," Caprice suggested as she slid off of Shu and to the ground. She brought the reins over Shu's head and began to lead him through the gaping archway. Shu hesitated, but then slowly followed his mistress inside. He glanced around cautiously as he did so, but he was following her, and that was what counted.

Elijah decided Caprice's method was a good one, and dismounted as well. Delilah trembled slightly as she looked at Elijah, who frowned and patted her neck firmly. "Come on, girl," he said, taking her reins in his hand and urging her to walk alongside him. "You gonna let that metal horse make you look yellow?"

Delilah warily obeyed Elijah, though she didn't stop shaking as she walked with him. He couldn't entirely blame her. The temple was turning out to be as huge and imposing on the inside as it was on the outside. The arches were big enough for giants to pass through, and the ceiling in the main corridor was vaulted even higher.

Elijah looked back at Stephen, who was also on foot and slowly guiding his motorcycle after the horses. "Guess you don't have to worry about that thing gettin' scared," Elijah remarked.

"You would think," Stephen replied. "But she apparently likes it here just about as much as your horses. I couldn't get her to go any further until I started leading her like this."

"You call it a 'she'?" Elijah asked with a cocked eyebrow. "Don't get weird on me."

"How's that weird?" Stephen asked evenly. "They call ships and cars 'she' all the time, don't they?"

"The hell's a car?" Elijah asked, puzzled.

"A boat with wheels that travels on land," Caprice replied in a very distracted tone of voice. She had spotted something ahead and was staring at it intently.

Elijah looked ahead to see what had Caprice so captivated, and saw an open doorway which led to a spacious chamber with a strange fountain in the center. The fountain was extremely tall and rather oddly shaped. It was made of black marble and gold like the temple around it, but it had a more delicate design than the looming building.

Black fluid overflowed a bowl of gold at the top of the fountain and trickled gently down the sides into a shallow, black pool with gold trim on the ledge. Watching it, Elijah realized the liquid looked an awful lot like the substance covering the portal he and the others had crossed through.

"What do you think it's for?" Stephen asked quietly. "Some sort of altar?"

"Hard to say," Caprice replied as she led Shu closer to the fountain. She reached out with one hand towards the thin, black fluid, and Elijah nearly had a stroke.

"Are you crazy?!" he hissed. "Don't touch that!" Caprice looked over at him, and Elijah wondered which horrible thing he'd done in life had cursed him to being a damn nanny.

39

"I wasn't going to touch it," Caprice insisted. "I just wanted to see if I could feel if it was hot or cold by putting my hand over it."

"Which is it?" Stephen asked, obviously interested. "Did you feel anything?"

Elijah slapped a hand over his face. He could just see this devolving into Caprice and Stephen trying all sorts of ill-advised experiments with that crap, and he wanted no part of it.

"Neither," Caprice replied to Stephen. She looked back to the fluid and put her hand over it again. After a pause, she shook her head and drew back. "It doesn't feel like anything."

"That is because it was not made for you," a deep male voice rumbled throughout the chamber. All three riders and both horses started at the sound and looked around in alarm for the owner of the voice. When they found him, part of the reason the building was so massive became very clear.

A man who stood at least nine feet tall was walking slowly and calmly into the chamber, with deep, black eyes firmly locked on the riders. He wore long robes of black and dark crimson, and his head was covered with the same type of cloth. The entire outfit looked as though it had been made to protect the man from the desert sun and sand. He even had a red cloth draped over his nose and mouth, exposing only those strange eyes which looked like they were filled with ink.

A large hourglass filled with glistening sand hung from a black and red rope tied around the man's waist. It had a fairly simple design, with the glass held in a rectangular frame of black wood, but something about it set Elijah on edge.

The man walked and moved in time with the rhythm of a loud and deep ticking the riders hadn't heard before the man's appearance. As the deceased visitors watched, Elijah somehow realized he knew exactly who the man was, and that he wasn't a man at all.

He was Time.

"You stand before the Well of Worlds," Time said gravely as he crossed the room to stand next to the fountain. "Here the blood of every inhabited land and sea collects, and serves as a window into the lives of all those who have ever been and ever will be."

Elijah had absolutely no idea what the hell that meant, but he was definitely not going to say as much. He simply stared at Time along with the other two riders. To be honest, Elijah was horrifically unsure if he should even speak at all.

"My wife has been waiting for all of you," Time informed them. "The dead live outside of my sands, but not outside of her reach."

Elijah, Caprice, and Stephen were still at a loss for words, but it was just as well, because that was when someone else entered the chamber. It was a woman as tall as Time, with grey skin, and black hair cascading all the way down her back and spilling over her shoulders.

Like Time, the woman was almost completely covered in cloth. She wore a dark, crystal-studded silk skirt which hung from her hips to the floor, and a long, sheer black veil which sparkled as it moved. The veil was draped over her head and face, trailing all the way down to the floor in the back, and down to her hips in the front. But despite how much it covered, the nearly-transparent fabric did practically nothing to hide the woman's unclothed torso. Her strange jewelry did a better job of that than the veil, though not by much.

As Elijah watched the woman, he noticed there were actually multiple colors in her skirt that swirled and shifted as the woman moved. One second the cloth was a deep royal blue, then it was a rich purple, then black, then green, and so on. It happened in such a subtle way it actually took Elijah a moment to even notice it. Caprice would later tell Elijah that the way the various hues combined with the small twinkling diamonds in the fabric reminded both her and Stephen of pictures of nebulae or galaxies. Elijah had never seen pictures of that sort of thing, so his thoughts were a lot less poetic. They mostly involved comparing the woman's skirt to drug-induced hallucinations he'd had in the past.

The woman kept her eyes closed the entire time she walked, but it didn't seem to affect her one bit. As she came closer, Elijah could see through the veil that her eyelids had been painted with intricate designs. He'd never seen anything quite like them before, but they were nice to look at all the same. The woman's overall appearance made Elijah wonder what her real eyes looked like. Though, of course, there was always the possibility she didn't actually have any eyes.

Which was a rather disturbing thought, actually, so Elijah promptly brushed it aside for the time being.

As with Time, Elijah knew almost instantly who the woman was. Unlike Time, however, this woman was a presence who instantly had Elijah setting his jaw and narrowing his eyes. After all, Fate hadn't exactly been what Elijah would have called 'kind' throughout his life.

"Three travelers so far from home, or so they think," Fate said with a faint smile as she crossed the chamber. She held out her hands, and Elijah could see she had what looked like tiny stars embedded in her palms. She reached out to gently touch Elijah's chin and smiled at him, never opening her eyes. "Hello, Elijah," she said. Her voice was low and soothing, and somehow Elijah had known what it sounded like for a very long time.

"Hello," Elijah said curtly. "I think you and me need to have a talk."

"Do we?" Fate asked, sounding amused. She lowered her hands and interlaced her fingers as she said, "Then by all means, speak."

Elijah could feel Caprice and Stephen staring at him, but he ignored them. "Why me?" he asked the towering woman before him. "Huh? Did you just have it out for me or what? If my life was your idea of a joke, it was in pretty poor taste, lady."

"Oh my God," Caprice muttered, dropping her face into her hand.

Fate, however, didn't seem bothered in the least. In fact, she began to laugh.

"It was no joke," she promised Elijah with a lingering chuckle. "It was your life, as it was determined. Nothing more."

Elijah gave Fate a flat look and said, "Real easy for you to say. You didn't have to live any of it."

"I did through you," Fate said patiently. "Did you think I would roll your dice and leave you on your own?"

Elijah hesitated at that. Part of him was relieved someone had watched him throughout his entire life and knew exactly how much bullshit he'd been through. Being told God was watching over him was never much comfort while Elijah was alive. It was the sort of thing you told children to make them stop crying. Elijah didn't consider it to be a credible ray of hope for adults. So having Fate standing in front of him and assuring him she understood where he was coming from was unexpectedly good to hear.

But Elijah wasn't going to be won over that easily. "Is that it?" he asked. "I'm supposed to just shake your hand and tell you, 'Thanks a lot'? 'Cause I can think of a lotta times I coulda used more than somebody knowin' I was in trouble, and not doin' anything about it."

"Should I have lived your life for you, then?" Fate asked, her smile still warm and gentle. "That might defeat the purpose of having a life. At least, I would think so."

"Not real convinced mine was worth livin'," Elijah griped. He didn't even care that he sounded like a defiant five-year-old at the moment. After thirty-three years of nothing but what he saw as bad luck, he thought he'd earned a pout aimed at the woman who made sure his luck never changed.

"A very bitter sentiment," Fate mused. She moved her head as though looking Elijah over, but her eyes stayed closed. "However, it is certainly a sentiment I cannot begrudge. You must all define your own lives. I cannot do that for you."

"Whatever," Elijah said, watching Fate a bit warily by that point. It was getting harder and harder to stay angry with her, and he couldn't help but think of the stories where beautiful women with hardly any clothes on lured men to a horrible fate. Like the time a prostitute had tricked him and tied him to a bed before robbing him. "I'm a little surprised you let us in here," Elijah remarked, trying to just move on from that paranoid line of thinking. "You're kinda leavin' yourself open for people to come in here and tell you off, y'know."

"The Overhead Domain is controlled by only One," Fate replied cryptically. "Only He determines who may step where and when. I use my tools to lay forth your path, but my tools follow His will."

"I'm sorry," Caprice interjected politely, "I don't really understand. You determine what happens to us and what we do, but then again, you don't?" Fate smiled at her and gave a small shrug, which was, as far as Elijah was concerned, a bit weird coming from a goddess (or whatever it was Fate should have been called).

"Balance comes from multiple points," Fate explained. "The world is not so simple that it runs in a single line." She turned her face towards Time and said, "Even my husband's sands may be scooped up and rearranged by those with the ability and the wisdom to know better."

"So we can change the future," Stephen guessed. "Is that what you mean?"

"What is the future?" Fate asked, turning to Stephen and tilting her head. "Is it a picture carved into stone with a knife, or one which slowly forms beneath the flow of water, relying on the drops to make their own course and shape a pattern?"

"You always this vague?" Elijah asked rather flatly. Delilah tossed her head as if seconding his question.

"Yes," Fate laughed, "I am. Except when I am not."

"Oh, okay," Elijah said with a roll of his eyes. "That helps." Fate laughed again, and Elijah wondered why her laugh made him feel a little accomplished. It was the same kind of self-satisfaction he used to feel when he was younger and made his mother laugh.

"Why did you come to our domain?" Time asked then. He seemed even more somber standing next to his quietly amused wife. "What compelled you to seek our counsel?"

"Curiosity," Caprice said honestly. "Mr. Pritchett heard rumors about your realm from other riders, and I heard stories about you from the Ervonians before..." She trailed off there and looked mildly disturbed by what she was saying.

"Before your death," Time said to complete Caprice's sentence. Caprice hesitated, then nodded, and Time hummed thoughtfully. "Mysterious that you would travel here and yet be untouched by the madness which has claimed others who have explored our realm." He looked at Fate and said, "There is always a reason. What purpose of yours pulls them here?"

"Meetings and opportunities," Fate replied with a smile that was almost sly. With graceful motions, Fate walked over to Caprice and gently brushed her fingers over Caprice's cheeks.

"The lust of others shall be repaid with the vengeful lesson that beauty is not a sin which will absolve them of their crimes," Fate said gently.

Caprice stared at Fate, too stunned to say anything. Something in her expression had changed, however, and Elijah could tell that what Fate just said had an impact.

44

Once Fate was sure Caprice understood whatever she was imparting with that statement, she moved on to Stephen. Fate leaned down and rested her hands on Stephen's shoulders as she said, "Kings with no thrones may find hunger serves them well."

Stephen hesitated, but then nodded slowly, realization dawning on his face like it had on Caprice. With a satisfied smile, Fate straightened and then moved to face Elijah.

"You told me something on the gallows," Fate reminded him. "Though you called me by another name."

"I called you Lady Luck," Elijah said, looking around the chamber to appear uninterested. He actually was interested, but he was good at being difficult.

"That's right," Fate said in a reflective tone of voice. "I always did like that name."

Elijah smirked slightly and then noticed the other two were looking at him with questions in their eyes. For once, Elijah decided to give them what they wanted without a fight. "I told her I better get a chance to sit down with that Death guy," Elijah told Caprice and Stephen, "'cause I was sure I'd like him better than her." He went back to looking at nothing and muttered, "Least he gets things over with quick."

"That's not always true, is it?" Stephen asked, watching Elijah carefully. "Plenty of people die slowly."

"Their bodies might give out slowly, but the dyin' part is always quick," Elijah pointed out. He turned to look at Fate again. "So do I get to meet him or not?"

"You already have," Fate replied with a chuckle. "Though you may meet him again if you like."

"Gonna flip my coin and see what I choose?" Elijah asked dryly. Fate laughed again and shook her head as she spread her arms out in front of her.

"The coin's been tossed," she assured him. "Discover which side looks upwards."

Elijah pursed his lips as he considered it. He stood by what he said to Fate on the gallows, but anyone who told anyone they weren't intimidated by the concept of meeting Death face-to-face was a liar in Elijah's opinion. Elijah looked over at Stephen and Caprice, expecting them to look terrified that he would bring Death in to see them.

Instead he found them looking intensely curious. It was good to know he wasn't the only one with a complete lack of self-preservation when it came to doing something interesting.

"Looks like the side facin' up says I meet Death," Elijah said, looking back to Fate. "Unless he's busy."

"His work never ends," Fate reminded Elijah. "So long as there are beginnings, there will be endings. And as long as there is anything, there has been a beginning, which will need an ending."

"Sure," Elijah said slowly. He didn't want to make it too obvious her words were sailing right over his head. He really only understood about every other thing that came out of Fate's mouth. "So where do I find him?"

Fate smiled and tilted her head without saying a word. Elijah wasn't sure what to make of that response and was about to say as much, but the sound of wind coming from the corridor outside the fountain chamber made him stop short.

Elijah glanced at Delilah, who was surprisingly calm despite her earlier apprehension. Her eyes were still wide and alert, but she had stopped shaking. At that moment, she was staring towards the source of the sound in the hall. Elijah followed the horse's gaze back towards the passage just as a figure swept in through the entrance.

# Chapter 6

The man who entered the chamber was the same height as Time and Fate, and he wore a hooded robe of grey velvet which covered everything about him except the mask he wore on his face. It was a simple, curved plate of mirrored silver with no features whatsoever. It didn't even have openings for the wearer to see through.

But that wasn't anything special, Elijah thought. It didn't matter what was between those eyes and any living thing. Death would eventually find anyone and everyone.

The riders and horses watched as Death crossed the chamber, a massive scythe in his hand. The scythe stood nearly as tall as the Embodied, and the blade seemed to be made of the sharpened pieces of a giant clock. Once Death was right in front of the deceased group, he stopped and brought his scythe in front of him to grasp it with both hands. Then he simply stared at the riders with his blank, reflective face.

Elijah was a bit surprised Delilah and Shu weren't losing their minds in Death's presence. Wasn't Death supposed to make animals go insane with fear? Elijah was pretty certain he'd read that somewhere. Or heard about it.

"Hey," Elijah greeted, watching the grey figure warily.

There was a pause.

"I have to admit," Death said at last, "I expected a little more than that." His voice was deep and his tone was somewhat clipped. Unlike Time, whose speech was very paced and rhythmic, Death's was sharper and more final. Not quite impatient, but one certainly wouldn't want to push it.

"Uh, right, guess I shouldn't keep you, huh?" Elijah said, rubbing his neck. He stood up a bit straighter and looked right at Death's faceless stare as he said, "I just wanted to say thanks."

Caprice and Stephen looked at one another, but when they realized they were equally puzzled, they looked back to Elijah and Death.

"Oh?" Death asked. Elijah could almost picture him raising an eyebrow behind that mask. Assuming Death had a face at all, of course. "And why is that?"

"Sometimes endings are the best part of anything," Elijah said with a shrug. It might have sounded shockingly philosophical for someone like him, but he had spent a good portion of his life contemplating death in general. It never stopped being strange to him that so many people loved the beginning of life, and yet feared the ending of it. They always said birth was a natural and beautiful thing, but they never said the same about death. Elijah found that a little two-faced. Dying was a natural part of life as well, wasn't it?

Death watched Elijah in silence for a while before remarking, "You know, you and those like you have always fascinated me."

"Why's that?" Elijah asked. He was considerably more relaxed speaking with Death than he had been speaking with Time or Fate. Even Elijah could see how that was more than a little twisted, but he didn't really care.

"When the humans were created, it was understood the vast majority would cling to my wife, whom you call Birth," Death replied calmly. He glanced between the riders and added, "I take no offense. She gives life. I take it away. I don't know if you've noticed, but humans tend to have a problem with a little thing called faith. You only believe something is good if you can see it right in front of you. It's why so many of you fear me. But even amongst those who are not actually afraid of me, there has always been a very notable division. And I can show it to you by asking one simple question."

Death turned to look at Stephen then and asked him, "What would you say your goal in life was?"

Stephen hesitated, as if he wasn't entirely certain Death was actually addressing him. Once he was sure he was, Stephen said, "Respect, mostly. Recognition for the things I accomplished or helped accomplish."

"For the things you accomplished in life," Death clarified with a nod. He looked to Caprice next. "And you?"

"Love," Caprice replied without skipping a beat. "In any way I could get it."

Elijah was finding himself with a lot of new questions about both Stephen and Caprice in light of their responses and what Fate had said to them earlier, but it wasn't exactly the moment to ponder all of that.

"And now," Death said, turning back to Elijah. "Tell us what you lived for."

"Nothing," Elijah said plainly and honestly. He hadn't found a single thing in life worth living for up to the day he died. "I just got by."

"So in a way," Death mused, "you were living for the end result of meeting me. If you aren't reaching for something in life, then really, there's only one remaining option." He spread an arm out to the side, presenting himself. "And isn't that a strange thing to live for when you've been granted a life on a world made for you and your kind?"

Elijah considered it and then nodded with a shrug. It wasn't even something he could get insulted over, because it was just a cold, hard fact. And Elijah knew he wasn't the only person to have lived that way. Death gave a deep hum and then leaned forward towards Elijah.

"Is there anything else you'd like to chat about?" Death asked.

With Death's leaning closer, Elijah suddenly realized the silver mask Death wore wasn't reflecting the room or the things and people in it at all. As Elijah stared at the mask, he was shown one person dying after another. It was like the death of every person who had ever lived was being played as a moving picture on the polished metal. Some were sad. Some were horrific. Some were even funny. But every death was somehow intimate and personal, even though the ones Elijah saw were of strangers.

"You ever get tired of it?" Elijah asked after watching Death's face for a few moments. "Takin' lives, I mean. Seems like a thankless job."

"You thanked me just now," Death pointed out flatly. Elijah was starting to wonder if all the Embodied were smartasses.

"It's just that it seems like it'd wear on a guy after a while," Elijah went on after giving Death an unamused look. "Most everybody I know's scared of you, or thinks they should be. They associate you with somethin' bad."

"Thankfully, I'm blessed with a lack of concern of what your lot thinks of me," Death replied, standing straight once more.

49

"That must be nice, not caring at all what people think," Caprice said quietly. When Death looked at her, Caprice asked, "Do you know what it's like? Caring what people think, I mean." It was a genuinely interested question, and Death took a moment to seriously contemplate it.

"I can imagine what it must be like," Death answered at last, sounding thoughtful. "A lot of trouble, mostly. But so many of you are so determined to make your own trouble that it's hardly surprising you would add yet another thing to the pile." He looked at Elijah. "No offense. It's not something limited to humans."

"Good, I was pretty worried you were bein' racist just then," Elijah said dryly. Caprice and Stephen both had to stifle their laughter at that, but the surprising thing was Fate actually *did* laugh, and Death gave an amused sort of snort. Time didn't do any of those things, but Elijah was quickly learning Time didn't react to much of anything.

"So now you have met Death," Fate remarked to Elijah with a smile. "Are you satisfied with this meeting? Have you found you truly do hold more affection for him than you do for me?"

"It's been interesting," Elijah said simply. To be perfectly honest, actually meeting Fate face-to-face and speaking with her had altered his stance on her a bit. He felt oddly comfortable with all three of the Embodied that he had met so far. Elijah imagined it was because they weren't really strangers; this was simply the first time he'd seen them in personified form.

"While we have you all here," Caprice said, obviously choosing her words carefully, "I was wondering if I could ask you a few questions. You know, about all this."

"You may ask," Fate responded with a nod of her head. "We may not answer, but you may ask."

Caprice smirked a little at that response and asked, "Why is it that we look like we did when we were alive? You know; our clothes and things like that."

"You personify your 'self' when you're alive," Death pointed out. "Why is it surprising that you do the same when you're dead?"

"I always did love this outfit," Caprice mused, looking down at her ensemble. Stephen snorted and shook his head. Caprice turned her attention back to the Embodied and asked, "Can you tell us why we never see any dead people except for other riders?"

"For now you will keep to your own," Death replied. "This little quest of yours isn't meant for everyone. You must find your way through this before you find your way to anything else. That is the arrangement."

"So when can she get to see her husband?" Elijah asked evenly. Caprice and Stephen both looked at him in surprise, but he ignored them and simply watched Death, Fate, and Time for an answer.

Fate's eyebrows went up, though her eyes remained closed, as she turned her face towards Elijah. "Is this a relationship in which you have invested yourself?" she asked, sounding genuinely curious.

"No, she just misses him," Elijah replied with a shrug. "You'd miss your husband if he was separated from you, right?"

"The living worlds would crumble," Time said in solemn response.

"Well, there you go," Elijah said, satisfied he had made his point. "So you got a time frame?" He paused for a moment. "Wait, look who I'm askin'. 'Course you do."

The Embodied simply looked at him for a moment, and Elijah could tell Caprice and Stephen were wondering if Elijah could be banished to Hell for making jokes with them.

"When the trial is over, and the tasks have been assigned, then you will reunite with those from whom you have been segregated," Time said finally, his voice as even and deliberate as ever. "It will be when it will be."

"Now," Fate said, before Elijah could open his mouth again. She swept over to Elijah and loomed over him somewhat ominously. Then she looked upwards and seemed to be listening to something, but Elijah couldn't hear anything besides the breeze still wafting through the temple. Fate stayed that way for a moment before finally tilting her head back down so she was looking at Elijah. Or, rather, would have been if she opened her eyes.

"You have many choices ahead of you, Rider," Fate said. "Ones which will not only affect you, but worlds beyond your present comprehension." Her face still held that lovely and cryptic smile, but her voice was even deeper then. It gave Elijah an old, familiar feeling of impending doom. It was the feeling he always got when he was about to be presented with multiple options leading to varying degrees of bad outcomes.

"You are all on this journey together," Fate went on, slowly turning her head to make it clear she was addressing all three riders. "Not only you here, but everyone else along your paths."

"Are any of us three going to win this competition?" Caprice asked. Fate turned to face her and tilted her head.

"If I give you assurance you will triumph, will it comfort you?" Fate asked Caprice. "Or will it make you complacent, which in turn will change your destination?"

Caprice didn't seem to have an answer for that. Fate's smile widened slightly and she looked back to Elijah.

"Beyond this place, behind the stars, there is a realm of great significance," Fate told Elijah calmly. "One awaits you there, though he does not realize. Find him and turn the key."

"Why are you tellin' me this?" Elijah asked cautiously. "If I didn't know any better, I'd say you're tryin' to help."

"This was the way the dice fell," Fate replied. Elijah frowned at her, and Fate laughed. "Do not stretch a mind not created to reach the width of our purposes," Fate advised, which Elijah knew was a fancy way of telling him he was too stupid to get it. Then Fate folded her hands in front of her and took a step back, apparently giving Elijah and the others room to leave. "Behind the stars," she repeated.

Elijah stood there for a second, waiting to be sure that was it. When it was apparent it was, he looked at Delilah, and then shrugged and led his horse out of the fountain chamber. Caprice and Stephen were close behind him, with their respective steeds in tow.

Nothing was said as the riders departed. The Embodied simply stood there and watched them go. Just before he reached the corridor, Elijah looked back over his shoulder and saw that all three figures had vanished without a sound.

"Well, that was something," Caprice whispered. Elijah wasn't sure why the hell she was whispering, but it somehow seemed appropriate, so he simply nodded.

"Any of you got a clue what the hell she meant by 'behind the stars'?" Elijah asked, keeping his own voice down as well. Why did they feel like they had to be quiet?

"None at all," Stephen replied. "I was rather hoping you knew what she was talking about."

"I'm surprised he even knows how to stay on his horse," Caprice remarked. Stephen snorted, and Elijah shot them both filthy looks.

"You better hope I don't figure it out without you, 'cause I'll leave your asses here," Elijah snapped, though he was still trying to keep his voice quiet. Quiet for him, anyway. Caprice waved him off, and the group walked in silence until they were outside the temple.

# Chapter 7

Back out under the strange night sky, the three riders stood for a moment and simply looked up at the stars slowly drifting overhead. It was peaceful, but in a strange sort of way Elijah couldn't put his finger on. It was as if there was more going on beyond what they could see, and that it was all going perfectly according to plan.

"Right," Stephen said at last, breaking the silence. He mounted his motorcycle and added, "Suppose we should be off, then."

Caprice and Elijah blinked a few times as if trying to reset their trains of thought, and nodded. Once all three of them were back in the saddle, they started off. Admittedly it was in a randomly chosen direction, but they were off all the same.

The trio rode out through the courtyard of the Embodied's temple and back into the empty glass plain stretching beyond. None of them were entirely certain what it was they were supposed to be looking for. "Behind the stars," Fate had told them, but it didn't seem incredibly helpful quite yet. There wasn't anything to see behind the twinkling lights overhead, or beneath their reflections on the ground.

There was a long silence as Elijah, Caprice, and Stephen rode across the landscape of star-brushed black. They were all trying to concentrate as hard as possible on their surroundings, but it didn't make much difference. Even after it felt like they'd been riding for ages, they didn't come across anything. No landmarks, no change in the horizon, not even any signs of anyone else living there. The world remained quiet and still and a bit eerie.

...And really boring. Elijah was close to throwing his hat at Caprice just to give himself something to do. Before he could actually do it, however, Caprice brought Shu to a halt and said, "Wait a minute. Look."

"Look at what?" Elijah asked irritably. He stopped Delilah and turned in his saddle to look at Caprice. "All I see is darkness, stars, more darkness, and more damn stars."

"Well, I knew you thought a lot of us, Mr. Blanco, but I had no idea you considered us stars," Caprice remarked. Stephen laughed.

"What?" Elijah said with visible confusion.

"Never mind," Caprice said with a wave of her hand. She looked up and pointed towards the sky. "Look past the stars. There's something out there."

Both Elijah and Stephen looked up and squinted as they tried to see what Caprice was talking about. At first they couldn't find anything particular eye-catching, but then Elijah saw it. There was a strange shift in the darkness beyond the sparkles overhead. It was almost like looking through glass during the day and noticing a faint reflection if the angle was just right.

Apparently Stephen noticed it as well, because he asked, "What is that?"

"Can't tell," Elijah replied. He looked over at Caprice and tossed a hand up in exasperation. "Not sure how it's gonna help anyway. Sure, we can see somethin' up in the sky, but what the hell are we supposed to do with it? Throw somethin' and try and break it?"

"That's the thing," Caprice admitted. She rested one hand on her hip and continued staring skywards. "I don't know."

"No point in just standing here, then," Stephen said. "Let's keep going and see if there's some sort of way to get up there. We might not have found quite what we need yet."

Caprice didn't seem to be listening. Instead, she was staring up at the sky intently. Elijah and Stephen looked at one another, then up at the stars, trying to see if there was something else that had Caprice's attention. When they saw nothing new, they looked at Caprice again.

"Are the voices in your head giving you advice?" Stephen asked.

"Something's not right," Caprice said, more to herself than her companions.

"It's a little damn late to start reflectin' on what ain't right," Elijah pointed out. "We'll be here forever if we start that. Look where we're at, for God's sake."

"We really need to work on your English," Caprice remarked as she gave Elijah a very distasteful look. "It was cute at first, but now it's getting a bit sad." She locked her eyes right back on the space above and lifted one hand to tap her lips with a finger. "It just seems like there's something staring us right in the face."

"It's likely obvious to people who know what to look for," Stephen agreed. "But how are we expected to—"

He never finished that sentence, because what Caprice did next made his question completely obsolete. With one swift, confident motion, Caprice reached up towards the sky above, and Stephen and Elijah watched in shock as Caprice's hand went past the stars and took hold of something. As soon as she had it in her grasp, she pulled down what looked like a large sheet of glass. The twinkling lights—which Elijah then decided were only *possibly* stars—swept out of the way of the movement and then realigned themselves to where they wanted to be.

The pane of clear material Caprice pulled down from the sky was wide and tall, but the material seemed to be quite thin. It certainly looked like glass, but it wasn't like glass Elijah had seen in the past. Little shapes made of light slowly drifted along the surface with no particular purpose, shimmering softly.

"Seriously?!" Elijah griped, throwing his hand up in the air. "Just reach into nothin' and pull windows outta the sky?! That's the answer?!"

"Apparently," Stephen said, staring at the glass.

Caprice ignored both men and gently tapped the surface of the glass with a finger. The glowing shapes there suddenly swept away and were replaced by a series of images which showed different locations.

"It's a Smart Mirror," Caprice said with surprise.

"What the hell's a Smart Mirror?" Elijah asked.

"It's technology that uses a special glass as an interface for a computer," Caprice explained as she started navigating the images on the screen. Elijah stared at her, at a loss, then looked to Stephen.

"It's...complicated," Stephen said. He was obviously trying to think of a way to put it so Elijah would understand. "Do you know about phonographs?"

"Saw one once," Elijah replied slowly. "Wasn't like this."

"Right, but it's still a bit like that," Stephen assured him. "Computers are things that read and play recordings of information, like a phonograph reads and plays sound recorded on a record."

Elijah frowned. It looked a hell of a lot more complicated than that. But he simply nodded and hoped it seemed like he got it.

It clearly didn't, because Stephen smirked and said, "You didn't understand a word I just said, did you?"

"I understood 'phonograph'," Elijah said dryly. Did both of his impromptu companions have to be smartasses?

"I think this is a portal control system," Caprice said, still completely absorbed in what she was doing. "Look. All these pictures must be destinations you can select."

"How many choices are there?" Stephen asked curiously.

"From what I can see, hundreds," Caprice replied with a small frown. "I don't know which one we need."

"Move," Elijah ordered. Caprice looked at him in surprise, but obediently urged Shu to step away, leaving the glass hanging in the air. Elijah had Delilah take him over to the console, and he squinted at the glowing images on the screen.

"You can scroll through the selections by putting your finger on the glass and sliding it to the side," Caprice prompted. "To choose one of the destinations, tap the picture."

"This is stupid," Elijah grumbled.

What followed next was a fairly comedic series of attempts by Elijah to try and navigate the interface. He kept accidentally selecting things he didn't want, scrolling too far one way and then the other, altering the layout of the options, and he even once managed to toggle the display into a three-dimensional feature that nearly caused him to fall off Delilah in alarm.

"You're a sad man, Elijah Blanco," Caprice commented as Elijah pulled himself up to sit properly on Delilah's saddle again.

"Shut up," Elijah snapped. "Not all of us come from fancy times with this kinda nonsense."

"Why don't you have one of us do the scrolling and selecting, and you tell us what to do?" Stephen suggested. It had gone well beyond being sad to becoming apparent there was a real chance of never getting out of there.

"Just keep quiet and let me figure this out," Elijah demanded. Stephen looked at Caprice, who shook her head.

"There's no point in arguing with someone who's as stubborn as they are stupid," Caprice muttered to Stephen.

"I heard that," Elijah said darkly. Caprice just rolled her eyes while Stephen did his best not to laugh.

After what felt like an eternity, Elijah finally pulled up the selection he actually wanted. "This one," he said, pointing at the image. "We want this one." It was a picture of a vast desert with smooth, red dunes of sand. The sky overhead was a deep blue, with a pearl white moon hanging near the horizon.

"How do you know that's the one?" Caprice asked as she examined the picture. "Something about it stick out to you?"

"I used to have this weird dream all the time when I was alive," Elijah said, keeping his eye on the desertscape. "It was always set in that desert."

"So that's all you've got to go on?" Stephen said dubiously. "A recurring dream?"

"Don't be an idiot, there's more to it than that," Elijah said with a glare. "When Fate was talkin' to us, that image just popped in my head for no damn reason. I had all kinds of dreams when I was alive, but I haven't exactly been dwellin' on 'em since I died. So why did this one come to mind?"

Stephen looked over to Caprice to see what her opinion was, and she shrugged. "Fate works in mysterious ways," she pointed out.

"I thought that was 'God works in mysterious ways'," Stephen said.

"Well, who do you think made Fate?" Caprice asked. Stephen didn't have a response for that right off the bat, so Caprice turned her attention to Elijah and said, "It can't hurt to check it out, right?"

"Actually, it could," Elijah said nonchalantly. "It could be a horrible place of nothin' but pain and sufferin'."

"Was it in your dream?" Caprice asked, unruffled.

"No," Elijah admitted after a pause.

"Then let's go," Caprice said in a satisfied tone. Elijah looked at the glass for a moment and then looked at Caprice again. "Oh, for God's sake, that's right," Caprice said as she put a hand to her face. "You don't know how. Here, move over."

Elijah and Delilah moved to the side, and Caprice rode Shu back over to the screen. She tapped the image with a finger and then selected an affirmative answer when the glass asked her if she was certain. Next to the glass, a hole appeared in the air that was about twelve feet in height and eight feet in width. It was clearly a portal, seeing as how it opened into the same desert which had been displayed on the screen.

"After you," Caprice told Elijah lightly. Elijah leaned over in his saddle a bit to get a better look at the world beyond, then signaled Delilah forward.

# Chapter 8

Like all horses, Delilah had always possessed an amazing sense of situational awareness and a keen intuition. It was something even crossing over into the afterlife couldn't take away from her. Although she was finding herself going into stranger and stranger depths of worlds her horse mind had never conceived, she was still keyed into the things that mattered. The blessing of being a horse was she didn't spend much time worrying about things not obviously important at any given moment. So all Delilah was concerned about as she stepped through the portal and onto the desert sands was whether or not something was going to leap out and try to eat her and Elijah.

She couldn't see anything that would.

She couldn't smell anything that would.

She couldn't hear anything that would.

So Delilah walked out into the strange desert obediently and resolved to keep aware just in case, since the moron on her back was pretty hopeless as a sentinel half of the time. There was a reason he trusted the important things to Delilah. Elijah knew for a fact Delilah was thinking all of that right then.

It wasn't as warm in the desert realm as the riders expected it to be. In fact, the weather was rather pleasant. The sands constantly shifted by the work of a cool wind sweeping over the dunes, making them almost seem alive. There was no sun Elijah could see, but it was bright enough to be daytime. Not even the full moon hanging low in the sky should have given off that much light.

Caprice, Stephen, and Elijah all looked around for a moment, soaking in the sights, and then finally set off into the quiet landscape. They weren't certain what they were supposed to be looking for, or what direction they needed to be going, so they simply rode straight ahead to see what they'd find along the way.

"Where do you think this is?" Caprice asked as she looked around. "A living planet or somewhere else?"

"I won't even try and guess," Stephen replied with a shake of his head.

They were only riding for a little while before they spotted something on a hill of sand in the distance. It was a massive black horse that was staring right at them. Its long mane and tail streamed out around it in the wind, and when it knew the riders were looking at it, the horse tossed its head as if beckoning them. The three riders hesitated for a moment before finally heading in the horse's direction. They had definitely seen stranger things, but it was still odd.

"Still like that dream I had," Elijah muttered as he and the others continued towards the horse. "Except I was alone."

"Maybe you actually came here via astral projection," Caprice said thoughtfully.

"What's that?" Elijah asked with a small frown.

"It's when you have an out-of-body experience during which you go to another place," Caprice explained. "Like visiting with nothing but your mind."

Elijah opened his mouth to say something, but then thought about it and shrugged, nodding his head. Honestly, at that point, it didn't sound terribly outrageous.

"If that's the case, I can tell you it only gets weirder from here," Elijah remarked. Caprice smirked slightly and Stephen chuckled.

"Not real comforting, Elijah," Stephen said.

No one in the group spoke as they approached the horse. The beast watched them with black eyes which looked more like polished marbles than anything on a living creature, and its gaze set Elijah somewhat on-edge. Most intelligent animals watched people in a thoughtful and careful sort of way, but this black horse had the cold, hard stare of someone bitter and critical. Why was it looking at them like that?

Once the three riders were several feet away from the black horse, they stopped and simply stared at it in silence. They all stayed that way for quite some time, and then the black horse actually spoke.

"Travelers of six," it remarked in a deep, rhythmic voice. "I saw you in the sands, as I saw the two awaiting."

"Six?" Stephen echoed. "Does that mean you're counting the horses and the bike, then?"

"All are counted," the horse replied. The three humans looked at one another and Caprice gave a little shrug.

"So who are you supposed to be?" Elijah asked, looking back to the horse.

"Who?" the horse echoed. It was honestly a bit difficult to tell where he was looking thanks to his doll-like eyes, which Elijah found slightly unsettling. "Not who. Where."

"Okay," Elijah said slowly. He looked around and then back to the horse. "Where are you?"

"Here," the horse answered, his voice still very plain.

"I know you're here, but where is here?" Elijah insisted with a growing frown.

"This place," was the simple and unruffled reply.

"But where is this place?" Elijah demanded, definitely ruffled.

"Where Here is."

"What?!" Elijah barked, throwing his hand up in frustration. Stephen put a hand over his face and Caprice decided to intervene before Elijah could try his hand at punching horses.

"Here," she said to the horse politely. "Can you tell us what we're looking for?"

"Two more travelers," Here replied. "The puzzle will not be solved until the eight convene."

"You mean us plus this other bloke and his horse," Stephen guessed.

"Time brings what Fate gives," Here said calmly.

"Don't anybody speak English around here?" Elijah groused. It felt like everyone spoke in riddles, and he was getting tired of it.

"You can barely speak English, so I don't see why you're complaining" Caprice said under her breath.

"Look, just tell us which way the other rider went," Elijah said to Here, pointedly ignoring the woman. "Or is that too damn hard for you?"

"Over the dunes and for the upward fall," Here said, still completely unmoved by Elijah's attitude.

"I guess it's too damn hard for you," Elijah said with another frustrated toss of his hand.

"Elijah?" Caprice said, but Elijah went on pretending he couldn't hear her. She was looking off to the side at something or other, and since she had displayed an occasional habit of staring at nothing like a cat, Elijah didn't think anything of it.

"I'm gettin' real sick of the people in this afterlife," Elijah went on ranting. "You all act like there's some grand scheme, but God forbid you actually let people in on it!"

"Elijah," Caprice tried again, but with as little success as before.

"It don't make you look wise, it makes you look like an asshole," Elijah declared.

"Elijah!" Caprice snapped, reaching over and slapping at his shoulder lightly. Elijah finally looked at her with a sharp glare.

"What?!" he demanded. Caprice just pointed where she was looking. Elijah followed her silent direction and his expression shifted from one of irritation to one of surprise.

"What the hell is that?" he blurted out. Off in the distance a steady stream of sand was pouring up into the sky, where it pooled and dissipated into nothing. It was a bit like watching the sand fall through an hourglass, except it was falling up instead of down.

"Do you think Here meant that?" Stephen asked Elijah with a quirked eyebrow. Elijah decided to ignore him too and signaled Delilah forward. Both Stephen and Caprice could stay there and talk to Here forever for all Elijah cared.

Stephen and Caprice both went after Elijah, though they were polite enough to say goodbye to Here first. Elijah ignored that fact as well and kept his eyes locked on the rising sand up ahead.

Who the hell named a horse "Here" anyway?

# Chapter 9

"I take it your dream didn't prepare you for that conversation," Stephen commented once he and Caprice caught up with Elijah. "Seeing as how you didn't quite handle it like a man who knew what was coming."

"I don't remember all the details of the dream," Elijah spat. "I remember the horse, but I don't remember the horse bein' a conversational jackass."

Both Stephen and Caprice burst out laughing at that reply. "Conversational jackass!" Caprice echoed, thoroughly amused. "I'm going to have to use that one someday."

As they got closer to the upward spout of sand, the riders noticed a man near it with his sorrel horse at his side. It was the Roman soldier Elijah had noticed when they all met the Angel. The soldier was sitting on the ground, staring up at the rising sand in silence. His helmet was off and resting on his lap, and he seemed to be lost in a trance. He didn't even look over as Elijah, Stephen and Caprice rode right up to him. His horse noticed, however, and she looked over and bobbed her head as if greeting them. She was a large and lovely animal, and Elijah could tell she was bred for hard work. It was no wonder she was a warrior's horse.

"Excuse me," Caprice said to the soldier politely. "I believe we were meant to come and find you."

The man didn't respond at first, but Caprice was hardly bothered. She simply kept watching him patiently with a very relaxed stature. Elijah supposed it was better to let Caprice handle that particular social situation, because he would have already been demanding an acknowledgment if it was left up to him.

Finally the man stirred and said, "Yes. I suppose you were."

He turned his head and looked up at Caprice, and then looked at Stephen and Elijah in turn.

"A strange fellowship," the soldier remarked. Elijah looked at Caprice and Stephen, and then shrugged and nodded. He couldn't argue with that commentary.

"If you mean his hat," Stephen said to the stranger, pointing at Elijah, "we completely agree with you. We've been trying to get him to get rid of it." Caprice laughed, and the Roman actually snorted. Elijah was far less amused and shot Stephen a glare. To be perfectly honest, Elijah was just relieved it was clear the stranger's remark wasn't said with any sexist or racist implications. He'd had to listen to that sort of bullshit regarding mixed company all too often while he was breathing. He didn't plan on putting up with it post-mortem.

But since he wasn't going to have to stick up for his companions, Elijah was absolutely prepared to turn on them for judging the way he dressed.

"I am Theocritus Atius," the soldier said before Elijah could start ranting about how practical his hat was.

"It's a pleasure," Caprice said with a smile. "My name is Caprice DeGaglia." She indicated the men next to her. "This is Stephen Pritchett and Elijah Blanco." Then she leaned forward in her saddle and patted Shu's neck. "And of course, this is Shu. The lady carrying Mr. Blanco is Delilah, and Mr. Pritchett is riding...um..."

"I call her Cleopatra," Stephen supplied.

"Oh, that's sort of funny," Caprice said. "I named my horse after an Egyptian god and you named yours after an Egyptian queen."

"This is Benedicta," Theocritus said, nodding to his horse.

"A blessing," Caprice translated with a smile. "She must be very wonderful to earn a name like that."

"It has always seemed the Gods smile upon her," Theocritus agreed as he looked up at Benedicta. The horse shifted her weight placidly, watching the newcomers with interest. At least she apparently didn't consider them a threat, Elijah thought.

"So what are you doing here, then?" Stephen asked. He was back to looking at the sand, which continued its silent stream into the atmosphere. "Just enjoying the scenery?"

"Something waits within," Theocritus replied dourly, following Stephen's gaze. "Something that must be unlocked."

"So what're you waitin' for?" Elijah asked. He looked away from the fountain of sand to watch Theocritus. "Unlock it."

The soldier didn't reply, simply continuing to observe the sand. Caprice frowned softly and tilted her head. "You don't know how, do you?" she asked in a gentle tone.

"I have known for some time that I was not to be the one to unlock it," Theocritus replied with a sigh. "I have come to wonder why I was brought here at all."

"Fate's got a real funny way of workin'," Elijah informed Theocritus dryly. Elijah still wasn't Fate's biggest fan. Meeting her had been interesting and somewhat enlightening, but Elijah was an expert when it came to holding a grudge. "Sometimes you don't know why anything's happenin' until it's too late for knowin' to make any difference. And you're left waitin' years for help to come along."

"I am hardly seeking assistance," Theocritus said, sounding a bit offended. "I meant why I was brought here for more struggle and war."

"You were looking for a little rest after death, weren't you?" Caprice guessed sympathetically. "I'm sorry."

Once again, Theocritus didn't reply. Elijah rolled his eyes and said, "Oh, come on."

"Elijah," Caprice scolded, staring at him.

"No, just hang on," Elijah insisted, waving Caprice off. He pointed at Theocritus. "What, you think you're the only one who was lookin' forward to a long sleep in the ground? Get in line. That don't give you an excuse to sit around and feel sorry for yourself."

Theocritus turned to glare up at Elijah hard. "I would advise you to choose your next words carefully," Theocritus said. Elijah was hardly deterred.

"Oh, I am," Elijah said irritably. "I'm real sick of people like you. You all right with rollin' over and goin' to Hell? Fine. But get the hell outta the way so you don't hold the rest of us up."

Theocritus got to his feet, and Caprice slowly raised a hand to put it over her eyes in exasperation. Stephen offered Elijah a sarcastic thumbs-up and then shook his head. But Elijah was back to ignoring his two companions, so he just watched Theocritus stand up to face him.

"And who are you to speak so confidently of things you clearly do not understand?" Theocritus asked with a dangerous edge to his voice. His tone made it clear he had been a commander when he was alive, but Elijah wasn't that easy to intimidate.

"Who says I don't understand?" Elijah asked, keeping a steady gaze right into the other man's eyes. "Not givin' a damn don't have a thing to do with understandin'. If you wanna sit and feel sorry for yourself, that's your business, but let's get the important shit outta the way first." He pointed to the sand. "What do we need to do with that?"

Theocritus glared at Elijah hatefully for a while, and it wasn't until Caprice gently said, "Please," that he responded.

"I have been told something beneath this stream waits to be unlocked," Theocritus said, tearing his eyes away from Elijah to speak to Caprice instead. "There is a structure within the sand, but I have not been able to discern its function."

Stephen stepped off his bike then. He flipped the kickstand down and left the motorcycle to go have a closer look at the skyward-falling sand. Caprice dismounted Shu and went to follow Stephen, but Elijah stayed where he was, opting to simply watch for the time being.

Stephen leaned in close to the sand and squinted as he tried to see through the stream. Finally he gave up on developing the ability to see between grains of sand, and reached out to part the rising sand with his hands. Caprice peered over Stephen's shoulder as he blocked enough of the sand to reveal a large stony surface with strange markings.

"What is it?" Elijah asked, leaning in the saddle to see what Stephen had uncovered.

"It's some sort of...oh, what's the word?" Stephen muttered, frowning.

"Column?" Caprice offered helpfully.

"No, that's not it," Stephen said with a shake of his head. "I mean, yes, that's what this is, but that's not the word I was thinking of. Hell, this is going to bother me..."

"Did anyone tell you how you're supposed to unlock it?" Caprice asked Theocritus as she kept staring at the massive, carved rock behind the sand.

"No," Theocritus replied. "But I have made a number of various attempts."

"What sort of attempts?" Stephen asked. He slowly moved his hands to get a better look at different parts of the column, trying to find some sort of clue.

"Spoken words, specific pressures on various points, turning the entire column, prying apart the cracks..." Theocritus trailed off and shook his head. "None of my attempts have had any sort of effect on the structure at all."

Caprice hummed thoughtfully and put a hand to her lips as she studied what she could see of the column. "Strange," she murmured.

"Let me look," Elijah said, swinging off Delilah and dropping to the ground.

"Going to shout at this too?" Stephen asked flatly.

"If I think it'll work, maybe," Elijah shot back. He barged his way past Stephen and put his hands into the sand to part it like Stephen had. The column seemed to be made of one giant piece of sandstone. There were the markings which looked like cracks at first glance, but Elijah couldn't see any part of the stone that had been pieced together. For some reason he had a mental image of the stone growing out of the ground like a tree and being shaped by the rising sand over time. He wasn't sure why. That was an odd thing to think.

"So what happens next in your dream?" Stephen asked Elijah.

"I could never remember the part after the weird horse," Elijah replied as he scratched his head. "I only know that it's weird and that I always wake up sweatin'."

"Helpful," Stephen said. "You think—"

Before he could finish his question there was a rumble from within the column, and some of the markings began to shiver within the stone. It was very brief, but it had all four of the riders staring at the column with wide, alarmed eyes.

"You see that?" Elijah asked without looking away.

"Yes," the other three replied in unison. Caprice glanced back at the horses and found them all staring as well, their ears pricked forward anxiously.

"I've got a bad feeling," she whispered. "Maybe we should leave it alone."

"Don't get yellow on me now," Elijah said, though he sounded distracted. He leaned in a bit closer to the stone and moved one hand so he could touch one of the markings with his index finger. "The hell are you?" he muttered to the column.

The stone rumbled again, louder this time, and all of the markings began to shift their position. Elijah pulled back, startled, letting the sand resume its steady climb into the sky unobstructed. However, the noise didn't stop, and even started to get louder. The four humans quickly moved back, and the three horses began nervously prancing in place.

"Did it ever do this before?" Elijah asked Theocritus over the roar.

"I should think the surprise written on my face would answer that question before you ask it!" Theocritus said as he stared at the fountain of sand.

"Simple 'yes' or 'no' wouldn't kill you!" Elijah griped.

Before Elijah could complain any further, the ground began to quake. Despite his anxiety, Elijah had the presence of mind to wonder how Caprice managed to stay on her feet in her ridiculously high, wedged shoes. He would have been impressed if she didn't irritate him quite so much. The horses were nothing short of panicked at that point, but they didn't run. Elijah was far more impressed by that than Caprice's agility.

"Now what?!" Stephen yelled over the rumbling as he struggled to keep his balance. "Elijah! Any of that dream coming back to you yet?!"

"If it was, don't you think I'd be doin' somethin' besides this?!" Elijah demanded. "I think—"

They never got to hear what Elijah was thinking. The surface beneath them abruptly stilled, as did the stream of sand. For a moment, all of the sand that had been rising in the air was completely frozen in place, like it was nothing more than a picture. Then without warning, the suspended sand dropped to the ground, revealing the column completely.

# Chapter 10

The column previously hidden by the rising sand was extremely tall. It climbed all the way up into the sky, just like the sand that had been concealing it. Far above, where the sand had pooled, the column flattened and extended out like a parasol overhead. The markings in the stone began to shift, and they arranged themselves in bizarre geometric patterns. Once they stopped moving, the lines in the column pulsed with an orange glow.

"What is it?" Caprice breathed after a moment of silence.

"Haven't a damn clue," Stephen replied. He looked at Theocritus. "Anyone tell you all that would happen?"

"No," Theocritus replied, unable to look away from the structure before them. "I was told nothing beyond it must be unlocked. And that it would pave the way to the finish."

The riders went back to staring at the stone in silence for a while.

"So let's do a quick review," Caprice suggested finally. "We've come to a strange desert, met a Roman soldier, and uncovered a strange pillar umbrella."

"Pillar," Stephen said, snapping his fingers. "That was the word I was trying to think of."

"And now we don't know what to do with the pillar umbrella," Caprice went on. "Does that sound about right?"

"Anybody think they can climb this?" Elijah asked.

"Sorry, left all my gear back in the world of the living," Stephen said dryly. "Feel free to give it a go with your hands and feet, though."

Elijah started walking around the column, looking it over thoughtfully. It was at least thirty-five feet in diameter, so there was plenty to see. Caprice and Theocritus took to wandering around it as well, while Stephen stayed in one spot and squinted up at the part of the pillar overhead. The horses had calmed down by that point, but they were still on high alert. Everything was quiet, but it didn't seem entirely safe yet.

"Hey, look at this," Caprice said suddenly. The others went over to her and found her pointing at a particular marking in the surface of

70

the pillar. It glowed like the other etchings, but in a pale green light rather than an orange one. Also unlike the others, its shape had curves rather than sharp lines and angles.

"Looks a bit like the arches back at that temple," Stephen commented.

"Speaking of," Caprice said, looking to Theocritus, "I forgot to ask. Did you meet the Embodied? Fate, Time, Death? Any of them?"

"I met a woman who called herself Birth," Theocritus replied. "She came to me in another world and spoke to me of this place."

"What was she like?" Stephen asked curiously. "We didn't meet anyone called Birth."

"Her laugh was like music," Theocritus said almost wistfully. "And she laughed often. Her hair was long, and brown like the earth, and wherever she stepped, delicate flowers began to grow."

"Where'd you meet her?" Elijah asked. He wondered why Birth hadn't been at the temple with the other Embodied, but he wasn't going to ask any of the people there with him at the moment. They'd most likely give him some smartass remark.

"In a field," Theocritus replied. "Since there was no ferryman, I sought out the places in which I had always been told the dead belonged. I wanted to see if I would find peace and rest there. She found me and told me there was still much to do. She said no death is the end of life."

"And she told you to come here?" Caprice asked with genuine interest. Elijah could tell Caprice found Theocritus fascinating. She must have been into Ancient History when she was alive, Elijah thought. He wondered if her husband would be jealous.

"She told me of a place called the Desert of Knowing," Theocritus said, turning his gaze back to the column as he reflected. "She told me of the rising sand which hid a stage to be unlocked. Though she warned me I would have to be patient. She said answers do not always present themselves in our preferred timing."

"Never been one for patience," Elijah piped up as he stepped towards the column.

"You know, he might not be done," Caprice said to Elijah, sounding vaguely irritated. Elijah ignored her and reached out to touch the glowing green mark on the stone. The column itself was warm to the touch, but the crack seemed to be expressing cool air from within.

"Weird," Elijah muttered to himself. He stooped down to see if he could see anything inside the carving, but all he could see was that sickly green light.

"What else did Birth tell you?" Caprice asked Theocritus. She was clearly giving up on corralling Elijah for the moment.

"That I should not seek endings so eagerly, because they are only mirrored beginnings," Theocritus replied a bit dourly. Caprice tilted her head and was about to ask him something else, but she was interrupted by a flash and a yelp from Elijah.

Elijah had been poking his fingers into the marking on the column to see if he could...well, make much of anything happen. It was clear they were meant to do something with the giant stone, but he wasn't sure what, so he was making wild guesses. Either he had been on the right track, or the pillar hadn't cared much for all the prodding, because the marking in the stone suddenly widened and the light became more intense.

If anyone had pointed out the fact that Elijah had just made a rather less-than-adult sound, he would have denied it up and down. Luckily for him, the others were more interested in the pillar than in his dignity.

"How did you do that?" Stephen asked Elijah as he frowned at the column.

"Just stuck my fingers in there," Elijah said, scratching his head. "It opened right up."

Caprice made an odd choking sound, and Stephen and Theocritus both gave her puzzled looks as she put a hand over her mouth and shook with stifled laughter. Elijah, however, kept his attention on the stone. After thinking about it for a while, he reached out and touched the edges of the mark again. Then he went about trying to pull apart the edges to see if he could make it wider.

It worked. The mark grew until it was larger than Elijah, who scrambled back and away from the stone, just to be safe. The riders and horses stared as the mark continued to grow larger and larger, spreading over the pillar and pushing the other carvings in the surface out of the way as it formed a massive doorway of sorts. The sight wasn't particularly loud or frightening, but it certainly was unsettling.

"Is this good or bad?" Elijah asked Stephen, though he didn't look away from the column.

"Don't think it's good *or* bad," Stephen replied. "Just weird."

"Weird's never good," Elijah proclaimed. Weird generally meant problems, or things Elijah didn't know how to handle. He didn't much care for either.

"Maybe not in your experience," Caprice said. She had to tilt her head back even more than the men to see from beneath her hat, and she was holding onto the hat to keep it from falling off. Naturally *she* would find weird an acceptable thing, Elijah thought.

Once the mark on the stone halted its growth spurt it looked like it was meant to be an entry into the column, but it was a bit excessive. Elijah figured its new height to be over twenty feet high and ten feet wide at that point. Despite its size, however, the group still couldn't see anything within the mark except for the green light. The riders and horses watched the pillar in heavy silence for a moment to make sure nothing else was going to happen.

"Just so you know! It's still weird!" Elijah called out to whatever higher powers he assumed were watching. "Still don't make sense! So thanks for nothin'!"

Everything fell into silent stillness once again, and the four riders frowned and looked at one another.

"What now?" Theocritus asked with a frown.

Stephen looked at Elijah and jerked his head in the direction of the light-filled mark in the pillar. "Go on, then," he encouraged.

"The hell—why me?" Elijah asked, rather shocked. "You go!"

"It's only been reacting to you!" Stephen reminded Elijah pointedly. "I can't speak for everyone, but I don't care to stand here staring for the rest of eternity. So if we have some sort of idea of what it is this thing wants, well, then..."

"Glad I'm so convenient for you idiots," Elijah said darkly. Despite his irritation with the situation, he marched back up to the stone. The others trailed behind him slowly, looking up and around the pillar as they went. Even the horses seemed interested in what would happen next, judging by the way they followed after the four humans.

"You see how deep this thing goes?" Elijah asked the group as he squinted at the green light.

"I can't really tell," Caprice admitted. "The light makes it impossible."

"Bit strange," Stephen murmured. "It's not as though it's all that bright."

Elijah contemplated everything in silence for a bit. The others glanced between Elijah and the mark, waiting to see what he'd do next.

The answer came in the form of Elijah walking into the mark.

"Elijah!" Caprice yelped, alarmed. "What are you doing?!"

Elijah pointedly ignored Caprice and disappeared into the light. He half-expected to walk smack into the stone, but he didn't. Instead he ended up standing in an empty space, surrounded by the pale green glow. Elijah blinked a few times and looked around, turning to get a complete view. It wasn't impressive. There was nothing to see but the light around him.

"You hear me?" Elijah called out to the others. He tilted his head to listen, but heard no response. Had he been transported somewhere else?

That was when it occurred to Elijah he couldn't see the way back out into the desert, and he couldn't help but wonder if he should be concerned. It was a bit hard to be concerned when it was so nice and quiet in there.

But then it hit him that he'd left Delilah back there with those idiots.

"Damn it!" Elijah said, slapping a hand over his eyes. He really needed to start thinking shit through.

# Chapter 11

Elijah explored the empty space with a lot less caution than he probably should have. It was fairly obvious he wouldn't be getting back to the others for a while, so he was better off doing what he'd gone in there for in the first place: figuring out what the hell he and the others were supposed to do.

"Well?" Elijah called out to the green void around him. "You wanted me to come in here, right? Not like I got a lot to do now, so might as well get this over with."

Nothing happened at first, but when Elijah turned to look behind him for about the fiftieth time, a pedestal of pastel green marble appeared. Interested, Elijah walked over to it. The pedestal stood about chest-high, allowing him to look at the top surface. A piece of glass was set there with glowing letters scrolling across it, though it wasn't in a language Elijah recognized. Next to the glass on the marble surface was a key resting in a lock. The top of the key pointed to an engraving that said, "BEFORE," though apparently it could be turned to an engraving that said, "AFTER."

After examining everything he could, Elijah looked around once more. Mysterious podiums with keys and foreign languages didn't count as a proper response to his earlier request.

"That it?" Elijah asked the nothingness. There was no reply.

But after another pause, there was a shift in the light next to Elijah, and suddenly Caprice was leaning through it. She didn't come all the way inside, and Elijah could see Stephen's hands holding onto her waist. Damn it, maybe he should have thought of having someone do that with him when he went inside the column.

"There you are!" Caprice said, tilting her head back to look at Elijah from beneath her hat. Her eyes were wide with worry, which was quickly turning into aggravation. "What the hell!"

"Come here and see if you can read this," Elijah ordered. Caprice drew her head back slightly in surprise.

"You can't just disappear without warning and then boss me around as soon as I find you again!" Caprice said, rather insulted. But she then looked at the pedestal by Elijah and asked, "What's that?"

"You gonna stand there all day or come and help me figure this out?" Elijah asked impatiently. Caprice made a face and pulled away from Stephen's grip to step closer, though she did take one of Stephen's hands in hers to be safe.

When Stephen felt Caprice moving away, he leaned in just enough to stick his head through the light and asked, "Everything all right?"

"Yes, we're fine," Caprice replied distractedly as she focused on the pedestal. "Don't come all the way in yet." She grabbed Elijah's jacket, clearly intending to yank him along if Stephen pulled her back to safety. Or, at least, what she perceived as being safety. Elijah wasn't convinced it was any safer out in the desert than it was in the green chamber.

"What the hell—let go of me!" Elijah said, trying to shove Caprice's hand away. "How many times I gotta tell you I ain't your husband?!" Caprice ignored him and kept a firm grip on both Elijah and Stephen as she examined the object in front of her.

"This looks like Greek," Caprice commented regarding the words on the podium's screen. She looked to Stephen and said, "See if Theocritus knows how to read Greek."

"Shouldn't we be able to read it even if it is?" Stephen asked with a frown. "I've been able to read and understand everything since crossing over."

"It didn't look like this before," Elijah interjected. Caprice and Stephen looked at him, and Elijah pointed to the podium's glass. "These words," Elijah emphasized, "they didn't look like that before you came in here."

"What did they look like?" Caprice asked, puzzled.

"Just scribbles," Elijah replied. He scratched his head and gave Caprice a shrug. "Maybe it's not actually words."

"Let's have Theocritus come and look anyway," Caprice suggested. She looked to Stephen and nodded to encourage him to go ahead and ask. Stephen pulled his head back and there was a slight pause before he leaned through again.

"All right," Stephen said, "He's going to come through and take your hand, then I'll take his hand, that way you can go in a bit further."

"This is stupid, just come inside," Elijah said in irritation. "We're already dead, remember?"

"Just," Caprice began, but she never finished her thought, choosing instead to make a frustrated sound and watch for Theocritus. Elijah wondered if Caprice would've shot him if she'd had a gun with her.

Theocritus finally stepped into the chamber of light, and Caprice released Stephen's hand to take Theocritus's, who in turn took Stephen's with his other hand.

Like kids going to school, Elijah thought.

Theocritus looked down at the podium and frowned. "I thought Stephen said this was Greek," he remarked. Caprice and Elijah looked at the scrolling inscriptions and found that the language had shifted again, and this time into a language they could read without help.

"Well, that's odd," Caprice murmured. Elijah frowned. He was getting the distinct feeling someone was toying with them.

"Can he read it?" Stephen asked as he leaned back in to check on their progress.

"We all can now," Caprice replied with a shrug. She looked back down at the screen. "Maybe it was a translation software glitch."

Stephen snorted, and Theocritus looked at Caprice blankly before turning that look to Elijah.

"Don't look at me," Elijah said, holding up his free hand in defense. "I never know what the hell she's talkin' about."

"So what's it say?" Stephen asked in an obvious attempt to try and keep them all on-topic.

"It is difficult to read when the words are in motion," Theocritus said. He was squinting at the glass, trying to keep up with the moving letters. Just like Elijah, he wasn't accustomed to words that moved.

Caprice, however, was apparently plenty accustomed to scrolling words. She took one look at the glass and said, "It looks like a user manual." She glanced at Elijah and Theocritus. "That's a set of instructions telling you how to use something."

"And?" Elijah said impatiently. This was getting boring, fast.

"It says if the game is to change, the key must be turned," Caprice said, reading the text with a frown.

"It must be referring to this," Theocritus remarked, gesturing to the switch on the pedestal. "But what does it mean by changing the game? What will happen?"

"It doesn't say," Caprice replied with an exasperated sigh. "Guess we're supposed to change it and find out."

"I'm not sure I like that," Stephen said apprehensively.

"So, what, you reckon we should just stand around and talk about what might happen?" Elijah asked Stephen flatly. "There's already been enough talkin' and not enough actin', in my opinion."

"*This* is not enough acting for you?" Caprice asked, exasperated. "Going into unknown worlds, finding weird devices, solving mysteries? For God's sake, Elijah, we've been following a trail of breadcrumbs since we died. What more do you want?"

Elijah responded by reaching out and turning the switch.

The other three would likely have suffered aneurysms if they hadn't already been dead. Elijah thought Caprice's face was going to actually split in two for a moment.

"Have you lost your goddamn mind?!" Caprice shouted as she grabbed Elijah by his lapels and shook him hard. So much for holding hands.

Before Elijah could respond, or wrestle Caprice off him, there was a flash above the pedestal, and a small figure made of golden light appeared above the glass. It looked like a miniature version of the Angel who had spoken to the dead when they first arrived. The projected image looked at the four riders, and then suddenly grew to over seven feet tall. It remained suspended above the pedestal and gave the humans a hard stare.

"You have chosen to escalate the game to the next phase," the Angel's voice boomed. "Confirmation is required to proceed."

The riders looked at one another. That was more than a little ominous, but Elijah could tell the other three were on the same page he was. They'd put in a lot of effort and taken some pretty massive risks to get to that point, so it was far too late to back out and say they didn't want to see what would happen next. In unspoken agreement, the four riders looked back to the Angel's image with similar expressions of determination.

"Confirmed," Caprice said decisively.

The Angel nodded solemnly and then winked out of sight. Nothing else happened quite yet, however, which made the riders' tense silence rather anticlimactic.

"Is that all?" Stephen asked cautiously, looking around.

"I am certain it is not," Theocritus replied as he continued staring at the place the Angel's image had been. He looked at Stephen and added, "Things here are never so simple."

"Well, I doubt we're supposed to just stay here," Elijah remarked. He turned and walked up to Stephen, and then turned sideways to edge around him and back into the desert. Caprice and Theocritus were close behind him, and Stephen pulled back out of the column completely once everyone else was out. As soon as he stepped out of the green light, Elijah found Delilah staring at him curiously. He gave her a shrug and walked over to her.

"Don't worry," Elijah told Delilah as he took her reins. "You didn't miss much."

Those words were barely out of his mouth when there was a deafening sound. Elijah wasn't sure how to describe it other than it sounded like a garbled and lower pitched train whistle. Whatever it was, it had him nearly jumping out of his skin. It equally startled the other riders and the horses, and they all began looking around frantically for the source of the sound.

"What the hell is that?!" Elijah yelled over the noise.

"Sounds like the game is on!" Stephen answered in kind. He ran over to his motorcycle and swung himself onto it as Caprice and Theocritus mounted their horses. "Time to figure out how to play!" Stephen added.

# Chapter 12

The four riders and their steeds raced back to the Hub on something of a whim. When asked, none of them could really say why their first instinct was to return to that place in particular, but when they arrived, Elijah and the others discovered they weren't the only ones who had felt that pull. All the dead riders were returning, and those who had arrived first were standing and looking around in varied mixtures of curiosity and confusion.

Once the stream of people and their beasts of burden trickled to a halt, the siren, or whatever the hell it was, went quiet. Its work must have been done, Elijah thought.

The group wasn't left to sit and wonder for long, because soon after the last rider entered the Hub, a vortex appeared in the air and opened the way for the Angel they'd seen at the beginning of the competition. He stepped out of the swirling lights, looking far more menacing than he had the first time the riders met him. His armor pulsed with a brilliant white light, and there was an ominous red light piercing through the slits of his helmet.

Elijah couldn't help but wonder if he and the others had made a mistake in turning that key.

"The next phase has begun," the Angel announced in a thundering voice. "The key has been turned, and what switch has been thrown cannot be pulled back."

"What key?" someone asked, completely confused. "And what switch? What are you talking about?"

The Angel held out his hand, and a massive gold spear flickered into view next to him. He took hold of it and slammed the dull end into the ground, sending a shockwave through the surface. Some of the sentient beasts of burden shied at the vibration and the sound, but Delilah was one of several who simply tensed and readied herself. For what, Elijah doubted she knew. He sure as hell didn't.

High above the crowd, the vaulted ivory ceiling began to fill with a cluster of angry storm clouds. The edges of the clouds flashed with light in a wide variety of colors, and thunder rolled throughout the corridor. Elijah shared brief glances with Caprice, Stephen, and

Theocritus. To his relief, they all looked as confused and concerned as he felt. At least he wasn't the only one.

The thunder began to get louder, and the flashes became more intense, but then suddenly everything went silent.

For about three seconds.

There was a deafening crack, and the clouds split violently, revealing a herd of demonic horses. They were larger and more monstrous than the ponies the riders had been wrangling before. Some were nothing more than skeletons with strips of rotting flesh hanging from their bones. Others looked to be constructed out of iron and flames. There were even some which were nothing more than dense shadows, snorting noxious fumes. Elijah was still trying to wrap his head around the nightmares in front of him when the herd charged.

The riders and their steeds drew back as the monster horses flooded down from the clouds and into the various portals. The creatures shrieked and howled as they passed, spooking more than a few individuals in the gathered crowd of the dead.

The Angel didn't move or speak as the horses passed him. He didn't even seem to be watching them. Elijah took the Angel's demeanor as a challenge and stared at him hard, trying to ignore the horses as well. It was admittedly difficult since every single one of the horses was hypnotically macabre. They caught the eye in the way a decaying murder victim attracted the focus of everyone who passed. All the disgust in the world couldn't keep a person from sneaking at least one peek.

When the last demon horse had left the Hub and the air was quiet again, the Angel finally stirred. He tossed the spear to the side and it vanished without a trace.

"You may want to begin your pursuit now," the Angel said in a dire tone. Then he was gone. A cold, black dread settled on the riders. Something was very wrong.

Since there was really nothing they could do about the game except play, the dead took off for the portals to chase the horses. There wasn't much to know at the moment, so Elijah couldn't imagine any of the riders having a real strategy beyond following the demons to wherever it was they were going. Elijah had to admit that with so little information at his disposal, he would feel better if he was accompanied by people he knew, so he checked around him to be sure

Caprice and Stephen were headed in the same direction he was. They were, and so was Theocritus, which was a little surprising. But not totally unwelcome, Elijah decided. Maybe extra backup would be good with that herd on the loose.

As soon as the foursome went through their chosen portal, Elijah could see things were different there as well. Although they had crossed over into a world of the living, things weren't just an abstract blur of watercolors. It didn't take a moment of pausing and focusing hard to make things shift into clear view. The city the riders landed in was as easy to see as the Hub or the world of the Embodied.

The riders landed on a path below the street level, next to a river which was lined with broad walkways. The outer portions of the walkways were hemmed in by stores, restaurants, and bars. It was all nestled in the heart of a city unlike any place Elijah had seen while he was alive, but he had learned since his death that it was common for Earth around the early twenty-first century. Traveling to a wide variety of locations and time periods was educational if you paid attention, and Elijah had paid enough attention to know the name of that particular place.

It was the Riverwalk in San Antonio, Texas. It was always a busy location, but Elijah couldn't recall having ever seen the crowds there screaming and running away from something. He and the other riders had dropped right into a scene of complete chaos.

One of the monstrous horses the Angel had released was charging down one of the paved riverbanks. It was large and angry, and it seemed to be made of molten rock. Liquid fire oozed from cracks in the monster's charred black skin and dripped to the ground. And because all of that apparently wasn't awful enough, the horse left a trail of flames in its wake, and white hot fumes poured from its mouth and nostrils as it shrieked.

But the strangest thing of all was the fact living people were fleeing in a panic from the hellish horse. None of the riders Elijah knew had ever witnessed a living person reacting to any of the ponies they'd been chasing. Clearly the demonic horses were different in more ways than the riders could see at first glance. The stakes had been raised.

"Back to work," Stephen said as he whipped out his Heaven's rope. He hit the throttle on his motorcycle and went straight for the horse that was thundering in the other direction. People began reacting to Stephen as well, diving out of his way in fear, and Elijah's eyebrows shot up.

"Hold on," Elijah said to no one in particular, "can they see him too? Hell, can they see *us*?"

His answer came in the form of a group of living people suddenly screeching to a halt in front of him and the other riders. The living humans immediately drew back with horrified screams and ran for another escape route, leaving the three dead riders staring.

"Apparently so," Caprice replied, thoroughly baffled. "I didn't think we looked all that terrible, though."

And to one another, they didn't. But apparently, to the eyes of the living, the dead riders looked very different.

It was hardly an appropriate time to dwell on that, however. Down the way, Stephen was still giving chase to the horse of molten rock. It screamed and kicked at him as it ran, knocking over tables, chairs, and even people in the process. It was clear Stephen would need help, so the other three riders and their horses went to join the pursuit.

Physical space itself wasn't an actual obstacle for any of the riders after death. They'd all discovered they could move right through almost anything in their way without feeling a thing. However, getting the nerve to do so was another thing entirely. After spending a lifetime moving around objects, it was difficult to grasp the concept of walking straight through a waist-high fence, let alone an entire building.

It had turned out to be even more of a chore to convince the horses they could do it. Elijah wasn't sure if the horses only saw the smears of color the dead humans first did or if they saw proper objects, but whatever the animals could see had proven enough to make them shy away from charging on through. The horses could be taught with patience, but it had never seemed like a necessary skill to perfect, so not too many riders had spent much time on it.

Elijah was really starting to regret having been one of those riders as Delilah fought to dodge things being thrown into her path. The monstrous horse ahead was leaving quite the trail of destruction, and

Delilah's ducking and weaving was slowing her down considerably. Theocritus and Benedicta looked to be having similar issues. The two mares were simply too accustomed to being careful. Being on a relatively narrow path next to a river wasn't helping anything.

Caprice and Shu, on the other hand, didn't seem to be having any trouble at all. Elijah wanted to assume it was because Shu wasn't a real horse and was therefore dumber, but a nagging voice in the back of his head said otherwise.

Since Shu wasn't a real horse, he most likely didn't think like a real horse. It was something that had to be a bad thing in most situations, Elijah thought, but was honestly probably better in situations like this one. Maybe Shu was able to see the situation more logically than Delilah and Benedicta. Or maybe Caprice was able to completely control what the horse did and didn't do. Whatever the reason, Shu barreled through the items tossed in his way like they were nothing more than clouds of mist.

"Come on, girl!" Elijah hollered at Delilah over the noise. "If that metal showboat can get this shit right, so can you!"

An odd thing happened then. Shu suddenly slowed and then came to a complete stop, looking back to the other two horses. Caprice looked back as well, though it was because she was surprised and trying to see what had caught her horse's attention. After a very brief pause, Shu snorted and tossed his head before lunging forward after the demon horse again. However, he was slower then, and seemed to be very pointedly moving through tables and chairs while glancing back to the pair following him.

Delilah and Benedicta slowed to a surprised halt for just a moment, watching Shu intently. It only took a split-second for Elijah to realize what was happening. Shu was showing them the ropes.

It was ridiculous, and yet it worked. After a brief observation, both Delilah and Benedicta started forward again. This time they went straight ahead without deviating to avoid anything. They were more hesitant and still unsure, but they were willing to leave their comfort zone. And Delilah proved as much when she came up to a table and hesitated, but then lunged forward with all the grit she had in her.

She passed through the table.

Nothing horrible had happened.

Her rider was still okay.

That seemed to be good enough for Delilah. She sent a kick back toward the table she had just conquered and took off at a run after Shu and the others. Elijah would have been prouder of her if that small buck hadn't nearly sent him flying over the horse's head.

Benedicta wasn't quite as quick in gaining her confidence. She was older and wiser than Delilah, but as a result she was admittedly more set in her ways. The seasoned warhorse was being more careful, and it was slowing her down a bit. But she was picking up steam, and the more objects she passed through, the more fearless she became. Gradually, the horses and their riders caught up with Stephen and his mercifully fearless Cleopatra.

# Chapter 13

With the timidity of the horses all but gone, the chase was very much on. The four riders pursued the galloping and screaming horse from hell through the terrified crowd, slowly but surely catching up to it. But there was still the hard fact there wasn't much they could do to corner the beast the way things stood at the moment.

"We need to drive it up there!" Caprice shouted, pointing to what Elijah knew from past experience was a street above. There were staircases every so often which led up, and there were also bridges which crossed over the river. Going up to the level above would give him and the others both the space and the opportunities they needed to end the chase for good.

"We must get around the creature first!" Theocritus pointed out. "Find a way to cut it off!"

"I can't get—" Caprice began, but then she stopped herself. After a slight pause, she cried, "Oh my God, we're idiots!"

Elijah was about to tell Caprice to speak for herself, but then she proved they really were morons. Without another hesitation, Caprice turned Shu and had him jump down to the water. Rather than sink, Shu stayed right on the surface and kept running as if it was solid ground, which really wasn't a difficult feat for a dead thing. Elijah wanted to kick himself then and there. Why hadn't they thought of that sooner?

Stephen noticed what Caprice was doing and slowed a bit. Elijah knew the man was hoping with a little less pressure, the horse ahead would also slow down and give Caprice more of a chance to get around it. The demon horse did slow down, but not because it thought it was getting a break. The monster had spotted a fifth dead rider up ahead, and it was sizing him up.

Elijah remembered the other rider from both the Hub and a rather unfortunate encounter in one of the living worlds. The man hadn't taken too kindly to being cheated out of a pony. Elijah seemed to recall the man introducing himself as Sanders, but he wasn't sure. It hadn't really mattered once Elijah went back on his word and roped the pony he'd helped the other man corner.

The-man-who-was-probably-called-Sanders was older, but less experienced on a horse. Elijah could see that a mile away. It was a shame, really, since the man rode a handsome bay gelding that seemed like he could do a lot better as far as riders went.

Experienced or not, Sanders and his horse were racing for the angry monster the others were chasing. The demon horse was apparently happy to meet the new opponents head-on, which was a switch. The ponies the riders had been wrangling before had never stood their ground or made offensive moves. They would snap or throw a kick as they tried to get away, but they weren't fighters.

The fact an already terrifying horse was ready to fight was concerning. Elijah had seen enough to doubt being dead exempted him from pain and suffering. Especially at the hooves of a beast made of molten rock.

When it was very clear Sanders wasn't going to back down from the impending confrontation with the snarling monster, Stephen called out, "Are you thick?! Get out of the way!"

Luckily for Sanders, his horse had more sense than he did. The gelding shied away from the beast lunging for him, and narrowly missed a bite to the throat.

"Goddamn moron!" Elijah snapped at Sanders irritably. But at least that display of idiocy had slowed the monster horse, and given Caprice and Shu the opportunity to get neck-and-neck with it. Caprice whipped out her rope as Shu charged for their target, though she didn't try to snare the horse just yet.

"I believe it's your turn for a catch, Mr. Pritchett!" Caprice called to Stephen. "You'd better be ready before I decide to take an opening!"

Stephen grinned and sped Cleopatra up to close in on the horse, but then it happened.

Instead of simply continuing on to try and evade capture, the demon horse stopped and whirled around to face Sanders and his horse again. It charged with a hellish scream and barreled right into the terrified bay gelding, snapping at his neck. Not only did Sanders and his horse topple to the ground, but there was a god-awful stench of burning flesh and hair. It took a second, but then Elijah realized what that meant.

Physical contact with the monster had seared both horse and rider.

Sanders was pinned and yelling as his horse flailed on the ground. The demon horse wasn't done however. It was rearing up and going for another attack. Elijah wasn't close enough to do anything, but Caprice was, and she swung her rope hard to crack the end of it like a whip right into the demon horse's face. The horse shrieked and pulled away, and Caprice whipped it again with a fierce cry of, "Back off!"

The monster staggered back a little, but pinned its ears back and bared its teeth to show it wasn't intimidated. Shu squared his stance and made an attempt to stare the horse down, while Stephen moved in from behind and threw his rope's lasso over the hell-horse's head.

What came next happened so quickly that none of the riders even had a chance to react until it was over. The fiery horse shrieked and bucked before darting forward, right for Shu and Caprice. Shu jolted and pulled back and away before any contact could be made, which was something the monster had probably been counting on, Elijah thought later.

It was the delay between being roped and being transported to Stephen's corral that even made the attack possible. Yet another thing Elijah was going to add to his list of reasons to pick a fight with God. The monster had just enough time to lunge forward and crush the heads of both Sanders and his horse with sickening crunches before finally vanishing in a flash of light. Delilah slid to a stop a few yards away from the scene, and Elijah stared in horror, barely even noticing Theocritus and Benedicta beside him.

In the blink of an eye, Caprice was off Shu and running over to the fallen horse and rider, but when she got there, she almost instantly pulled away again with her hands pressed over her mouth. Stephen dismounted Cleopatra and hurried to grab Caprice and turn her away. He looked over at Elijah and Theocritus, and asked, "Since when can the dead have their brains bashed out all over the pavement?"

"Got me," Elijah replied, unable to take his eyes off the remains. The only thing left of the heads of both man and horse were piles of smoldering gore. The living bystanders who hadn't fled the scene completely were screaming and chattering in horror, but Elijah didn't really pay any attention to them.

That is, he didn't pay any attention to them until he heard one of them yell, "What the hell are you?!" It seemed like an odd question

88

since the crowd had just seen a horse from Hell made of nothing but molten rock. What made people on horses and motorcycles so terrifying to witness? Elijah turned his head to ask that very question, but then he caught a glimpse of himself and the other riders in the reflection of a restaurant window.

The first words that came to mind were "walking nightmares." Though if he was honest, Elijah could recall plenty of nightmares which had been less horrifying than how he and the rest of the little group of deceased looked in that window.

Theocritus and Benedicta loomed like menacing statues carved from sharp, blood red rock. When Theocritus turned his head to look at the crowd around him and the others, red dust fell from cracks that formed in the surface of his skin. The same thing happened to Benedicta when she pawed at the ground with a front hoof. Red light spilled from the cracks in both horse and rider, but then the little openings closed up again, locking the glow inside.

Stephen still looked like he was made of flesh and bone, but his eyes were black and empty, and there were dark, shriveled holes where Stephen's mouth and stomach should have been. It looked like something had sucked them away from the inside. The flesh at the edges of the holes was rotted, and flies crawled in and out of the tissue like they were having the time of their lives. The motorcycle Cleopatra didn't look much better. She was blacker than night, and thick, dark smoke poured from her exhaust. Chains and barbed wire were wrapped around her, and pieces of her looked like they had been eaten away by years of decay.

Caprice's reflection was less revolting, but still unsettling. She was still wearing the white, glittering bodysuit and hat like always, but she was bathed in a ghastly white light which made her nothing short of ominous. What could be seen of her skin on her hands and face was like white pearl, and her fingers were long and thin like claws. When she tilted her head back to look at Elijah from beneath her hat, he could see in the reflection of the window that all of her facial features were gone, save a pair of oval blue lights where her eyes should have been. Shu was as white and ghoulish as Caprice, and he was shrouded in wisps of white fog which shuddered as he stamped a hoof.

And then there was Elijah himself. The man had never actually wondered what his corpse would look like decades after being thrown in the ground, but he was being given a pretty good idea right then. His flesh had all but rotted away, and his clothes were hanging in tatters off his bones. Empty sockets stared from beneath the brim of his damaged hat, though Elijah could see a sickly pale green light flashing where his eyes had once been. Delilah was also nothing but a skeleton, and her bones glowed with the same pale green light Elijah saw in his own eye sockets. She chomped on the bit of her bridle, which was somehow still intact despite the rot that had taken it as well, and she seemed to be no more aware of her appearance than the others. Or maybe she was and simply didn't care.

Elijah was so morbidly entranced by what he saw in the reflection of the window that he didn't even notice anyone was speaking to him until Stephen yelled, "Blanco! You listening?"

Elijah blinked and looked at Stephen, somewhat dazed. At least the others still appeared to be normal when Elijah looked at them directly. "Huh?"

"I said," Stephen replied slowly and carefully, "let's get back to the Hub and see if we can get some answers."

"If you think anybody's gonna tell you anything useful, you're crazier than I thought," Elijah said flatly. The way he saw it, the best way to forget about everything he just saw was to lash out at the others. Besides, Elijah wasn't in the mood to watch the others see themselves and stand around looking horrified, so he wanted to keep their attention firmly away from their reflection. "Name one person we've met so far who knew shit and was actually helpful."

"Fate was helpful," Caprice pointed out, sounding a little insulted. "You were just too impatient to listen."

"Because I ain't got time to solve riddles with all this goin' on," Elijah shot back.

"You have no time?" Theocritus asked with a cocked eyebrow. "You're dead. You have all the time in the world now."

"And who the hell said you could ride with us?" Elijah demanded, glaring at Theocritus. Yes, he had been fine with Theocritus a few moments ago, but that was when they had bigger problems on their plates. And no, he didn't care how ridiculous that was. "This is turnin' into a damn circus. We gonna pick up a juggler and a clown next?"

"If you're so miserable, feel free to strike out on your own again," Caprice said coldly. She went over to mount Shu once again, adding, "I would hate to have the idea of holding you back weighing on my conscience."

"Maybe I will," Elijah replied, his eyes narrowed. "I was doin' just fine without any of you before, you know. At least I got some damn peace and quiet."

"All right, all right, let's not do this," Stephen sighed with an exasperated wave of his hand. "We've all got questions, so let's go and start asking. If the people we ask first won't give us any answers, we'll ask someone else."

"And if none of them give us any answers?" Theocritus asked a bit dubiously.

"We've got an eternity to wear them down until they do," Caprice replied, guiding Shu back to the portal.

# Chapter 14

An argument inevitably broke out when the four riders returned to the Hub. Elijah had assumed they were going to track down the Angel who'd been directing them, but Caprice found that to be one of the worst ideas on the table.

"And what are you going to do when he shows up?" Caprice asked Elijah in a flat tone. "Demand he give us answers? I doubt he'll take very kindly to being bossed around by someone like us."

"If you've got a better idea, let's hear it!" Elijah shot back, throwing a hand into the air. "Anybody! Be my guest! How 'bout you, Pritchett?"

"Well," Stephen replied slowly and carefully, "if I'm honest, I don't think we'll get much from the Angel. I'm not convinced he's even allowed to speak to us unless he's told."

"He appears to be a foot soldier," Theocritus agreed. "He might not even know enough to tell us."

"So what now?" Elijah demanded, thoroughly irritated. Mostly because a part of him had to admit the others were right. That was really annoying. "You wanna ask Fate and her posse? What makes you think they'll talk to us?"

"They might not talk to us, but I think I know with whom they will," Caprice said thoughtfully. She tapped a finger against her lips as she considered it a moment longer, and then said, "Come on. Let's go to Ervonia."

"Ervonia?" Elijah echoed in confusion. Caprice didn't pay any attention to him, and was already guiding Shu for the portal she wanted. Elijah and the other two riders followed after her, but Elijah wasn't done trying to get more information. "How are the livin' gonna help us? It's not like they're gonna know much of anything."

"Now, now, Mr. Blanco, your ignorance is showing," Caprice chastised lightly. She halted Shu by the portal and looked back at her companions. "How much do any of you know about the Ervonians?"

Elijah, Stephen, and Theocritus looked at one another as if silently comparing answers, and then looked back to Caprice.

"Not a thing," Stephen replied simply.

"I wouldn't suggest going to talk to them if I didn't think they'd be able to help," Caprice promised. "They're known for their connections to the worlds beyond ours." She nodded to Elijah. "Remember those abilities I was telling you about? That there are some with talents even more advanced than Nigel's being able to see the dead?"

"There is a man there who is able to see us?" Theocritus asked in surprise.

"Yes," Caprice said with another nod. She urged Shu forward, and called over her shoulder, "Come on, gentlemen. This race isn't going to wait for us forever."

Since it was worth a shot, and they were admittedly curious, the other three riders went after Caprice and followed her through the streets of Ervonia. It didn't take as long as Elijah had been dreading it would, because Caprice clearly knew where to look for her friend.

They found Nigel near some sort of dome made of iron and glass. It was just as lovely as the rest of the structures in Ervonia, but in Elijah's opinion, it didn't quite look as though it had been made by the same people. Metal framework curled and looped like vines around the clear panes, while the other buildings Elijah had seen looked like they were completely carved out of crystal.

Nigel didn't seem to be terribly surprised to see the four riders. He watched them placidly from his place on a bench, waiting for them to come closer before saying anything. "Quite the group you've assembled," he remarked to Caprice at last. "I'm almost certain I've heard a joke that begins with the four of you walking into a bar."

"Very funny," Caprice said, brushing the jest aside. She brought Shu to a halt and gave Elijah quite a surprise by actually taking off her hat. For the first time, he was able to see she had long, blonde hair pulled back and knotted behind her head. Elijah had started to wonder if Caprice wore the hat to hide a complete lack of hair, so that was one mystery solved.

"We need your help, Nigel," Caprice told the Ervonian gravely. "Things have been happening that don't make any sense, and we need answers."

"I've already told you there are some things the living should not know," Nigel reminded Caprice as he watched her, unblinking. "The same goes for the dead. The Embodied didn't give me this sight to help you cheat your way through some design of Fate and Death."

"But they might have given it to you to help us get answers from them," Caprice countered. "You and yours understand the Embodied a lot better than we do, Nigel. Please hear us out."

Nigel didn't reply for a moment. He just sat there and watched Caprice without any discernible expression on his face. Before Elijah could become so impatient he snapped, Nigel turned his attention to the other riders.

"Have I met the rest of you?" he asked calmly. Elijah lifted an eyebrow. Nigel didn't even recognize him? Sure, if the guy grew up seeing dead people he probably didn't remember every single ghost he ran into, but it was still a little insulting.

"Not that I recall," Stephen replied. "I'm Stephen Pritchett. This is Elijah Blanco and Theocritus..." Stephen trailed off and looked at Theocritus with a frown. "Sorry, what was your last name?"

"Atius," Theocritus replied flatly.

"Right, right," Stephen said with an apologetic wave of his hand. "Sorry, the only reason I remember Elijah's is because Caprice uses it so often."

"Pleasure," Nigel said in response to the introductions. "I'm Nigel Cairnahm, in case Caprice didn't bother to tell you."

"Hold on, so you really don't remember me?" Elijah interjected. Nigel blinked at the sound of Elijah's voice, and recognition dawned on his expression.

"Oh, that's right," Nigel said simply. "We did meet before, didn't we? Apologies. You didn't say anything."

"You have to be told every time you've met someone before?" Elijah asked incredulously. Great. Caprice had them seeking the help and advice of someone not quite all there.

"No, it's not like that," Caprice answered for Nigel. "Almost all Ervonians have a hard time recognizing most people until they hear their voices."

"What, like face blindness?" Stephen said curiously. Elijah didn't have a clue what face blindness meant, and it was clear Theocritus didn't either, but Nigel apparently did.

"A bit, I suppose," Nigel replied with a shrug. "Not really. But if it makes it easier for you to wrap your head around it, let's go with that." He looked at the two confused riders from the past and added,

"Some humans have an inability to distinguish one person's facial features from another's. It's quite rare."

"Are you gonna help us or not?" Elijah asked a bit impatiently. Things were getting more and more confusing, and that was the last thing he needed at the moment. Had the others completely forgotten there was a competition going on where the dead were dying?

Nigel watched the group with careful consideration for a moment before finally sighing and getting to his feet. "All right," he said as he began walking towards the street. He motioned for the riders to follow him, only speaking again once he was sure they were moving. "Tell me what you must of what you've seen. But only what I absolutely need to know and nothing more. After that, I'll tell you what I think you should do."

"Would seeing the death of a man who has already died be something you would consider necessary information?" Theocritus asked. Nigel looked at him in surprise, which was something Elijah took as a bad sign. When people who were supposed to know more than he did looked confused or surprised, it was never an encouraging thing.

"Well, I like you," Nigel remarked to Theocritus. "You certainly know how to get to the point. To answer your question, yes, I would consider that necessary information. What killed him?"

"This monster of a horse an angel released," Caprice replied. "It's part of this competition we're all involved in. It started out simple enough, but it's gotten really horrible." She was trying to keep the details sparse, Elijah could tell, but he had to wonder how Nigel could keep from wanting to know more. Elijah didn't have that sort of willpower.

"Is the horse still loose?" Nigel asked, his gaze wandering as he walked.

"No, I caught it," Stephen said. "With a lot of help, but it's locked up now."

Nigel kept walking without a word, obviously deep in thought. Elijah could practically hear the Ervonian's brain working. He was wondering more and more about what sort of situations people in Ervonia dealt with on a regular basis for Nigel to be taking everything in stride as gracefully as he was.

"There are many more of those beasts," Theocritus added when Nigel didn't say anything else. "Their variations appear limited only by one's dark imagination. In order to stop a foe, one must learn of their strengths and weaknesses. We will stand no chance if we remain in the dark as we are now."

"I agree," Nigel murmured thoughtfully. He continued looking around distractedly as he considered everything. Once he'd reached whatever conclusion he'd been searching for, Nigel looked up at the riders and said, "We will speak to Maral. She may not have the answers you need, but if anyone will know who to ask and how, it will be her."

"Who's Maral?" Stephen asked. Elijah just hoped the answer would be that she was someone like Nigel, which would mean she could see and speak to them as well. Hell, Elijah could admit that it was rather nice to be able to talk to a living person again. Even an inhuman one with glowing eyes.

"She is our Mother Priestess," Nigel replied, looking at Stephen. "She is our Voice to the Embodied, and one of the two who remain from the First Days." He looked out ahead of him again and added, "And she's extremely persistent, which will help you immensely in this little quest for knowledge." Nigel waved a hand to Caprice blindly. "That one has met her before."

"'That one'?" Caprice echoed with an arched eyebrow. "You know how to make a girl feel loved, Nigel."

"It's a long walk to the temple," Nigel continued, ignored Caprice's feigned indignant remark. "I would suggest you find yourselves a shortcut to avoid boredom."

"What do you want us to do?" Elijah asked with a frown. "Think real hard and show up in a place we've never been?"

Nigel stopped in his tracks and looked at Elijah in surprise. The rest of the group stopped along with him and stared at him with confusion written all over their faces. After a pause, Nigel's surprise gave way to some sort of realization, and he nodded slowly. "Well, I suppose you wouldn't have had the opportunity to learn about that," he admitted. "Apologies. It seems your experience with Death is proving quite different than most others'."

96

"What do you mean?" Caprice pressed, no less confused than the others.

"Most who die and cross my path have had nothing to do but learn their new environment and how to utilize their lack of limitations," Nigel explained. "Many have goals and aims, yes, but any tasks and purposes they have are those they've appointed themselves." He pointed to the riders. "Your little group marks the first time I've seen departed souls assigned some mission by higher powers. And it's given you little to no opportunity to know Death as well as you could."

Elijah felt a strange sinking feeling inside him at that, and it was clear by their expressions the other three riders did as well. It seemed like even in death they weren't being given a very fair break. Why were they pulled into one hell of a mess while others got to rest and explore on their own time?

"Right," Nigel said, looking around. "Since you're all so new to this, it can't hurt to give you a hand." He took off his gloves and slid them in his coat pockets, and then held up his hands. Strange, pearly white veins crisscrossed the skin of the Ervonian's hand in intricate patterns, and Elijah couldn't be sure if the marks had occurred naturally, or if they had been tattooed on somehow. Then Nigel said something in a language Elijah didn't recognize, which was strange. It marked the first time since his death Elijah couldn't immediately understand what someone was saying. Elijah would have asked about it, but then the marks in Nigel's hands began to glow a turquoise similar to the color of his eyes.

Before anyone could comment, Nigel turned and grabbed what looked like nothing at all, and motioned like he was tearing wrapping paper wrapping from a box. Apparently he hadn't been grabbing nothing at all, because as Nigel pulled his hands back, the scenery pulled away as well, leaving a jagged hole into blackness.

"There we are," Nigel said, stepping back and brushing off his hands. The marks on them faded back to white, and Nigel put his gloves back on as he looked at the riders. "What you're seeing is a sort of shortcut. Since you're dead, you aren't limited to rules of space. Once you're in a particular world, you can quickly travel from location to location. You may have once heard the term 'mind over matter'. Well, you're all mind now; you have no matter. So quit minding, and you won't even notice matter."

"If that's true, then why do we need that?" Stephen asked, pointing to the hole.

"To learn," Nigel replied with a shrug. "Seeing is more effective than listening to me go on and on for ages." He held a hand out to the opening. "Go on. I've given you a direct line to the temple. Don't worry about timing. It doesn't matter for you. Assume I'll already be there, and I will."

The riders glanced at one another. Really, it was no stranger than anything else they'd encountered up to that point. Caprice shrugged and put her hat back on her head, and then took Shu's reins in both hands and kicked him on. The others weren't far behind her.

# Chapter 15

The change in scenery was rather jarring. In the blink of an eye, the riders went from the streets of Ervonia to the foyer of a massive, black and gold structure. The style of the architecture reminded Elijah of the home of the Embodied. Smooth, black walls went up and up, and peaked into vaulted ceilings at least thirty feet high. Sharp-edged arches of gold were set into the walls, running all the way from the floor to the ceiling.

Straight across the room from the riders was a set of stairs which led to a pair of towering black doors. To the left and right, empty corridors stretched and then curved into a bend, making it impossible to see how far they went. When Elijah turned to look behind him and Delilah, he found a tall archway which led outside the building. Black drapes hung from the opening and wafted in ripples with a lazy breeze.

All of it would have been strange and daunting on its own, but then there was the liquid pooled in the ceilings. It looked like some kind of black oil, and it swirled and lapped at the walls gently. When Elijah looked at it, he could see the fluid reflecting something, but it wasn't him or the others. He couldn't tell what the reflection was showing, but it made him uncomfortable.

"What is this place?" Theocritus asked quietly, staring around him.

"It's the temple of Time and Fate," Caprice whispered back. "This is where their Mother Priestess lives and communicates with the Embodied."

"Did the Embodied tell them to build the temple like this?" Stephen asked. "Or do they just share an architect?"

Before Caprice could reply, the doors at the top of the stairs opened, and Nigel stepped out onto the landing. He looked down at the riders and said, "There you are. Come along. You may bring your horses, regardless of their shape, but I would ask that you dismount first."

There was the slightest of hesitations, but all four riders were too curious to linger too long. They all dismounted and led their horses and motorcycle up the steps. Elijah was simply thankful the stairs didn't seem to be a problem for Stephen's bike. As funny as it would've been to watch the man struggle, Elijah really didn't have the patience for it right then.

Through the doors Elijah and the others entered an even larger chamber. Two grand staircases stood on opposite sides of the room and curled as they ascended up into the black liquid overhead. Unlike the foyer, there were no gold arches in the walls. The only gold was in the railings on the staircases and on the edges of the steps themselves.

In the center of the room stood a fountain strikingly similar to the fountain in the home of the Embodied, but it was smaller, and the liquid flowed up instead of down. Dark fluid trickled in rising streams from the pool and into an upside-down bowl held up by small poles.

Behind the fountain, a portion of the room had been sectioned off by black curtains stretched between pillars. Elijah wondered if it was some kind of confessional. Or maybe a sacrifice room. He really wasn't sure what to think at that point.

As the group went inside, a woman walked out from behind the fountain. Her face was wise and somber, and she stared out in front of her with eyes that glowed a vivid yellow. She had long, black hair trailing all the way to the ground, and she was covered from neck to toe in a black gown. The sleeves of her dress were so long they fell over her hands and all the way down to the floor, but Elijah could tell underneath the fabric, the woman was holding something in each hand. She must have been the priestess Nigel had been talking about, though she looked more like a mourning widow than a priestess to Elijah. Of course, to be fair, he'd never seen a priestess before, so for all he knew, they all dressed like that.

The woman's eyes didn't move to watch any of the group as they approached her. She just continued staring past them toward the doors. It was clear she knew they were there, however, because she greeted them, saying, "Four who ride beyond Time's reach and yet still within his purpose. Welcome. It is a strange night which will grow stranger still."

"Don't know if I can handle much stranger," Elijah remarked flatly as he and the others approached the woman. "I might be dead, but that don't mean I can't go crazy."

"Is that such a concern for you?" the woman asked, still not looking at any of the riders or Nigel. "Some find the pools of insanity a relief."

Nigel looked at Elijah, Stephen, and Theocritus, and said, "Gentlemen, this is Maral: Daughter of the Embodied, Mother Priestess to my people...and a walking book of riddles."

"I walk with answers," Maral corrected. "It is no fault of mine if others have not the questions." She tilted her head slightly and said, "Caprice. Songbird of Ice. Much of Time's sand has passed between us."

"Hello, Maral," Caprice said with a smile. She took off her hat and hung it on Shu's saddle before bowing to Maral. "It's good to see you again."

"It is a strange thing," Maral remarked. "You should be beyond my sight, and yet you stand as more than past shades."

"So you do see us?" Stephen asked slowly.

"See?" Maral echoed. She hummed a musical note and said, "What I see is not by eyes, so my yes is your no."

The three male riders looked at Maral in silence for a moment, and then looked to Caprice and Nigel for a translation.

"Maral's physical eyes have not worked for a very long time now," Nigel explained nonchalantly. "But she sees streams of Time. Things that have happened, things that are happening, and things that will happen."

"Are you a goddess?" Theocritus asked Maral, genuinely interested. Elijah figured it was a fair question. Even he was starting to wonder if all those religious stories and folktales were actually accounts of people from distant worlds and dimensions.

"We are all gods and goddesses of some thing or another," Maral replied. "Even you, soldier, undoubtedly strike fear and awe into some men's hearts."

"Maral," Caprice said respectfully, "I don't know if Nigel's already told you, but we need your help." Maral looked towards Caprice and nodded slowly.

"You have traveled far to seek this help," Maral commented. Her voice always held the same even pace and soothing rhythm every time she spoke. It was relaxing, which concerned Elijah. Mermaids were supposed to have relaxing voices too, and that never ended well for sailors in stories.

"Death has a way of making distance simply melt away," Nigel reminded Maral.

"And grow that much larger," Maral countered. She looked in Elijah's direction then, and she asked, "What would you ask of me, Prodigal of Fate?"

Elijah felt rather put on the spot by that question. Why was she singling him out? And what was "Prodigal of Fate" supposed to mean?

"Just a wave in the right direction would be nice," Elijah replied a little cautiously. "Feels like we've been run in circles ever since we kicked our buckets."

"There are many directions which could be considered correct," Maral informed Elijah. "You must be more specific. Why are you here?"

Normally Elijah would have been snappy right about then, but something held him back with Maral. He wasn't sure what it was, exactly. There was just something reverent about her, even though he generally wasn't bothered by titles and status.

"I guess that right there is the real question that needs answerin'," Elijah said frankly with a small shrug. "Why are we here in all this nonsense? Seems a bit odd to me that God would snatch up only some of the dead and go about killin' some of 'em again."

Maral nodded and turned her head to the side. "Would you all agree this is your question?" she asked the other three riders.

"Yes," was the unanimous reply. One corner of Maral's mouth curved up slightly in the smallest hint of a smile for a moment.

"Then you must all find your answer together," Maral said, her expression grave once again. She turned her face back to the riders and assured, "I know of one you should consult. One of you here has already met her." Maral lifted one hand and held it out towards Theocritus. "Your laughing Mother. You knew her then. Know her better now."

"The Lady Birth?" Theocritus asked in surprise. Given that reaction on top of how Theocritus had spoken of Birth when they first met him, Elijah was plenty curious about her by that point. Maral simply nodded her head once, slowly.

"So should we go back to the home of the Embodied?" Caprice asked Maral.

"We must find where Death's wife has wandered," Maral replied. She sounded the slightest bit exasperated as she added, "The laughing Mother and her children are known for their capricious nature. As you would know, Songbird."

Elijah looked at Caprice and found her looking as puzzled as he felt. Good. There was no one-up on insight at the moment.

"To find, we must search," Maral went on. The blind woman turned and walked for one of the two large staircases without even a hesitation. At first Elijah was a bit surprised, but then he realized Maral had probably lived there long enough to memorize the place. Though he did think she would be better off being a little more cautious in case someone put a chair in the way for a laugh or something.

As Maral walked, she beckoned for the others to follow her, though she said, "You must wait, my Timeless child. It is not yet the moment for you to see beyond the waters."

Maral must have been addressing Nigel, because he replied, "I'll wait right here. Though if this is going to take a year, a little warning this time would be nice."

"Patience will reward you more bountifully in a lack of assurance," Maral said with a dismissive wave of her hand. Nigel just looked straight up in something of an eye-roll. Elijah wanted to know if Nigel had actually been left waiting on Maral for an entire year in the past, but he had a feeling he wouldn't get a direct answer if he asked.

"Should we leave the horses to wait?" Theocritus asked, not following Maral quite yet. Maral halted at the question and turned her head a bit so the riders could see the side of her face.

"You are all travelers on this path," she said rather ambiguously. "You should all walk as you will."

With that, Maral continued on her way. It was enough of an answer for the riders, who all fell in line behind the priestess, with their respective steeds at their sides. The staircase was wide, but only allowed one person and their horse (or motorcycle) at a time. As a result, the group went on with Maral in the lead, Caprice and Shu behind her, Elijah and Delilah behind them, then Theocritus and Benedicta, and finally Stephen and Cleopatra bringing up the rear.

Maral took the group all the way up the stairs, never once touching the railing, and simply passed through the strange liquid overhead without a word. Elijah leaned to the side slightly to watch from his place behind Caprice and Shu as Maral disappeared into the fluid. He still couldn't tell exactly what the substance was. It was thicker than water, but didn't move the same way as oil. It reminded him more of blood, really. It was just the wrong color.

Caprice looked back to the others behind her and asked, "You ready?"

"Not sure that makes much of a difference," Stephen remarked. But all the same, he gave Caprice a nod. "Go on, then."

Caprice smiled slightly and then turned and led Shu up into the liquid. Elijah briefly glanced back at Theocritus and Stephen before going on after Caprice. They weren't going to get any closer to the answers they needed by standing there, he figured.

# Chapter 16

When Elijah was much younger, he used to wonder what it would be like to be very small and somehow get inside a soap bubble. He imagined he would push through the surface and immediately be in a safe little world, completely surrounded by a sphere of swirling colors.

Walking into the black liquid at the top of the Ervonian temple was almost exactly like that. Only, instead of having a shield of white and prisming colors overhead, he was surrounded by a living dome of black with whirls of silver dust.

The area around Elijah and the others was massive, and it wasn't completely vacant. Strange, glittering clouds hung in the air and drifted by slowly, but that wasn't what left the four riders staring in dumbstruck wonder. Weaving gracefully between the clouds were two giant creatures which swam through the air like it was nothing at all. They looked like some of the whales Elijah had seen in drawings and paintings, though he was pretty confident real whales weren't brilliant iridescent blues and greens with traces of gold. Whatever the creatures were, they were gently guiding the clouds with their flippers and tails, and they watched Maral and the riders carefully as they entered.

Maral turned her head to look in the direction of the whales, and flicked her hands and forearms up sharply. The motion sent her sleeves flying up and back, exposing her hands and the things she'd been holding the whole time. In her left hand she held a die and a coin, and in her right she had the hands of a clock and a bit of sand. She held the objects up towards the whales and said, "Peace find you, Guardians. I walk with company, and also with purpose."

The whales looked at Maral's hands, and then gracefully arched back and rolled onto their sides, waving their flippers as if beckoning the group forward. Maral looked back towards the riders and said, "These are the Shepherds of Passages. Old Swimmers in the Oceans of Worlds."

"So are all of these nebula things portals to other worlds?" Stephen asked. Elijah had no clue what a nebula was, but he assumed Stephen meant the clouds, going by where the man was looking.

"Other worlds, and worlds within worlds," Maral replied with a slow nod. "Much of what you see here will remain beyond your understanding even an eternity from now. Ponder and reflect, but do not wallow."

Maral looked back to the whales and held her hands up to them as if offering what she held as gifts. "We humbly request guidance," she told the whales somberly. "The Great Cycle has finally spun us hence. Not all are as wise as the Knowing."

"Is she even speakin' English?" Elijah whispered to Stephen with a baffled look. Stephen just shrugged, clearly at a loss.

Fortunately, the whales seemed to understand Maral perfectly well. The airborne giants slowly drifted lower so they were level with Maral's hands, and one of them gave a low, musical hum. Once the note died away, Maral curled her fingers around her tokens again and gently set her fists on the whales' snouts.

"Birth," Maral said simply.

The creatures Maral called Guardians bobbed their heads, and then gracefully turned and swam through the air towards the clouds surrounding them. While the riders watched and waited, the Guardians moved around the clouds, occasionally dipping their flippers or noses through the swirling colors. It took a while, but finally the Guardians found what they were searching for. They honed in on a cloud of silver and guided it over to Maral with gentle pushes. Once the swirling cluster was in front of her, Maral slipped the objects she'd been holding into the pockets of her gown. She lifted her newly freed hands and carefully touched the silver cloud, exploring it with her fingertips.

"The Mother has wandered far," Maral remarked after a thoughtful pause. She pulled her hands away from the clouds and turned towards the riders. "I know where you must go, but it will not be easy. You will need guidance."

"We cannot travel there from this place?" Theocritus asked, a bit disappointed.

"No," Maral replied. "This is a place of viewing and communication. Not access." She started back for the stairs leading out of the strange bubble, and added, "Fear not. I know just the person to take you on your quest."

The riders frowned at one another and looked at the Guardians one more time, then fell in line behind Maral once again. It wasn't as much progress as Elijah had hoped, but it was a lot more than they'd had before.

Down in the temple, they found Nigel waiting right where they had left him. He watched the group descend the stairs and asked, "All set?"

"Nearly," Maral said calmly. She dropped down to the floor from the bottom step and walked right for Nigel, reaching out to take his face in her hands. Nigel let her, gently taking hold of her elbows. He looked somewhat puzzled, but before he could ask anything, Maral said, "You must abandon your body and accompany them."

The riders were rather shocked by that statement. After all, it sounded an awful lot like Maral had just told Nigel he needed to die. Nigel, however, merely looked exasperated.

"Oh, for God's sake," he said irritably. "Is that all I'm good for these days? Do you think hopping in and out of the world of Death is like going to the shop?"

"Listen, we don't need all that," Elijah interjected cautiously. He might have had a reputation for being heartless, but he wasn't about to let Nigel off himself, even if it was to help the riders out. "Just tell us what to do."

"Even if I described to you the things which must be done, and even if you somehow understood all I said, you would still need to take one who is known by those who will watch your passage," Maral informed Elijah. She continued holding Nigel's face in her hands and stared at him with sightless eyes. Nigel stared right back at her for a while and then finally sighed.

"Yes, all right," Nigel said to Maral. He still sounded like it was more of an inconvenience than anything else. "You don't have to look at me." Nigel looked over at the riders and said dryly, "Hope you don't mind a fifth wheel for a while."

"Don't this worry you at all?" Elijah asked Caprice. She looked at him with a frown and nodded, though it was hesitant.

"It does, but he's done this sort of thing before," Caprice answered. The other riders stared at her, and she held a hand up with wide eyes. "Well, it's not like I tell him to do it!"

"I hate to cut in on all this talking about me like I'm not here," Nigel said with a raised eyebrow, "but I'd like to offer my input. Assuming you don't mind, of course." The riders said nothing, so Nigel went on. "It isn't as drastic as it sounds. And as Caprice said, it certainly isn't the first time. So let's just get on with it, shall we?"

No one replied at first. It was clear all four riders still felt like leaving one's body to run around in the afterlife was a much bigger deal than Nigel seemed to think. His flippancy alone was a bit disturbing for normal, albeit deceased, humans.

"We would be disrespectful to be anything but gracious for your assistance," Theocritus told Nigel after a moment. He looked to the other riders. "After all we have seen, should we be so wary of what may be a common thing for another?"

The soldier had a point. That mental acknowledgement must have shown on Elijah, Caprice, and Stephen's faces, because Nigel nodded and swept for the foyer.

"Come along, then," he said over his shoulder. "Peace find you, Maral. I'll be in touch."

"Peace find you, my Timeless child," Maral replied, lifting her hand in farewell. "And peace find you as well, wanderers." She looked towards the riders and swept her hand out as if blessing them. "May Fate's Star-Herders keep your paths clear."

"Thank you, Maral," Caprice said with a smile and a bow of her head. Shu bobbed his head as if mimicking the gesture, and then Caprice turned and led Shu off after Nigel.

"Yes, thank you," Stephen said to the Ervonian priestess. "It's a shame we can't stay longer."

"Longevity means little to you now," Maral reminded Stephen. "You have no Time and yet all Time could ever give. We will meet again when it is right."

"I look forward to it," Stephen said sincerely. "Take care, Maral," he added before taking Cleopatra away to catch up with Caprice. Maral nodded and then looked to Theocritus, even though he hadn't said anything.

"Your laughing Mother awaits," she assured him. "The coin has flipped for you now. Enjoy her as you enjoyed her husband in life."

Theocritus looked at Maral in silence for a moment, and then bowed and said, "Ervonia is blessed to have such graceful wisdom in its house."

Maral actually smiled at that and waved Theocritus on. As Theocritus and Benedicta went after the others, Elijah and Delilah went as well, but Maral apparently wasn't done with Elijah yet.

"It is a good fellowship you have assembled," Maral called out. Elijah drew Delilah to a halt and looked back at the black-shrouded priestess.

"I didn't really assemble 'em," he said with a shrug. "They just sorta stuck."

"Being bound does not always equate restriction," Maral promised. "It can also strengthen."

Elijah watched Maral carefully. He wasn't sure if she was trying to give him some encouragement or a life lesson. "We've made it this far," he conceded at last. It was the closest he would come to admitting the others helped him get to that point.

"Ride on," Maral urged gravely. "You will find your true name, even if it is after the rider in black is shrouded in pale."

Maral had gone from poignant reassurance to indecipherable weirdness, so Elijah decided it was time to just go before it became obvious he had no idea what the hell she was talking about.

"Right," he said slowly. "Thanks." He walked Delilah along again and told Maral, "I'll keep that in mind."

Maral simply waved in reply, and Elijah continued glancing back at her occasionally as he and Delilah continued on toward the temple's foyer.

"What do you think the chances are of us meeting someone normal for a change?" Elijah asked Delilah quietly. Delilah snorted and tossed her head, and Elijah sighed. "Yeah, that's about what I figured."

# Chapter 17

Nigel took the group down one of the long corridors they had seen upon entering the temple, and led them to a large bedroom which looked practically untouched. There wasn't much to it in terms of furniture and décor. There was only a bed, a bookshelf, and a small table with an empty glass bowl resting on top. As Nigel went into the room, the four riders followed him in, leaving the horses and motorcycle out in the hall.

"This will only take a moment," Nigel promised as he took off his coat. He hung the coat carefully on a hook on the wall and went to lie down on the bed. Without the extra layer, Elijah was actually able to see how thin the man actually was. He wasn't quite emaciated, but it was obvious Nigel tended to forget a meal or five.

"Shouldn't you have someone nearby in case something goes wrong?" Stephen asked with a frown.

"If I can't get back into my body, I'll simply throw things around the temple like a poltergeist until Maral comes to assist," Nigel replied flippantly as he made himself comfortable on the bed. He didn't sound like he was joking, either. Elijah wondered if Nigel had actually done that in the past.

"So how does this work?" Elijah asked. "I'm guessin' you don't blow your head off or slit your wrists."

"Since I would like to actually come back to life, that is correct," Nigel confirmed. He looked at Elijah from his place on the bed, flat on his back with his hands folded over his chest. "My kind practices something often referred to as bioregulation. We learn to master our bodies with great focus and hard work. It allows us to control things such as physical strength limits, pain tolerance, and even our pulse and brain activity."

"So you stop your body from living?" Stephen asked. "How do you start it again?"

"I put it on a timer, so to speak," Nigel said. He sounded patient enough, but he was somewhat fidgety. It was clear he just wanted to get everything over and done with. "I only have to be dead long enough to separate my soul from my body. Time doesn't matter once I'm out, after all."

The riders nodded slowly. At least Nigel's confidence was somewhat reassuring.

"Anything else?" Nigel asked, watching his dead audience carefully. When he received headshakes as a response, he rested his head back on the pillow and closed his eyes. "Caprice, if you do anything to my body while I'm out, know that I will find a way to kill you in the afterlife."

It was an interesting choice of last words, but it definitely amused Caprice, if her smirk was any indication. Nigel went completely still, and no one moved as they waited to see what would happen next. Would they see his soul come up out of his body? Would there be some sort of flash?

"You can stop your figurative breath-holding," Nigel's voice said behind the riders rather abruptly. "It's an extremely anticlimactic process."

The four riders turned to look behind them in surprise and found Nigel standing there, once again in his coat, hands in his pockets. He looked at them with no discernable expression for a second, and then turned and started down the hall.

"Now then," he said as he walked, "let's get you to Birth's doorstep, shall we?"

There really wasn't anything to do but follow him, so the riders retrieved their horses and motorcycle, and did just that.

"Where are we going?" Caprice asked as she climbed onto Shu's back.

"Some dimensions must be entered in specific ways," Nigel explained calmly, looking back at Caprice. "Just as in the world of the living, there are limits in the world of the dead which require a certain sort of finesse to circumvent."

Nigel turned his attention back to where he was going, and put his hands out in front of him. He said another strange phrase Elijah couldn't understand, and flicked his hands out to the sides. A split appeared in the space in front of the group, and Nigel started to go through the opening, but Elijah said, "Hey, hang on a second."

Nigel stopped and looked back at Elijah with a confused frown. "Yes?" he asked.

"How come when you talk like that, I can't understand you?" Elijah asked. "I thought Death did all the translatin' for us."

"Death only translates what you need to understand," Nigel explained. "Rest assured, if I speak words that apply to your person, you will know what I'm saying."

"But what did you say?" Elijah pressed, far too curious to let it go at that.

"An Ervonian Word of Alteration," Nigel said. He finally turned away from the opening completely so he could face Elijah properly. "I don't like using the word 'spell', but I suppose that's the easiest way to describe them. Whatever one might call them, they're not words meant for your ears."

"Weird," Elijah said, rubbing his chin thoughtfully.

"Many things are," Nigel remarked. Then he turned and went through the opening without another word.

"He would know, wouldn't he?" Caprice said lightly. The others snorted, and the four riders headed off after Nigel.

Once through the passage, the riders found themselves standing in a field of wheat which stretched as far as they could see. The sky overhead was blue with fluffy, white clouds drifting in a peaceful breeze. Scattered across the field were towering, white structures Elijah recognized as windmills, even though they didn't look like any windmills he had ever seen. They were slim and white, and looked like they were built out of metal rather than wood.

"Welcome to Doorfields," Nigel said passively. He was standing several yards ahead of the group, giving them a moment to take everything in. "Theocritus, I imagine you've heard stories of it, thanks to the Greeks. Though they generally leave out the bit about the windmills."

After the group had a little more of a chance to look around, Nigel started walking again. "I'm afraid the name is rather literal," he said as he went. "I don't care for literal names, myself. Sort of unoriginal, isn't it? Anyway, as you can see, each of these windmills has a door. By using those doors, one is able to access just about every possible world and dimension. Normally the dead are quite familiar with it, but it's obvious at this point that your deaths aren't of precisely common fare."

"So it's like the Hub," Stephen said, still looking around even as he rode Cleopatra after Nigel. "That's the place we often meet up in. It's got portals that take us to different worlds. That's how we got to Ervonia in the first place."

"I would imagine it's basically the same, yes," Nigel replied without looking back. "I have no doubt there are many nexus spots like this you could access. After all, Death opens doors. Most living people never realize just how much their physical body holds them down until they finally lose it."

"Why give us this much freedom only *after* we've passed?" Theocritus wondered aloud. "Our scope of knowledge was so limited in life. Why hide such opportunities from those who still breathe?"

Nigel hummed quietly and looked back over his shoulder at Theocritus. "That's the question, isn't it?" he remarked. "Unfortunately, giving you the answer isn't how this works."

"So you know the answer?" Caprice pressed curiously.

"I know the answer for myself," Nigel said, looking out in front of him again. "That doesn't mean it's the answer for you."

The riders frowned, but said nothing. Elijah couldn't help but think back to the days when his mother would tell him he'd understand when he was older. He'd always thought that was a stupid thing to say. Why not just give explaining things a shot? Wasn't it better to teach people things sooner rather than later?

Despite his dissatisfaction, Elijah kept his thoughts to himself and continued riding along with the others in silence. As they went, Elijah began to wonder how anyone could tell their way around the place. Everything looked exactly the same, except for the shape-shifting clouds overhead. He had to figure if a person had nothing else to do for a very long time, they'd be able to get the hang of it, but it was a daunting concept.

Nigel certainly wasn't bothered. He walked along with his eyes locked on a particular point ahead of him, never hesitating even once. It was becoming clearer and clearer exactly how common this was for Nigel. Elijah also noted that Nigel seemed less distracted than he'd appeared back in the land of the living. While they were in Ervonia, Nigel's eyes had been almost constantly wandering off to the sides, like he was watching things the others couldn't see. But there in

Doorfields, Nigel either didn't have the same distractions, or he was so focused on what he was doing that it was harder to derail him.

Curiosity finally getting the better of him, Elijah asked Nigel, "So how many times you been here?"

"Many," Nigel said, glancing back at Elijah briefly. "I'm afraid I stopped counting a long time ago."

"Why do it?" Elijah asked with a raised eyebrow. "I find it pretty hard to believe it's not at least kinda unpleasant to die and come back over and over."

"Because it's part of my purpose," Nigel said as patiently as ever. "In my home, we believe that if one has a certain talent or ability, the only way they can find true happiness is to contribute it to the world as the Embodied intended. Harmony can only be found through the participation of all."

"So you're obligated to help the greater good by killin' yourself?" Elijah pressed, a little disturbed. That sounded almost like brain-washing to him. Nigel blinked as if having a realization and looked back at Elijah.

"Ah," Nigel said after a thoughtful silence. "I see."

The Ervonian stopped walking and turned to face Elijah properly. At first Elijah was wondering if he'd pissed the man off, but Nigel was still calm as he said, "I know our society must seem strange. I've been amongst your kind enough to understand why you would think that way, so allow me to try and explain how we see things."

Elijah looked at the other riders briefly just to make sure none of them were getting ready to punch him for distracting their guide. Once he was sure he wasn't about to be attacked, Elijah looked back to Nigel and nodded to prompt him to carry on.

"In your society, various classes and demographics of people are often stacked, like so." Nigel put one hand flat out in front of him and put his other hand above it, then brought the hand below over the hand above. "This leads to the belief that one is higher than another. It creates a hierarchy rather than a unity. However, in Ervonia, our classes are seen as a connected, functioning unit." He put his hands out side-by-side and then swept them around in a circle. "We all have many purposes, but one common goal."

"And what goal is that?" Elijah asked. Nigel tilted his head and looked at Elijah as though it should have been obvious.

"To make the best world we possibly can," Nigel replied simply. He paused for a moment to let that sink in before asking, "Is there anything else you would like to know?"

"Actually, yeah," Elijah replied, scratching his chin thoughtfully. "How'd you get the name Nigel?"

Nigel looked surprised for a second, and then just appeared baffled. "What?" he said in obvious confusion.

"Well, that's a pretty human name, right?" Elijah pointed out. "Are human names common for you folks?"

Nigel stared at Elijah, and then looked at the other riders, only to find Stephen and Theocritus looking as curious as Elijah. Caprice was doing her best to hide the fact she was grinning by putting her hat back on, but it wasn't working terribly well. Nigel narrowed his eyes slightly at his extremely unhelpful friend, but then turned his attention back to the other riders.

"Is that really important?" he asked a bit irritably. "We have a living incarnation of Birth to find, after all."

"I'm just curious," Elijah said, holding his hands up. "Your last name and first name don't really match, that's all."

"Plenty of people have mismatched names," Nigel said in a tone that was dangerously close to sulky.

"Oh, Nigel, come on," Caprice cooed with a chuckle. "It's really not that bad. Just tell them."

Nigel shot Caprice a filthy look before looking back to the others in defeat. "Maral thought it would be funny," he said flatly. "Can we carry on now?"

"She thought it would be *funny*?" Stephen echoed, making it obvious he wasn't sure he'd heard that right. "What do you mean?"

Nigel pinched the bridge of his nose and said, "She saw a variety of jokes made on Earth—" He cut off there and threw his hands up in exasperation. "Listen, that's what happens when a nearly omniscient being who thinks she's witty is allowed to select your name." Nigel let his hands drop back down to his sides and gave the group a hard stare. "Now. Shall we continue?"

That question was met with four separate valiant attempts to keep from laughing. Really, it wouldn't have been so hilarious if Nigel

115

hadn't been so angry about it all, but since he was, it was hilarious. Even Theocritus was having trouble maintaining a straight face.

"Right," Stephen said finally, after clearing his throat. "Sorry. On you go."

Nigel gave the riders one last hard stare before turning and heading on his way again. "We're going to that door over there," he announced, pointing to a specific windmill quite some distance ahead. "It's one I'm not certain you would be able to open without assistance, which is part of the reason I'm here with you at all."

"How are you able to tell one door from another?" Theocritus asked, voicing the question which had been plaguing Elijah earlier. "They all look the same."

"Spend part of an eternity here and you'll be able to tell the difference as well," Nigel assured. At least Elijah had been spot-on assuming that. "What may seem wondrous to one is often a honed skill to another. For instance, I'm not able to tell one puppy apart from its littermates, and it bewilders me that anyone can"

"He's not lying," Caprice piped up. "He really can't tell the difference. It's one of the saddest things I've ever seen."

"I've come to know this place extremely well," Nigel went on, pointedly ignoring Caprice. "It never changes. It's always just as I—" He stopped talking rather abruptly and halted to stare at something. "What the hell is that?"

# Chapter 18

Surprised, the riders followed Nigel's gaze to see what was so shocking, and they spotted what looked like a cloud of black smoke rolling towards them. It moved along the ground at a fairly impressive speed, and it was flashing with what looked like lightning. As the cloud got closer, the group could see a shape inside. It was one of the demonic horses that had been set loose in the Hub. The horse was running with its teeth bared, and it was glaring right at the riders and their escort.

"Oh, you've gotta be kiddin' me," Elijah said, exasperated. It just figured they couldn't enjoy a simple trip from point A to point B without some kind of hang up.

"What's *that* doing here?" Nigel asked in disgust as he watched the horse approach. He seemed more insulted than anything else.

"Well, I would guess they're able to go across any dimension," Caprice said with a casual shrug. She reached for her Heaven's rope and added, "No rest for the wicked, right?"

"I suppose not," Nigel said flatly. Before any of the riders could do or say anything else, the Ervonian started marching right towards the charging monster with a set jaw and narrowed eyes.

"Whoa, what are you doing?" Stephen asked, concerned.

"Setting a precedent," Nigel replied with an edge. The four riders looked at one another, and then back to Nigel to watch and see exactly what the hell that meant.

While Nigel continued to walk with a dark calm, the horse only became more infuriated. It screamed and kicked as it ran, and the flashes of lightning in the black cloud around it became more intense. The display didn't affect Nigel, however. He simply continued forward, glaring at the horse.

When horse and Ervonian were about three yards away from one another, Nigel took off his gloves and shoved them into his pockets. As soon as that was done, Nigel said what must have been another Ervonian word, and then swung a fist right for the horse's face.

Nigel's fist made contact with the horse's muzzle, and the resulting explosion of light and sound from the impact startled the

117

bystander riders and their horses. The demon horse staggered and fell with a crushed jaw, obviously as surprised as the deceased audience.

"Shall I repeat myself?" Nigel asked the creature as it fought to stand again. The horse finally made it up to its feet, and reared at Nigel with a loud and eerie scream. Nigel watched without reacting for a moment, and then said the same word he'd spoken a moment before and punched the still-rearing horse in the chest. There was another explosion, and the horse fell to the ground with a pained wail.

Nigel let the creature kick around helplessly for a moment, waving away the wisps of black cloud still surrounding the horse. Once he'd seen enough, Nigel stooped down and placed one hand firmly on the horse's head. The monster finally gave up and let its limbs flop limply on the ground.

"Time for you to leave," Nigel said simply. He said another Ervonian word, and the horse faded away, along with its black cloud. With the horse gone, Nigel stood up and pulled his gloves out of his coat pockets. As Nigel put the gloves back on, he turned to face the riders again, and blinked when he saw the way they were staring at him. "What?" Nigel asked.

"What do you mean, 'What?'" Elijah said in disbelief. He pointed to where the horse had been and asked, "What did you do to it?"

"I sent it away," Nigel replied with a shrug. The riders stared at him some more, and Nigel raised an eyebrow. "Just because something *can* go anywhere it pleases doesn't mean it *should*. I don't like strange dogs in my house, and I certainly don't like horses with behavioral problems in peaceful nexus dimensions."

"Where did you send it?" Theocritus asked.

"A place you don't want to visit," Nigel said plainly. Apparently that was all they were going to get on the subject, because Nigel turned and continued for the windmill he'd indicated before. "Enough chitchat. Things to do, remember?"

The group went after Nigel, though Elijah leaned over towards Caprice and asked, "You ever seen him do that before?"

"I've seen him do some pretty amazing things, but not that in particular, no," Caprice replied in a hushed voice. "I told you, he's one of the warriors of Ervonia. I never pictured him punching a monster horse in the face, though."

118

"I have to admit," Stephen remarked, "Didn't think a skinny guy like that could do that much damage."

"Benefit of being Ervonian, I suppose," Caprice said with a delicate wave of her hand. She watched Nigel for a second and then shook her head. "You should see him in a bar fight."

The group finally reached their intended windmill, and Nigel turned to face the riders. "Who would like the honors?" he asked placidly. He looked at Theocritus and said, "How about you? You've met Birth before, yes?"

Theocritus seemed somewhat surprised, but nodded and dismounted. Once on the ground, he went up to the large door set in the massive windmill and took hold of the handle. Elijah was expecting some grand show of Theocritus heaving the door open and revealing a strange world beyond. Instead there was just a very sad display of Theocritus pulling on the door and not being able to move it at all. In fact, Theocritus nearly fell over since he had been fully expecting the door to move with him.

"Ah, so you can't open it after all," Nigel mused.

"Wait, you knew that would happen and you told him to do it anyway?" Stephen said, staring at Nigel.

"I didn't know for a fact it would happen," Nigel protested, though he seemed to be only pretending to be offended. Which meant yes, Nigel had known for a fact it would happen. "I'm not a fortune-teller, am I? I can't see the future, unlike certain individuals in my life."

"He could have pulled his arm out, Nigel," Caprice said reproachfully, taking on the look of a disapproving mother. "What the hell's the matter with you?"

"Do you hear how little faith they have in you?" Nigel asked Theocritus. "I'd be offended if I was in your place."

"I try to refrain from striking men who have not struck me first," Theocritus informed Nigel darkly, "but I am willing to make exceptions."

"All right, all right," Nigel said as he moved to the windmill door. "No need for violence. We've had more than enough of that today." Theocritus glared at Nigel as he passed, and for a moment Elijah was hopeful Nigel would get punched by a Roman soldier, but it didn't happen.

The Ervonian pulled the door open, revealing a world Elijah hadn't expected to see. He was pretty sure the others hadn't expected it either. When Elijah had imagined what sort of place Birth would be wandering, a barren industrial landscape hadn't been his first guess. Or any of his guesses, really. What was she doing in a place which looked as if it couldn't even grow grass?

At first Elijah thought the world might look better once they were through the door, but it didn't. The only things that could be seen for miles were looming scaffolds made of thick steel beams, and strange machines Elijah had never seen before.

"The hell are those things?" Elijah asked quietly, squinting at the machinery.

"They look like different kinds of construction equipment you might find in my time," Stephen replied. He frowned a bit as he added, "Though I don't see any seats or controls. They must be fully automated."

"That's how most construction equipment is in my time," Caprice chimed in with a nod.

The group fell silent again as they went back to taking in the strange world around them. A faded sun shone bleakly through thick clouds like a lantern about to go out. It didn't provide much light, and the massive lamps flickering here and there among the scaffolding weren't any better. In fact, what little light there was only served to make the place look more dead and abandoned. Elijah couldn't be sure, of course, but he imagined if he could feel the air, it would be hideously stagnant.

Nigel seemed completely unaffected by their surroundings, and he resumed the confident and steady pace he had set back in Doorfields. The riders followed, but somewhat hesitantly. Even though the place looked entirely unable to support any form of life, it practically stank with hostility.

"What is this place?" Caprice asked Nigel quietly as she looked around.

"An alternate," Nigel replied without looking back. "It's a place you really shouldn't be able to enter, which is why Theocritus couldn't open the door."

"Are we going to make worlds collapse or something by being here?" Stephen asked. Elijah's eyebrows went up. Now there was a concept he hadn't even thought to be worried about. Could that happen?

"So long as you stay close to me, and don't do anything that would compromise the integrity of reality, everything should be fine," Nigel said nonchalantly. His passive attitude was most likely meant to be reassuring, but Elijah didn't feel very reassured. The other riders weren't acting very reassured, either. Elijah looked down at Delilah to see what she thought of everything and found her looking around with interest. Whatever was making Elijah uneasy apparently caused no concern for the mustang, which was just plain odd. Weren't animals supposed to be sensitive to that sort of thing?

As they went on, Nigel began stooping down and stretching up to look under, around, and over obstacles off to the sides of his chosen path. Every so often he would mutter things to himself like "Where are you?" or "Oh, don't do this. I know you're here." It was like watching a game of hide-and-seek. It ended when Nigel suddenly came to a stop by a large beam which had come loose on one end and fallen to the ground. He squinted at the shadows beyond, and asked, "Is that you?"

A female voice laughed from within the shadows, and Nigel looked back to the riders. "There's our answer," he said.

"Answers, answers, it's always answers you seek," the woman's voice lilted happily. There was a shimmer in the shadows, and a grinning woman emerged. She was as tall as the Embodied whom Elijah, Caprice, and Stephen had met before, with deep brown skin and thick brown hair which fell past her hips. Her dress was light and gauzy, and her eyes sparkled green as she surveyed her visitors. "Didn't I tell you that you would make friends?" the woman asked Theocritus with another laugh. Her voice was light and joyful, which honestly made her all the more out of place in such a bleak and lifeless world.

"You did," Theocritus conceded. To Elijah's surprise, the normally somber soldier was wearing a warm sort of half-smile as he said it.

"Your hearts already know me, but I will say despite: I am Birth," the woman informed the other riders, a musical ring in her tone. "And I am so happy to see you here."

"High Mother, we have questions," Nigel said to Birth. He had the tone of a man who was thoroughly prepared for a lengthy and confusing conversation. "What do you know of a competition among dead riders?"

"Competition?" Birth echoed. She swayed in place like a tree in the wind as she considered the question. "I know of the shaping."

"Whatever you'd like to call it," Nigel said patiently. "There's something odd going on with that, isn't there?"

"Everything's odd," Birth laughed. She swept her arms out to indicate the world around them and said, "Connected, but not. You found me in a place you should have never been able to enter. The dead can't cross our barriers between one universe and another."

"But we did," Elijah blurted out incredulously. "You can't say the dead can't cross your barriers, because we just did. That's how we're even here in the first place."

Birth looked at Elijah with a broad grin, and put a finger to her lower lip. "Dead?" she lilted. "Or not dead?"

The entire group stared at Birth. Even Nigel looked shocked.

"What are you saying?" Theocritus asked cautiously. "We aren't really dead?"

Birth's grin twisted into a cryptic smile, and she turned and walked into the shadows of the towering scaffolding around her. Elijah watched her go with a baffled expression, not having a clue how he and the others were supposed to react to that.

Caprice, on the other hand, pushed up in her stirrups and gracefully dismounted Shu. She looked at the horse once she was on the ground, and firmly told him, "Stand." Shu bobbed his head as if acknowledging the order, and Caprice started after Birth on foot.

Elijah watched Caprice go for a second and then moved to get off of Delilah. "Come on," he ordered the others. "I ain't gonna play messenger for any of you, and I doubt she will either."

122

# Chapter 19

As soon as Elijah crossed into the labyrinth of steel with the others, he was fairly surprised to find he could actually touch and feel things around him without even trying. Physical contact with anything that wasn't another one of the dead had been more trouble than it was worth in dimensions of the living, so having access to yet another world he could actually interact with was almost nice. "Almost" because the framework was posing a tricky obstacle course. It got annoying, fast.

Caprice and Theocritus were having no problems navigating around and between the beams. It was fairly clear they had both lived lives which allowed them vast amounts of experience solving navigational problems on the fly. On the flipside, it was fairly clear Elijah and Stephen hadn't. It slowed them down considerably, to the point Stephen called ahead, "If you leave us behind and we get lost, we're going to have real problems!"

"*You* might, but I don't see how that's *our* problem!" Caprice called back. Despite her words, she stopped and looked back at the slower pair. "Come on," she encouraged. "Just do what we do."

"Hold up," Elijah said, halting and looking around. "Where the hell did Cairnahm get to?"

"Here," Nigel's voice replied. The riders looked over in the direction of the sound, and found Nigel standing a ways ahead and to their left. "Come along," Nigel added. "Just because we have an eternity doesn't mean I care to spend it here." He pointed ahead. "She went this way."

After quite a time of ducking and weaving their way through the industrial labyrinth, the group finally found Birth. She was stooped over a tangle of metal limbs attached to what looked like a huge spider made of clockwork. Other clusters of various metals and hard vinyl were scattered around the area in heaps. It was like a bizarre battlefield after a fight, littered with mechanical corpses.

"What is all this?" Theocritus asked Birth as he and the others approached her slowly. If it had been eerie before, it was nothing short of chilling at that point.

"It is where life will begin once more on this sweet little planet," Birth replied fondly. She stood straight and smiled at her visitors. "I am called here once every few decades."

"That rarely?" Stephen said in surprise. "Being born doesn't happen here very often, does it?"

"There is only one mother on this entire planet now," Birth explained, "And she is particular."

"Are these robots?" Caprice asked, still looking at the metal bodies all around.

"They are called many things," Birth lilted. "As is your kind."

"What are robots?" Elijah asked Caprice with a puzzled frown.

"They're machines that can do things on their own," Caprice replied. She paused to consider it a little further and then amended, "Actually, there are a lot of different meanings the word 'robot' could be used for, but that's the usual definition."

"Then they are manmade," Theocritus guessed. "How can a machine have life?"

"How can lumps of flesh have life?" Nigel countered from his place off to the side. He tore his gaze off the motionless thing on the ground he had been examining and looked at Theocritus. "Origins mean little in the scope of one's importance to any given world."

Before anyone else could say anything, there was the soft wail of an alarm of some sort in the distance. Birth's face lit up with delight and she lifted her arms towards the sky.

"Here it comes," she sang out joyfully.

More lights snapped on all around the group, and an electric hum throbbed through the air. Birth reached into a silk pouch tied to her waist, and pulled out a large pink egg encrusted in gold and gems. She cracked the egg hard against a nearby beam and split the shell in two. Once the egg was open, Birth flicked her hands outwards to scatter the contents. A surprising amount of sparkling powder flew out of the broken egg and spread out to hover over all of the fallen robots. Once every machine was beneath the cloud of glittering dust, the strange substance dropped all at once and seemed to disappear.

"Wake up, wake up!" Birth called out with a laugh. "I may dust your eyes, but my sand is no bringer of sleep!"

With that, the robots' eyes flickered to life with a variety of colored lights. One by one, they began to stir and rise. Some were similar to the one the riders and Nigel had found Birth standing over. Others looked more human. Still others looked like nothing Elijah had ever seen before. But regardless of their appearance, they were all definitely alive, and none of them seemed aware of Birth, Nigel, or the riders.

"Just as my husband is there for every end, so am I there for every beginning," Birth chuckled to the riders. "If it lives, I know its name and its soul, for I am the one who gave it both."

"But what exactly is your definition of living?" Stephen asked. He gestured to the metallic beings who were still finding their feet and beginning to explore. "Because I'll be honest – this seems to be a lot different from how we would define 'living' back home."

"Does it?" Birth asked, tilting her head with an inquisitive expression. "I think that definition would depend very much on the person you asked. After all, did you not bond with your machine version of a horse? Would you not call her a living thing in your mind?"

Stephen fell silent at that, and Birth smiled kindly. "It's very tricky, isn't it?" she said sympathetically. "There are many things you've never had to consider before."

"What's the point of all this?" Elijah asked, getting impatient. "I don't get why you led us all the way out here. You just feel like showin' off?"

"You must be the one to ask the questions," Birth explained. She began swaying slowly and gracefully as she added, "But I can guide you to the questions which will actually give way to answers."

There was a pause as the group considered that. Then it suddenly clicked.

"You gave life to the horses we've been battling," Theocritus realized aloud. "You can help us find out who made them and why."

"Good," Birth said with a gentle chuckle. "There's the revelation. Now all we need is the question."

"Will you take us to the place where all of this began?" Caprice asked with eagerness in her hazel eyes. Birth's smile widened into a grin and she beckoned for the humans and the Ervonian to follow her.

"Come," she said. "Let us find your steeds. There is much to see."

Once the riders had their horses again, Birth escorted the group back to Doorfields. Even while she was just walking along, Birth was joyful and lively, often laughing and singing about nothing. Normally that sort of thing would have driven Elijah up the wall, but for some reason he found himself not minding it so much with Birth. She was cheerful, but she managed to not be irritating about it.

The group had barely stepped back into the field of wheat and windmills when Birth turned to Nigel with a smile and held up a hand. "This next part of the journey is not yours to see," she told him kindly.

"You'll hear no complaints from me," Nigel assured Birth. He looked to the riders and gave them a small nod. "Good luck, then."

"Will we see you again?" Caprice asked Nigel from her place on Shu's back.

"I imagine so," Nigel replied. He walked over to Caprice and Shu, and gently patted Caprice's knee. "And probably sooner than you would think."

Caprice nodded, but even with the hat in the way, Elijah could tell she was trying to swallow back sadness. She reached out and gently tousled Nigel's hair, though it wasn't like she could make it more of a mess than it already was.

"You be good," Caprice told Nigel firmly. Nigel rolled his eyes and then gave her a look.

"Funny, coming from you," he remarked. Caprice smiled a bit, and Nigel reached up to touch her cheek just briefly. Then he looked at each of the other riders in turn and said in monotone, "It's been a pleasure. Can't wait to see how this turns out."

"Careful," Stephen said with a grin. "Your overwhelming enthusiasm might be too much for us to handle." Nigel snorted and then turned and started away.

"Thank you for your assistance," Theocritus called after Nigel.

"Of course," Nigel said as he tossed a wave over his shoulder. "Peace find all of you. And thank you, Mother Birth."

"Kindness for kindness," Birth laughed, waving after the Ervonian. Then she turned to the riders and spread her arms out with a smile. "We must journey far in this place," she informed them, "But I will guide you. Even if it seems I am not."

"What do you mean?" Theocritus asked with a slight frown. "Will you not accompany us?"

"I will," Birth said. "But not as you see me now. This must continue to be your path. I must guide, not dictate."

She paused there and looked up to the sky. The riders followed her gaze and saw that the white clouds which had been drifting lazily overhead were slowly transforming and joining together in an angry storm. The blackening sky flashed with red and white light, but there was no sound of thunder yet.

"What is in motion is gaining momentum," Birth murmured. It was hard to tell if she was talking to herself or if it was intended for the others. "Soon all places will be covered."

With that, Birth clapped her hands together and disappeared into a flock of pink and orange butterflies. The butterflies swirled around one another for a moment, and then began to fly off ahead of the riders.

"Praise the Lord," Elijah said dryly. "For a second there, I thought we were gonna go fifteen minutes without somethin' weird happenin'."

"Don't be stupid," Stephen said as he revved his motorcycle's engine. "There's no such thing as minutes for us anymore."

Stephen took off on Cleopatra to follow the butterflies, shooting Elijah a grin. Caprice and Theocritus went after Stephen, and Elijah sighed and shook his head. Was it a good thing or a bad thing that they were getting less thrown off by the surreal things happening around them? He wasn't sure. At any rate, he was still curious enough to urge Delilah after the others. There was no telling what they would find with Birth's help.

# Chapter 20

As the riders followed the butterflies, the sky continued to darken. The gentle breeze which had been sweeping over the hills of wheat turned into a gusting wind, causing the sails of the windmills to spin faster. But there was something far more concerning than the gathering storm.

The butterflies didn't seem to be terribly affected by the wind, but they began to occasionally disappear. Sometimes they flew around a windmill and didn't reappear where they should have. Other times they simply faded out of sight. They always turned back up after a brief pause, but it put Elijah on edge. If they got lost, he could imagine spending the better part of an eternity trying door after door in an attempt to find somewhere they recognized. And finding a place they recognized probably wouldn't help them get any closer to their goal.

Gradually the moments the butterflies were missing became longer and longer. Elijah decided if it was Birth's idea of a joke, it was a pretty damn mean one. There was an unspoken agreement among the four riders to just carry on in the same direction while they waited for the butterflies to reappear. Their course had been pretty straightforward so far, after all.

"I don't get why she's makin' this more difficult," Elijah muttered at one point.

"I do not think she has much choice," Theocritus said. He looked over at Elijah. "It seems to me she may be close to breaking some type of rule simply by leading us as she is. Perhaps she is attempting to stay within a limit to avoid drawing attention to our journey."

"But whose attention would Birth be worried about?" Caprice asked with a frown.

"I am still pondering that," Theocritus replied, turning his attention back on the fields ahead. "None of you can deny there appears to be a division in the ranks of this world beyond worlds."

"What makes you say that?" Stephen asked.

"Why else would the Mother be taking us to this place of origin?" Theocritus asked, as if it was obvious. "She has no obligation to show us anything, and yet she believes there is something worth our seeing."

"That could be part of the plan," Caprice pointed out, though she was intrigued, and so was Elijah. He had uncovered more than a few conspiracies in life, and the idea of that sort of thing not being limited to living humans was interesting. Did Heaven have its share of scandals too?

"It could," Theocritus conceded. "I suppose we will not know for certain until we reach our destination. Wherever that may be."

"God knows when we'll actually get there," Elijah remarked, throwing up a hand in exasperation. "Anybody see her yet?"

"No," Stephen said with a sigh. "Haven't seen her in a while now." He looked up to the sky, which had become as black as night at that point. "And these clouds aren't making it any easier to spot her."

"Why don't we stop for a bit?" Caprice suggested. "I don't know about all of you, but I haven't had a rest since my heart stopped."

"Ain't this supposed to be the eternal rest?" Elijah asked. "Didn't think the dead needed to take breaks."

"Our bodies might not, but even though we don't have those anymore, we still have our minds," Caprice said reasonably. "And our minds need just as much rest as our bodies once did. Maybe even more of it."

Elijah didn't really feel like arguing with her, and actually sitting for a while sounded like a nice change of pace. So the group went around the side of a nearby windmill for some shelter from the wind, and dismounted. As the four humans sat down, they heard the first soft rumbles of thunder from the sky above. The lightning had been flashing pretty consistently since the dark clouds first appeared, but there hadn't been any thunder to go along with it.

"I hope it doesn't rain," Caprice sighed. "That's the last thing this situation needs."

"Out of the three of us, you're the best prepared for it," Stephen pointed out, gesturing to Caprice's hat. "That thing's practically an umbrella."

"It doesn't cover all of me," Caprice said, though she wore an amused smile as she said it. If there was one thing Elijah could give Caprice credit for, it was that she generally had a good sense of humor about herself.

"You are all dressed strangely in my eyes," Theocritus commented as he leaned back against the windmill. He pointed at the cloth patches with various symbols and phrases on Stephen's leather vest. "But though Caprice wears small stars, I find your adornments more intriguing. What do these decorations mean?"

"These?" Stephen asked, pointing to a patch. "They mean a lot of different things. People can tell what group I ride with and what I stand for by these patches. Hell, some patches will tell you what sort of bike a person rides."

"What does the one on your back signify?" Theocritus asked. "It is by far the most eye-catching." Elijah agreed with that one. He'd wondered about the large design on the back of Stephen's jacket as well. On it was embroidered the head of a rotted corpse, which glared as it clenched a pair of scales between its teeth.

"That represents the club I belonged to back home," Stephen explained. "People where I lived saw this, they really stayed out of my way."

"I get the impression your club wasn't the kind to sit around and decide how to decorate town hall for a parade," Elijah remarked dryly. Stephen just gave him a smirk, so Elijah had to assume that was all he was going to get for the time being.

"Out of curiosity, where are you from?" Caprice asked Stephen, taking off her hat.

"London," Stephen replied.

Caprice smiled as she set her hat on the ground next to her. So much for her worry about rain. "Lovely city," she complimented.

"Depending on what part of it you see," Stephen half-agreed. "Unfortunately, not everyone gets to see the lovely side of it."

"What side of it did you see?" Elijah asked, watching the sky overhead.

"Thought I saw the best of it until my little girl was born," Stephen said plainly.

"You are a father?" Theocritus asked in surprise. Though he seemed to realize that could sound pretty demeaning, because he added, "I do not mean to offend. I simply would not have guessed."

"Dads don't wear leather and ride steel horses with wheels where you're from?" Stephen joked. Then he waved a hand and shook his head. "I'm not offended. If I'm honest, I wasn't as good at being a father as I should have been. If I was, I would have done a lot of things differently a lot sooner." He looked between the other three riders and asked, "Any of you parents?"

"I am," Theocritus replied. "I have two sons and a daughter."

"How old are they?" Caprice asked, resting her elbows on her knees and propping her chin up on her hands.

"My eldest son is fifteen," Theocritus said, his tone an awful lot more pleasant than normal. "My daughter is thirteen, and my youngest son is ten." Theocritus looked at Stephen and asked, "What about your daughter? How old is she?"

"Seven," Stephen replied fondly. "Going on twenty-one, it seems."

Caprice chuckled and Stephen turned his attention on her. "You mentioned a husband some time ago, didn't you?" Stephen asked.

"Yes," Caprice said with a lot of affection in her voice. She looked up to watch lightning streak across the sky. "But we didn't have any children. We had only just started trying."

"I hope you don't take this the wrong way," Stephen said, "but I never would have guessed you were married."

"Why is that?" Caprice asked, looking back to Stephen. Luckily for the biker, she looked amused rather than insulted. Elijah had a feeling Caprice had been told that before.

"You're very independent," Stephen replied thoughtfully. "Most women like you that I've met don't care for the idea of getting tied down."

"Love shouldn't tie you down," Caprice said with a laugh. "It should make you better. It seems like some people think you have to give up pieces of yourself when you're with someone, and I don't think that's true. I think you just need to find someone whose pieces fit in with yours and make you better as a whole. When John and I are together, we fit and we work. It's as simple as that."

"You are very wise," Theocritus complimented with a solemn nod. "I should hope my wife feels the same of my relationship with her."

"What about you, mate?" Stephen asked Elijah. "Leave any family behind?"

"I did that a long time before I died," Elijah replied carelessly. "Never had a wife and kids, and I doubt any of the folks who still knew me were sad to see me go."

"Is there anyone you miss?" Caprice asked with a curious tilt of her head. Elijah actually took a second to think about that, listening to the angry storm for a moment, and then shrugged.

"No real point in missin' people who don't care about you," he pointed out. Caprice looked a bit sad, but Elijah wasn't sure why. It wasn't like it was her problem.

The group fell silent for a while, thinking to themselves and letting the storm fill the silence. There was still no rain, but the wind and rumbling thunder wasn't letting up. Elijah wondered a bit spitefully if something or someone wasn't happy with the way things were going and had decided to take it out on the weather.

He looked up at Delilah, who hadn't moved from her spot standing behind him. She was being patient enough, but she was watching the world around them with wide eyes and pricked ears.

"Listenin' to ghosts again?" he asked the horse. It briefly occurred to Elijah that he should probably alter that metaphor a bit, seeing as how he and Delilah were the ghosts then, but whatever. Delilah swiveled one ear in Elijah's direction only briefly before turning her full attention right back to where it had been before.

"I think they all are," Caprice said, looking at Shu and Benedicta. The two of them were staring in the same direction as Delilah, watching something the riders couldn't see. Theocritus rose from his place on the ground and moved to Benedicta's side. He took a moment to squint out into the distance to see what the horses were looking at, but quickly gave up and moved to get up on Benedicta's back.

"Let us go and see what is so attractive or foreboding to their gaze," Theocritus suggested.

# Chapter 21

The four riders saddled back up and found the horses all too eager to go after whatever it was they were seeing. Even Cleopatra the motorcycle refused to turn in any direction besides the one the horses chose. They were all heading right for one windmill in particular, and it didn't take the riders long to see why the horses were so keen on it. Fluttering in front of the windmill's door was Birth's flock of butterflies.

"*There* you are!" Elijah called to Birth in exasperation. "We've been waitin' for you to show up for ages! Have you been here this whole time?"

Birth didn't say anything, but Elijah could have sworn he heard a distant laugh. The butterflies swept up to hover above the windmill's door, and Stephen said, "It looks like this is our stop."

"It better be," Elijah said as he dismounted and dropped to the ground. "I'm sick of bein' out in this storm."

"It's not like it's raining or anything," Caprice pointed out, watching Elijah walk over to the door. "It could be worse."

"Yeah, and I'd like to get outta here *before* it gets worse," Elijah said flatly. He heaved the door open and found a strange indoor stable built with pale marble. It was dark and quiet, and it didn't look or sound like any of the stalls were occupied. To be honest, Elijah wasn't completely sure it actually was a stable. It was far too clean and cold, in his opinion. What sort of person kept animals in a place like that?

Standing there and peeking in certainly wasn't providing any answers, so Elijah turned and got back onto Delilah. While he did that, the butterflies overhead swooped down to the ground and swirled, turning back into Birth's woman form. She smiled at the riders and waved for them to follow as she began sashaying into the eerie stable within the windmill.

As the four riders crossed into the hallway, bright white lights snapped on in the ceiling. It made the place look even colder and stranger than it had in the dark. Elijah stood up in the stirrups as much as he could to peer over the tops of the stalls' half-doors, but there wasn't much to see. Each stall had an empty trough made from the same marble as the rest of the building, but nothing else. There was no hay, no water—no sign of life at all, honestly.

Then, suddenly, a male voice with a strange, metallic drone spoke. It seemed to be coming from the ceiling, but when Elijah looked, he didn't see anyone up there.

"Ah, good, there you are," the voice said. It had the tone of a person who had calmly resigned themselves to being bored of the whole world a long time ago. Elijah was a little worried he'd get depressed just by listening for too long.

"I heard you'd be coming through here," the voice went on. "You've caused quite a fuss, you know. I hope you're willing to make more of one. This little experiment has grown quite dull."

All four of the riders were beyond confused, and plenty apprehensive, but Birth smiled and beckoned them onwards.

"Come along!" she encouraged. "All the way to the end of the hall. You've traveled far for this meeting."

She had a point. And the way Elijah saw it, Birth seemed like the Embodied who was least likely to try and pull one over on all of them. So the riders continued down the corridor of the stalls, heading for the end of the hall a fairly impressive distance away.

"Oh, hold on," the disembodied voice said then. "I have to prepare another shipment. Try not to let it put you off."

There was a loud warning tone throughout the corridor, and the stalls' ceilings began to open like hatches. A variety of things began dropping down into each of the stalls, and just like that, the stable became an exhibit of horrors.

One stall became home for a collection of hissing and striking cobras with venom dripping from their fangs. Another held a cloud raining liquid which steamed and hissed as it sizzled on the floor. There was a stall with a rabid dog, a stall with a small tornado, and even a stall with a man cutting up another man with a knife. It was as if someone had taken every possible human fear and nightmare, and separated them into display cases.

There was another tone overhead, and the hatches in the stalls' ceilings closed while panels in the walls slid open. Automated metal arms stretched out from the previously-hidden openings in the walls and reached in toward the things being held in the stalls. The arms, along with their claw-like hands, began squeezing and molding whatever horror show they had been given, shaping them into something else. It only took Elijah a fraction of a second to guess what was happening.

This was how the demonic horses that were killing the dead were made.

The riders stared around them as they continued on, mesmerized by the sights and sounds. Slowly but surely, the nightmare elements were shaped into angry, thrashing horses that did their best to try and break out of their cages. For all their effort though, none of them even dented a wall or damaged a mechanized arm. They weren't going anywhere. Yet.

Possibly even more disturbing than all of that was the way Birth continued to smile and even laugh as she led the way down the hall. She sometimes reached into her pouch and tossed glittering sand towards the horses-in-progress, and there were moments when she waved her fingers at them cheerfully like they were beloved pets. Elijah understood that Birth was as unbiased as Death, but it was still unnerving to watch her become so gleeful over those nightmares.

Finally Birth and the riders reached their destination at the end of the corridor, which appeared to be some type of office. Twin glass doors slid open to let the travelers inside, but before they could cross the threshold, Birth said, "It's only right to take this step with your own feet. Make the universes know this choice is yours."

No one spoke for a moment, and then Stephen asked, "That means you want us to get down and walk, right?"

Birth laughed and nodded.

"Right, just checking," Stephen said as he and the others dismounted.

The entire group went into the office and found it empty, except for a large desk made of the same marble used for everything else in the building. Resting on a gold stand on top of the desk was a piece of porcelain shaped like a large egg with an indigo light set in the front of it. The light roved around as if watching the group as they approached, and Elijah couldn't keep from looking horrified when he realized it was actually an eye rather than a simple light. Christ, he thought, did the same people who designed humans design those sorts of beings? Because the jump in weirdness was pretty significant.

"There we are," said the egg in the same voice that had been coming from the ceiling. Elijah wasn't sure how it was speaking, because he didn't see a mouth anywhere on the egg. "Welcome. It's been a very long time since anyone's come just to chat. It's a nice change from simply being given more to do. Sorry about the chaos out there. Quotas to fill, you understand."

"How do you know why we're here?" Caprice asked cautiously.

"I know a lot of things," the strange object replied, still sounding quite bored. "For instance, I know the four of you are going to cause quite the stir for a good deal of people who thought they knew what they were doing."

"You supposed to be God?" Elijah asked as he watched the glowing eye skeptically.

"Do I look like God to you?" the egg asked a bit impatiently.

"Can't say a whole lot of what I've been seein' in these alternate dimensions has looked like anything I'd expect," Elijah replied frankly. The other riders nodded their agreement.

"Well then, to set your minds at ease, rest assured I'm not God," the egg said. "You may call me Porus, if you really must call me anything. That was a human name for me at one point, if I'm not mistaken."

"So you run this place?" Caprice asked, looking around. "Is there anyone else here?"

"Not at the moment," Porus replied. "The inventions have already been approved, so all there is left to do now is continue inventing according to the submitted criteria until the inventing is finished. I assume you've already run into the product."

"Yeah," Elijah said flatly. "Thanks for that."

"We were hoping you might be able to explain a few things," Stephen said. "Like why the hell no one thought to tell us that we'd be running a risk of a second death if we turned that key to change up the game."

"Yes, that was a rather interesting development," Porus mused, almost to himself. "I can't lie to you; I was surprised when the request came in for that alteration. I'm afraid I can't be held responsible for information relay, however."

136

"Wait, hold on," Elijah said, holding up a hand. "You mean the whole killin' the dead thing wasn't the plan from the beginning?"

"If it was, they certainly never let me in on it," Porus replied. His nonchalant attitude about the matter was irritating, but Elijah knew he shouldn't have been surprised. It was becoming more and more apparent that all of the riders had been going around with the wool pulled over their eyes the entire time.

"Why don't you start from the beginning?" Theocritus said. It would have sounded like a suggestion if his tone wasn't so dark. Porus hardly seemed offended, though.

"Originally the horses were meant to be like the ponies," Porus explained. "More terrifying and oppressive to the soul than the little ones, certainly, but not lethal."

"But how can *anything* be lethal to us?" Caprice pressed. "We're supposed to be already dead." She glanced at Birth. "At least, that's what we were led to believe before."

"First of all, the belief that you can't be destroyed just because you're dead is a load of human nonsense that's been passed for no reason but your own ignorance," Porus said. "Of course, we're talking about a race who also believes only one point of view can be correct, so therefore anyone who thinks differently is wrong and should be punished for it. No offense, but you haven't had the most open-minded of upbringings. It's time you started thinking outside humanity's box."

"Yeah, we get it, we're idiots," Elijah said with a glare. "You gonna tell us what the hell's goin' on here or not?"

"Think back," Porus urged. "Has anyone actually told you that you're dead?"

The riders looked at one another. Now that Porus mentioned it, they couldn't remember being explicitly *told* they had passed away.

"Now, hang on," Stephen said, frowning at Porus. "I don't know about the rest of them, but I remember being killed. Quite clearly."

"Well, naturally you were all killed," Porus said dismissively. "How else would you be here?"

"Wait," Stephen said. He paused. Then he said, "What?"

"You are all here under special circumstances," Porus explained. "Think of it as being given a day pass to the world beyond that of the living. You are under no real obligation to stay. However, depending

137

on your actions in this place, you may end up beginning your eternity, or you may be sent back to your world of the living with a new being and a new purpose. Just like in life, there are countless possible outcomes for you over the course of this journey you're on."

"So we aren't actually dead?" Theocritus asked.

"Oh, no, you're quite dead," Porus replied bluntly. "And depending on how you were killed, you're going to find yourself in quite a lot of pain if you end up being revived."

"How long have we been dead?" Caprice asked, looking fairly concerned. "There's a time limit on when you can be brought back to life, right?"

"Ask Lazarus," Porus scoffed. When he got blank stares in response to that, he said, "What—really? You know, the man Christ brought back to life after being dead for days? No? All right, moving on, then. Keep in mind that you're outside of Time's domain here. Should you go back into it, he'll place you when you need to be. You'll likely find that not even one second has passed. And anyway, you should be far more worried about those new and improved horses on the loose. After all, the chances you'll ever go back to the world of the living have decreased dramatically with them running around."

"Let me just make sure I'm gettin' this right," Elijah said, rubbing his face. "Right now we're only sorta dead. If we get killed by those horses, we'll be really dead. There's a way to get back to our bodies and go back to livin', but we gotta survive all this nonsense to do that. Is that about right?"

"Basically," Porus said. "Though I'll be honest, I didn't realize the odds were going to be stacked so high against you."

"Let's get back to those horses you made," Caprice said. It was proving extremely difficult to keep Porus on track, but she was going to keep trying. "You said earlier that you were only just recently told to make them lethal. Who told you to do that?"

"You don't know his name," Porus replied. "But he's the Angel you've been taking guidance from since you first came here."

"What?" Elijah said, his eyes narrowing. That confirmed a whole lot of bullshit he'd been suspecting from the very beginning of the game. "Did somebody send him?"

"He didn't specify," Porus said flippantly. "But he brought me an intriguing idea. I have to admit, I struggle to turn down the opportunity to create or reinvent something compelling."

"You created something deadly just because it fascinated you?" Theocritus asked with a disgusted look.

"Yes," Porus said without any hint of remorse. His eye looked at each the riders in turn. "Haven't humans done that?" he asked.

No one replied. Elijah knew for a fact that no matter what time period they were from, each rider could think of something awful humans had done in the name of war, or even just for the simple reason that it was possible. He'd seen enough in the living worlds of different times to know humanity never changed in that regard.

"Is there anything else?" Porus asked after a silence. "I imagine you have quite a lot to do. Probably quite a bit of catching up to work on, as well."

"You're awful honest about all this," Elijah pointed out warily. "What makes you wanna help us?"

"Boredom," Porus replied. "That and I haven't been fond of my job ever since they decided to lock me up in this place. If they wanted me keeping my figurative mouth shut, they should have specified."

"So this is some kinda revenge?" Elijah asked, lifting an eyebrow.

"Of course not," Porus said with a chuckle. "It's just more entertaining than the alternative."

"If you have nothing else to offer us, perhaps we should be on our way," Theocritus commented, glancing at the other riders. "We will take Birth and leave you to your—" He stopped talking as he looked around for Birth and realized she was nowhere to be seen.

"Oh, crap, where'd she go?" Elijah asked, looking around as well.

"It's hard to say with that one," Porus mused. He didn't seem terribly concerned, but that hardly served to reassure Elijah at all. "I'd see you all out, but, well, that's hardly practical, as you can imagine."

"We'll manage," Caprice said. She turned to lead Shu back towards the hallway and told Porus, "Thank you for all your help. It's been enlightening."

"My pleasure," Porus replied, watching her and then the others as they followed her out. "Assuming this business doesn't end wretchedly for you, I do hope you'll pop by for another visit sometime. Things do tend to drag around here."

The riders simply gave Porus a wave in farewell and continued on their way. It was quiet once again out in the corridor of stalls. Apparently the horses had been finished and transported to wherever it was they needed to be. As a result, everything was eerily silent and still, as it had been when they first arrived.

Without a word, the four riders began guiding their horses and motorcycle down the long hallway. Elijah just hoped Birth would turn up on her own, because he had no desire to start checking each of the stalls to see if she was hiding in one of them. He'd already had enough close encounters with nightmares.

Not that it mattered. It was painfully clear the nightmares were only going to get closer.

# Chapter 22

None of the riders spoke until they were quite a ways down the hall from Porus's office. That was when Elijah stopped in his tracks, halting Delilah in the process, and said, "I dunno about you three, but I'm done."

The others stopped and looked at Elijah in surprise.

"What do you mean, 'Done'?" Caprice asked.

"I mean I'm done," Elijah replied flatly. He waved a hand around. "With all this. Gettin' jerked around, bein' told to do stuff that don't make any sense, findin' out that folks are still stabbin' me in the back even after I'm dead. Or half-dead. Or whatever the hell we are."

"So, what, you've decided to just give up?" Stephen asked dubiously. "That's not very American of you."

"It's plenty American," Elijah said, thoroughly irritated. "Shut up. And anyway, I didn't say anything about givin' up."

"So what is it exactly you intend to do?" Theocritus asked.

"Well, I figure since they've been cheatin' us, it's only fair that we cheat 'em back," Elijah said simply. He paused to note the way the others were staring at him in disbelief and then asked, "What?"

"Elijah, I know this has been rough on all of us," Caprice said slowly, "but have you lost your goddamn mind?"

"No," Elijah replied, a little offended. "I think this is the sanest idea anybody's had so far."

"You're talking about cheating Heaven, mate," Stephen pointed out. "As far as ideas go, I wouldn't put that on the list of sane ones."

"Oh, come on," Elijah groaned. He dropped Delilah's reins and started counting on his fingers. "This is a crowd that's pulled us here against our will, lied about what's goin' on, set things up so we get murdered, and who-knows-what-else that would go against the Bible."

The other three riders stood in silence as they contemplated that information. They had to admit, it really was a shady set of circumstances.

"They do say that the devil comes as an angel of light," Caprice pondered aloud. She looked at Stephen and Theocritus. "Honestly, after everything we've learned, I'm starting to wonder if this really is the Heavenly plan they said it was in the beginning. After all, the Embodied never even explicitly vouched for it, right?"

"Birth is the one who revealed we are not even truly dead in the first place," Theocritus agreed. "I doubt the Angel would have wanted that to happen."

"See, there ya go," Elijah said. He went to get on Delilah's back. "Either way, I figure since we're already damned, sendin' a message can't make things much worse for us. And anyway, who better to organize cheatin' than the guy who's been doin' it to half the crowd in this race?"

"I just have one question," Stephen said, frowning thoughtfully. "How can we be certain we're fighting the right side? What if we've been thrown by the real liars? We can't really know which side is good and which is evil."

"I'm not so convinced there's a good side or an evil one," Elijah replied honestly from his place back in the saddle. He shrugged. "I think everybody's just tryin' to figure out the right thing to do, and I think sometimes everybody gets it wrong. Even gods and angels. God said we were supposed to stone sinners until He changed His mind and sent Jesus, who said nobody should throw stones, right?" Elijah had been to church a few times. There was a reason he'd stopped going.

"That's one way of interpreting Christianity," Caprice said with a raised eyebrow. "I can't wait to hear your take on Hinduism."

"Whatever," Elijah said, mostly because he didn't know what Hinduism was. He signaled for Delilah to start walking and said, "Come on. I've got an idea, but we're gonna need help."

The other riders simply stood and watched Delilah and Elijah go, but Elijah had no doubt they wouldn't be standing there long. They had remained with one another that long, and besides, there was nothing like uncovering a huge conspiracy to persuade people to continue sticking together.

Sure enough, it was only a moment before Elijah heard the others mounting up and following him and Delilah. They might have suspected he'd gone off the deep end, but they were willing to hear him out.

Elijah's plan was simple enough in concept, but it was almost impossibly ambitious. Caprice, Stephen, and Theocritus were thankful they had an eternity to carry it out, because it would probably take them that long to simply get things in motion.

The way Elijah saw it, the Angel's plan relied on everyone playing the game as instructed. The winners would give the Angel tools to use in the Apocalypse he wanted so badly, but if no one played, there could be no winners, which meant there would be no tools. So the four riders had to convince all of the other dead riders that the best course of action was to take no action whatsoever.

In order for the plan to work, they needed every single rider who had crossed over to cooperate and work together. That meant tracking them down and gathering them together in one place for a discussion. Elijah was confident if things got at least that far, between him, Caprice, Stephen, and Theocritus, they would have a good shot at winning everyone over. After all, the four of them were different enough that they could appeal to all sorts of folks if they had a mind to do so.

"We're going to have to split up," Stephen said over the thunder booming overhead. Elijah was beginning to regret his decision to lead the other three back to the Doorfields so they could talk. The storm had only gotten louder there.

"I don't think that's a good idea," Caprice said with a frown. "We have no concept of time now. What if we lose track of one another and something happens? We wouldn't even know if something was wrong and someone needed to be tracked down and helped."

"She's got a point," Elijah commented. He was resting with his elbows on the horn of Delilah's saddle, watching the sky as he let the others discuss things. It would be a lot easier if they all agreed on something, so he was going to let them figure out what it was they should be agreeing on. He'd just keep throwing out little remarks here and there so the others would know he was still listening.

"There are benefits to both of these approaches," Theocritus said thoughtfully. "However, given the unpredictability of these places we must travel..."

"Yeah, all right," Stephen conceded, rubbing his head. "I hadn't really thought about it that way."

"So we're stickin' together?" Elijah asked, finally looking away from the storm.

"Looks like it," Caprice replied. She gave Elijah the smirk he had learned to really dread. It always came right before she said something to piss him off. "Were you afraid you'd be missing us?"

"I was afraid of gettin' some peace and quiet, yeah," Elijah shot back.

"Where should we bring the other riders?" Theocritus asked. "It does not seem wise to meet in the Hub of portals. The Angel most likely keeps his eyes turned to that place."

"There's no guarantee he's not keeping an eye on every other place we visit," Caprice pointed out. "But this seems as good a place as any, if it would make you feel better."

"We'll tell 'em to come here, then," Elijah said decisively. "Come on. The sooner we start, the sooner we get done."

"Wait a second, there's one last thing," Caprice said with a frown. "How close are you three to catching all of your sins?"

The riders fell silent as they all thought back to their last tally. The grim expressions pretty much said it all.

"Me too," Caprice assured the men with a sigh. "And the others have been riding and catching all this time. So I think before we focus too much on getting everyone here, we should catch up a bit."

"Or even better, surpass all of the others" Theocritus said. "I think it would serve our cause to be much closer to our goal than they. It could prove to be useful leverage if there are those who refuse to assist us."

Stephen sat back in his seat and thought about that. "Have to admit, that would be more convincing," he said, and it was true. Giving the other riders a choice of helping them or losing to them could prove to make things a lot easier than trying to plead with them.

"All right," Elijah said after a pause. "Then let's do that." He pointed at Theocritus and said, "Pick a windmill." It wasn't like it really mattered. They simply needed to find a door they could open which would take them to a realm connected back to the Hub.

Theocritus nodded and guided Benedicta in his chosen direction. The others followed, occasionally glancing up at the angry sky overhead. They still weren't sure what had triggered the storm. Elijah sort of wished Nigel was still around so they could ask him if this had happened there before. Elijah doubted it had. Nigel had said Doorfields never changed, after all.

Theocritus didn't lead the group terribly far. The windmill he'd set his sights on was just beyond a small hill, and once they reached it, Theocritus reined Benedicta to a halt and dismounted. When he opened the door, the riders stared at what was waiting for them on the other side.

"Well, that was a lucky pick," Stephen commented.

Just beyond the door, a large herd of monstrous hell horses was anxiously milling about. They were restlessly snapping and kicking at one another, but they were staying in a relatively contained group. It was impossible to tell if they were taking a break or if they were simply waiting for their dead opponents to come to them, but whatever the reason, it was awfully convenient for the four wandering riders.

"Hey, shut the door real quick," Elijah urged in what he considered to be a whisper. It wasn't easy for Elijah to be quiet.

Theocritus obliged, and he, Stephen, and Caprice all looked at Elijah curiously.

"What's wrong?" Caprice asked.

"Before you morons go in there and scatter the herd, I think we should come up with a plan," Elijah replied. He got three rather insulted looks.

"Nice to know you aren't making assumptions about us or anything," Stephen said flatly.

"Look, I never know what people who ain't me are gonna do," Elijah pointed out. "Anyway, if we coordinate, we'll be able to make this work to our advantage even better, right?"

"Very well," Theocritus said. "We will surround the herd to keep them in one group. And we will collect them one at a time. Is that what you were going to suggest?"

"Yeah, that sounds good," Elijah said, satisfied.

"Wait," Theocritus said with a frown. "You are forgetting something." Elijah gave him an impatient look, and Theocritus pointed towards the door. "Those monsters outnumber us at least twenty to one. I do not know if you recall the disaster by the river, but these horses are not what I would call timid."

145

"Hey, if you wanna sit this one out, be my guest," Elijah offered, holding up a hand. "More for us."

"I am not saying that," Theocritus said with a shake of his head. "I am saying we should try and catch them by surprise."

"You don't think they'll be surprised when we rush them from an invisible doorway?" Elijah asked sarcastically.

"I think they will see us all coming at once and try to surround us," Theocritus replied. "My suggestion would be to send in just one person to hold their attention and get them looking away from the entrance. The rest of us will follow once the horses' backs are turned. Two riders will move to flank the herd from either side and prevent them from scattering. The third will stay behind the herd to drive the beasts forward while the first rider works to keep the attention of those at the front. Then we can begin taking individuals wherever we can reach."

"That's a good idea," Caprice complimented.

"I would not have survived as many battles as I did had I not known how to handle being outnumbered by the enemy," Theocritus said matter-of-factly.

"So we need to send in some bait," Stephen concluded. "Give those things out there something to chase."

The group looked at Elijah.

"What—Oh, *hell*, no," Elijah snapped. "Why me?!"

"None of us said anything!" Caprice argued. "Good God, you're just ready to fight at any moment's notice, aren't you?"

"Then why the hell are y'all lookin' at me?" Elijah demanded. He didn't believe Caprice for a second. They might as well have just voiced a unanimous vote to send him and Delilah through the door.

"All right, I'll go first," Stephen said in exasperation. "Bloody hell, we'll be fighting here all day if we leave it to you two."

"No, you know what?" Elijah said. "I'll go. Since it's so damn obvious you want to get rid of me, I might as well give you bastards what you want."

"Oh my God, it's like we're traveling with a six-year-old," Caprice remarked bitterly. "No one wants to get rid of you, Elijah."

Elijah's response was to turn his nose up at Caprice and wave a hand at Theocritus, who was still standing by the windmill door.

"Come on, hurry up," Elijah ordered. "If I'm gonna get killed twice, let's get it over with."

Stephen and Caprice rolled their eyes, and Theocritus stared at Elijah for a moment. Theocritus then looked at Caprice, who said, "Oh, just give him what he wants."

With a frown, Theocritus obeyed and opened the door to the other world once again. Elijah kicked Delilah on, and the mustang reared and then took off straight for the demonic herd waiting beyond.

# Chapter 23

It was definitely a diverse group of monsters that had gathered beyond the door, though Elijah shouldn't have been surprised. The time Elijah spent in the hellish stables had opened his eyes to just how wide the variety was when it came to things that scared people. After seeing the nightmares in action, it suddenly made sense why all the demon horses looked so different from one another, and yet still managed to be haunting to watch. Even the horses embodying things Elijah had never considered frightening in the past made him want to lock himself in a small room and never let anyone in again. Elijah had a feeling he wouldn't be scoffing at anyone's phobias again anytime soon.

The monsters Elijah found particularly disgusting were the ones based on different kinds of toxin. Horses of airborne pollutants snorted fumes and made wet rattling sounds as they breathed. Acid-covered horses had the liquefied remains of their flesh sliding off their bones and dripping to the ground in steaming pools. Poisoned horses frothed at the mouth and kicked at their stomachs in agitation.

But they were just the beginning. The more Elijah looked, the more there was to see. Horses embodying torture, sickness, accidents, and even natural disasters were all right there for the viewing. It was quite the sight, but something beyond the horses' horrific nature was bothering Elijah.

Why were so many of them in one spot?

Elijah had all of about seven seconds to think on it. That was how long it took for several members of the herd to notice him and Delilah. The creatures screamed and howled an alarm, and all of a sudden Elijah had about eighty horses of Hell looking right at him and Delilah. Elijah knew there was no need to tell Delilah to veer off to the side, so he just held on and let the mare decide which way she wanted to go.

Delilah tore off to the left and began attempting to get around the herd without making contact with any of the monsters. It was predictably difficult. The horses were frenzied with rage, but they were still clever. As Delilah rounded the group, horses from the far side of the herd began racing around, trying to head her off. Elijah saw what the horses were aiming to do, and he urged Delilah further away from the herd. They were going to need a much wider berth if they wanted to survive this plan of Theocritus's.

Counting his lucky stars that it was as easy to see here as it had been at the Riverwalk, Elijah began looking around for some sort of advantage he and Delilah could use. Further off to the left, there was a towering wall which seemed to go up for miles and wrapped around what Elijah had at first assumed to be a mountain. But upon a closer look, Elijah realized it wasn't a mountain at all. It was a messy stack of buildings stretching up into the clouds. It looked like a city that had been haphazardly constructed upwards instead of outwards.

Elijah tore his eyes off the strange series of structures and looked back to the herd. Things were getting worse, fast. The horses were attempting to form a circle around him and Delilah, and it was going to work unless Delilah changed course.

Swearing loudly, Elijah signaled Delilah to race for the city to the left of them. He could see an open gate he and Delilah would be able to pass through.

That was when Caprice, Theocritus, and Stephen tore into the world. Stephen and Caprice guided Cleopatra and Shu off to the sides to try and get around the herd, their Heaven's ropes out and swinging. The horses shrieked and bellowed in anger, but they seemed to be having a hard time deciding the best course of action. When Caprice and Stephen each roped a horse, the herd became even more frantic.

Whether it was part of a larger plan or simply what felt like the smartest thing to do for the time being, the monstrous horses began to band back together in a tight group. But they were continuing to race for Elijah and Delilah, who were in turn still aiming for the city gate.

"Elijah, wait!" Theocritus called after capturing a horse.

"What do you mean, 'Wait'?!" Elijah yelled incredulously. "Do you see what's happenin' right now?!"

Theocritus didn't have time to respond. Elijah and Delilah made it through the gate and into the multi-leveled city.

There was no doubt the people there could see Elijah and his mustang. As the horse and rider thundered through the gate, there was a lot of running and ducking for cover, as well as a lot of screaming and yelling. Most of the citizens Elijah caught glimpses of appeared to be human, but there were others who were something else entirely.

Elijah recognized most of the other races of non-humans from his world hopping while still alone, but he had never learned any names. All he knew was the sort of worlds they came from. The people with large eyes and scaly blue-green skin came from a place with a lot of jungles. The extremely tall and bulky people with strange mouths, dark red skin, and bright emerald green eyes lived in a world with grand structures of brownish red stone.

It wasn't every day Elijah got to terrify multiple species at once, and he had to figure that it wasn't every day the people of the city had an undead horse and rider nearly running them over. Elijah wondered how many of them would write a book about the experience later. Especially since not three seconds after he and Delilah crossed the city threshold, an entire herd of crazed, demonic horses tried to enter as well.

The gate into the city was wide enough to let in seven horses at a time, but that apparently wasn't good enough for the herd. They fought and shoved one another, trying to be the first to enter, and as a result, multiple demon horses crashed into one another and slammed into the sides of the gate. Some of the horses staggered, and others actually fell to the ground, but the gate and walls were having a far worse time of it.

Infuriated by the concept of having to wait their turn, several horses began deliberately smashing against the wall to force a wider opening. The group still wasn't able to come in all at once, but the horses that got the chance to enter did so without hesitation.

Over the chaos, Elijah heard Caprice scream, "God *damn* it, Elijah!" He didn't have to guess why she was so pissed. He already knew, and his mind was acknowledging that, yes, he was an idiot. He had just led a herd of demons into a populated area, and he'd done it through a passage so narrow that it was impossible for the other riders to keep the monsters in check.

"Yeah, yeah," Elijah muttered in response to Caprice's fury. He figured it would be better to start redeeming himself right then, so he reined Delilah in, turned her back towards the monsters behind them, and whipped out his rope. A horse covered in grotesque spikes was closing in fast, giving Elijah the perfect opportunity to take his first capture of the escapade.

Elijah threw his lasso over the monster's head, eliciting a wrathful scream. The horse wasn't going down without a fight, and it lunged for Delilah's throat to prove it. Delilah darted to the side to avoid the creature's teeth, lunging toward its flank where she would be safe. The horse thrashed, but it was too late. It disappeared in a flash of light and was transported to Elijah's corral.

It was an all right start. Elijah kicked Delilah on, and she tore off to take on the other monsters storming into the city.

While Elijah and the other three riders did their best to take what horses they could, the majority of the stampede continued to wage war on the wall protecting the city. Even the creatures that managed to fit through the gate were smashing down the barrier keeping the rest of the herd from entering at once.

Gradually, the demons were becoming more organized. They alternated between breaking the wall and attacking the riders, forcing them to back off. It was quickly getting out of hand. Elijah and Delilah were eventually forced to turn tail and run from the beasts threatening to overtake them. Thankfully, the retreat incited a chase, which cleared more of a path for the other horses trying to enter the city. It wasn't good news for the city, because there was now a steady stream of monsters running down the street, but it meant that the herd wasn't putting as much effort into completely demolishing the wall.

Between the charging, shrieking demonic horses, and the terrified, fleeing citizens of the city, it was quite the commotion. But suddenly Elijah heard a familiar voice boom over all the noise like a clap of thunder.

"Have the four of you lost your *goddamn minds*?!"

Elijah turned his head to find an infuriated Nigel Cairnahm storming through the crowd of fleeing bystanders. The Ervonian's eyes were locked right on Elijah, who reined Delilah in and gave Nigel a look of surprise.

"Howdy," Elijah said. He turned in his saddle and threw his Heaven's rope over the head of a monster that was lunging for him, and then turned back to Nigel as the horse reared back and screamed.

"'Howdy'?" Nigel echoed, ignoring the protesting and then vanishing demon horse Elijah had roped. "You've brought Hell to an innocent and already struggling city, and all you have to say is 'Howdy'?!" Nigel waved his arms at the chaos around them. "I could banish you to a pit for this!"

One of the horses set its sights on Nigel then, rushing for him with its teeth bared. Nigel rounded on the horse, but before he could do anything, Elijah yelled, "Wait, don't send it anywhere! We need all the horses we can get our hands on!"

Nigel stared at Elijah just briefly before focusing back on the horse. He said a word and held up his hands with his palms facing the horse, and the monster suddenly hit an invisible wall. It staggered, dazed, and Nigel took the opportunity to glare back at Elijah.

"So this is part of your grand plan, is it?" Nigel asked dryly. He put on an expression of feigned enthusiasm and said with sarcastic cheer, "Let's chase a herd of destructive beasts into the living world! It'll be fun! If we're lucky, we'll ruin people's lives!" Nigel's face and voice fell flat again as he finished with, "Idiots."

"You ever been punched in the face by a dead man, Cairnahm?" Elijah asked with narrowed eyes. Before he could learn the answer to that question, the other riders managed to get through the city gate.

"Nigel!" Caprice called in surprise. She whipped her rope around a horse's neck and held on as it thrashed, asking Nigel, "What are you doing here?"

"Visiting," Nigel said irritably. "Thank you for making it so memorable."

There was a crash nearby, and Nigel and the riders looked to see one of the horses had slammed into a store, ruining its door and windows.

"Damn it!" Nigel barked. He whipped around and pointed at the riders fiercely. "You've all got some cleaning up to do," he said in a dark tone. "If you don't want me sending all of these things to a place where you'll never catch them, I suggest you get busy. Now."

The riders took off to obey, having ultimately decided they could try and justify themselves later. Nigel was obviously too pissed to listen anyway.

The demonic herd had spread out through the city streets, but it was hardly difficult to track them. They were about as stealthy as steam engines. And that was a good thing, because Elijah could tell there was more going on with the herd than he would have guessed at first glance. They were all going in the same direction, and they made strange calls to one another as if passing on directions. It was almost like they were searching for something specific. Individuals closest to the riders still snapped and kicked at them aggressively, but the assaults weren't nearly as fierce as they had been a moment ago.

All the riders could really do was keep after the herd and continue roping every horse they could. They were putting a dent in the monsters' numbers, but as the horses began to regroup, Elijah got the sinking feeling it was taking far too much time.

"Don't let them join together!" Nigel called suddenly. "For God's sake, break them up!"

Elijah wasn't sure how Nigel was even able to see what was going on since they had pretty much left him in the dust, but that was something he would worry about later. There were more concerning things going on up ahead.

The demon horses continued to move closer and closer together until they were actually pressed up against one another. Elijah thought they were just trying to make it harder for any of the riders to capture them, but then it got weirder.

# Chapter 24

Slowly, the demon horses were beginning to meld together. It reminded Elijah of multiple candles melting into one another as their wicks burned down. All four riders watched with widening eyes as the horses gradually transformed from a group of individuals into one giant, hideous body with several legs and heads.

"What the hell is that?!" Stephen yelled to no one in particular. He turned his head to stare at Theocritus and asked, "Do we just rope it? Pick a head and go for it?"

"We should try and surround it!" Theocritus replied. "Caprice! Go left and circle to its front! I shall take the right and do the same!" He pointed at Stephen and Elijah. "Stay behind it! We shall make it stand and fight!"

"Got it!" Caprice called. Though that was apparently easier said than done. The mass of horses was leaving very little room to pass it on either side. As a result, Caprice and Shu got closer, only to hesitate uncertainly.

That was when the four riders heard Nigel's voice again, this time yelling, "For the love of God, you're dead! Go through the walls! Hell, go up them! If you don't mind gravity, it won't matter anymore than anything else!"

"Ugh, where *is* he?" Caprice demanded, looking around. "You're the most irritating fairy godmother ever, Nigel!"

"*What?!*" was the extremely insulted reply. Elijah actually laughed. It was a shame he couldn't see Nigel's face for that.

Before Nigel could start cursing and threatening to leave, Caprice and Theocritus directed their horses off to the sides, heading toward the buildings on either side of the street. While Benedicta and Theocritus opted to pass through the walls as though they weren't even there, the temptation of defying gravity was apparently too much for Caprice and Shu to pass up. The metal horse leaped up onto the building off to the left, and landed on the structure as easily as he would have on the ground.

"Okay, we need to try that later," Stephen announced. Elijah snorted. He had to admit it was pretty intriguing. "Does it feel weird?" Stephen called to Caprice curiously.

"Not really," Caprice replied, looking around from her sideways vantage point. She whipped her rope out to lash it around one of the conjoined horses' necks and added, "Oh, look! It doesn't throw off your aim, either!"

"Oh, it doesn't throw off her aim," Nigel's voice muttered darkly. "Let's talk about that while that thing destroys the city."

"Fuss, fuss," Caprice said disapprovingly as she tried to keep the rope from slipping out of her hand. Meanwhile, Theocritus and Benedicta managed to get around the other side of the clumped horses, and Theocritus threw his Heaven's rope over one of the nearest heads.

It was a bizarre scene, with a nasty cluster of horses being leashed on one side by a futuristic horsewoman riding sideways on a building, and then on the other by a Roman horseman half-engulfed by a solid wall. With the conjoined herd roped, both Caprice and Theocritus reined in their horses in an attempt to force the group to slow down. It worked a bit, but it also did something else.

The clump of monstrous horses began to shift, moving more like a single beast than a collective. It started to tighten together even further, and then began to rise up. As Elijah and the others stared, the conjoined horses transfigured into an even stranger creature with a large head and four thick legs. Even though most of the individual demon horses were then completely absorbed into the shape of the beast, a few heads and kicking legs still stuck out here and there, including the heads Caprice and Theocritus had roped.

"Damn, I didn't think they could get uglier," Elijah remarked to Delilah.

Once it had transformed, the beast bellowed, and it shook itself and reared onto its hind legs in an attempt to break the hold Theocritus and Caprice still had on it. The two were doing an impressive job of hanging on, but they weren't going to be able to manage that forever.

"You two take hold of it as well!" Theocritus ordered Elijah and Stephen. "Aim for the heads of the horses we can still see!"

"I'll take the back right, you take the back left," Stephen directed Elijah before taking off to do exactly that. Since he wasn't really given

155

the chance to respond, Elijah directed Delilah off to their designated side and began scoping out a head to rope.

Once Elijah settled on the head of a horse that looked like it was made of sharp rock, he threw his lasso. The nice thing was that the horse couldn't try to kill him for roping it. The bad thing was that Elijah was now connected to a really big, really pissed-off monster thing.

The beast bellowed and swung a front leg towards Elijah and Delilah. The motion damn near yanked Elijah right out of the saddle, but he shoved his heels down and clung to Delilah with his legs like his immortal soul depended on it. Which it probably did.

Somehow Elijah stayed on, and he managed to keep a grip on the rope. He glanced over towards Stephen and found the biker had gotten a rope around a stray horse head as well. For better or worse, all four riders now had a hold on the giant monster.

"Now what?!" Stephen yelled. It was a good question. Especially since not two seconds after he asked it, the monster began to fight back.

There was something a bit odd to Elijah, and it wasn't the fact they were trying to take down an abomination that had no business even existing. What was odd was that despite the size of the thing and how strong it must have been, none of the riders were being pulled into the air. Sure, they were holding on for dear life, but they were lashed to a creature bigger than an elephant. How were they strong enough to fight its pulling?

Regardless of how they were doing it, simply holding on wasn't making any progress. So the question stood.

Now what?

That was when Nigel came walking down the street. He didn't look any happier than he had when he first showed up on the scene of the stampede, but Elijah was still glad to see him. Despite Nigel's sour attitude, he was generally extremely helpful. And besides, being able to hear Nigel's voice while not being able to see him had been sort of unnerving.

Nigel looked over the scene with pursed lips and critical eyes, and then asked, "What have we learned so far?"

"Oh, go to hell, Nigel!" Caprice snapped. "Do something helpful!"

"My going to Hell wouldn't be terribly helpful," Nigel informed her. Even though his voice was calm and level, it was remarkably easy for Elijah to hear Nigel over the chaos. Was that another Ervonian talent? Voice projection?

"Then what would?!" Stephen demanded. Elijah imagined Stephen was having the hardest time of all of them holding onto his rope since he also had to direct his motorcycle. But then again, there had been moments in the past when Stephen would release Cleopatra's handlebars and have absolutely no trouble at all. Maybe he wasn't as bad off as Elijah thought.

"I told you not to let them join," Nigel reminded the foursome flatly. Before the riders could lose their minds at him, Nigel added, "So as it is, you'll have to undo it."

The four riders looked at one another. At first that sounded impossibly vague, but somehow it wasn't. Elijah knew exactly what to do, and he could see the others did too. He weren't sure how they knew it, but they did.

"Pull!" Theocritus commanded. In unison, the four riders directed their horses and motorcycle to stop short and then back up as quickly as they could, taking the ropes—and the clump of monster horses—with them. The massive beast screamed with several voices at once as it stretched like taffy in the four directions it was being pulled, until it finally tore apart. The pieces that split away spilled to the ground and turned back into the individual demonic horses they had once been. The horses didn't move much at first, apparently dazed. It was taking time for them to reorient themselves and struggle to their feet.

"Now take them!" Nigel ordered, his voice thundering throughout the entire area. Shu and Benedicta reared with fearsome war cries of horses newly empowered, and barreled toward the crippled herd. Delilah kicked up her heels as she went to follow, and even Cleopatra seemed excited, her engine roaring louder than ever.

The riders made quick work of the remaining demon horses. It wasn't long before Elijah was roping a shrieking horse of rotting plague, only to realize it was the last. Once the horse had vanished and all was quiet again, the riders looked at Nigel. The Ervonian looked around for a moment, making sure there were no monsters left, and then turned his luminous, turquoise eyes to the dead riders.

"This is something you'd be far more likely to hear my husband say," Nigel warned, his voice back to being calm and deadpan. "But seeing as how he's not here to say it, I suppose I should. That was rather 'cool'."

Caprice burst into hysterical laughter, nearly falling off her horse. "I don't think he'd say it quite like that!" she wheezed, still laughing.

"You're married to a man?" Elijah asked in surprise. Nigel looked at him blankly, as if he wasn't sure whether or not the question was a rhetorical one.

"Does it make any difference if I am?" Nigel asked after a slight pause. He didn't sound offended or anything. In fact, he sounded more confused than anything else.

"Nah," Elijah replied with a shrug. "Just never heard of a guy havin' a husband before."

"Fair enough," Nigel said placidly. He looked at each of the riders in turn. "You realize it's been somewhere around four years since I saw you last?"

"Really?" Stephen asked, enough shock in his voice for all four humans. "Hell, it seems like it's only been a few hours for us."

"That's normal," Nigel assured. He turned to survey the damage to the city streets and made a face. "And frankly, it will be no great loss if you try to space out your future visits by a few years as well."

"That is for the best, for we cannot stay," Theocritus said. "There is much left to do. Though I hope I do not give the impression your assistance was not valuable."

"Oh, not at all," Nigel replied with a passive wave of his hand. "Just assure me that you now know what to do with any future herds like this."

"Yeah," Stephen said dryly. "Don't let Elijah act as bait."

"Hey, shut the hell up," Elijah snapped, pointing an accusatory finger at Stephen. "You assholes are the ones who made me go!"

"You really have a funny way of remembering things," Caprice said with a glare. Nigel held up his hands to stop the argument before it could go any further.

"I'm going to take that as a 'yes, Nigel, we learned very valuable lessons and will be on our way now'," Nigel informed them. "Now please." He waved them off. "Just go."

"It was good seeing you too," Caprice said nonchalantly, signaling for Shu to turn and start away.

"Thank you for your assistance," Theocritus added with a raise of his hand in farewell.

"Happy to do it," Nigel replied, tossing the riders a wave in return. "For the most part."

# Chapter 25

As the four riders continued their wrangling marathon, they discovered it was a fairly common thing for the demonic horses to gather in herds, and that it was just as common for those herds to join together and become one giant monster. Some were tougher to break apart than others, but they were all taken down in the same basic way. Rope whatever horse heads were still visible. Pry the beast apart. Capture the horses that fell out of the monster.

To be perfectly honest, it was proving to be a lot more efficient than tracking and catching lone ponies. Rather than only gaining one point per chase, the four riders were now walking away from a single encounter with as many as twenty-five points each. By the time they ran into another fellow dead competitor, Elijah, Stephen, Caprice, and Theocritus had all increased their score by a decently impressive amount. But it wasn't their current score that shocked the woman who found them in a bleak, snowy world of the living.

"How did you do that?" the woman asked from the back of her equally surprised camel. She was staring between the spot where the giant mass of horses had been torn apart and the four riders who had done the tearing. "You just...pulled it apart. How...?"

"You have never seen this done?" Theocritus asked, watching the woman carefully. She looked at him with wide, brown eyes and shook her head.

"I've tried to catch them before," the woman explained. "But they don't go to your pen when you've caught them when they're like that. They just stay joined to the others."

"That's why you gotta pull 'em apart," Elijah said with a shrug.

"I've tried, but I've never been able to do it," the woman insisted. "I haven't met anyone who has. Until now, obviously."

"Hang on," Stephen said, holding up a hand. "You mean no one else has been taking those things down?"

"If they have, news of it never reached me," the woman replied.

"What's your name?" Caprice asked.

"Senet," the woman said. "And before you ask, yes, like the game Senet."

"Senet," Caprice said with a smile. "I'm Caprice DeGaglia. This is Stephen Pritchett, Theocritus Atius, and Elijah Blanco." The men greeted Senet with silent waves, and Caprice went on to ask, "Are you riding with anyone else?"

"I was," Senet replied a bit tightly. "I'm not anymore."

"Had some problems with some assholes, huh?" Elijah drawled. Caprice gave him one of her "why don't you try a little sensitivity" looks, but he acted like he didn't see it. Senet's only reply was icy silence, so Caprice took over the conversation again.

"Senet, we have a proposition for you," Caprice said in a tone that was undeniably enticing. Elijah wondered if Caprice used that sort of voice on her husband when she really wanted something. "It's going to sound very strange, but not any stranger than what we've already been through."

"What is it?" Senet asked, still suspicious, but interested.

"We're trying to gather everyone together for a little talk," Caprice explained. "The four of us here have learned some things about this race that have us worried about just how secure our little arrangement with Heaven really is."

"Why should I trust you?" Senet asked rather snidely. "You could be trying to trick me. That's a popular pastime for people in this thing, you know."

"Because you can't even defeat one of those giant congregations," Theocritus replied. Senet clenched her jaw, but looked down to her camel with an air of defeat.

"Where do you want to meet?" Senet asked after a brief pause.

"There's a wheat field where you can access other worlds by going through windmills," Stephen said. "Have you been there?"

"A few times," Senet said with a nod. Though she frowned and added, "I hope you don't expect me to just go there and wait for you."

"Unless you're gonna be helpful, yeah, we do," Elijah said flatly. If everyone was going to be a pain in the ass about this, he wasn't going to be terribly pleasant. Not that he usually was, but still.

"I'm confident I can be more helpful than sitting around a wheat field, counting the stalks," Senet snapped.

"All right, all right, tell you what," Stephen said in a placatory voice. "Why don't you help spread the word? God knows we've got our work cut out for us. Not to mention there will probably be plenty of people who need help getting to Doorfields."

After a silence, Senet finally nodded and said, "I can do that. But what do I tell people?"

"Just ask 'em if they're interested in a little payback for gettin' treated like pieces in a game they never agreed to," Elijah suggested. "Tell 'em you met some folks who might have a way of gettin' outta here without winnin' or goin' to Hell."

Senet looked surprised. "You really think we can do that?" she asked with a hint of hopefulness.

"We think we have a much better chance than we did before," Caprice said, adjusting her hat. "But it's going to take everyone working together if we have any hope of leveling the playing field."

Senet seemed to light up a bit. With just that flash of sunshine in her eyes, Elijah could tell it had been quite a while since the last time Senet allowed herself a little optimism.

"I'll see you there," Senet said as she kicked her camel on. The four riding partners watched her go for a while before looking at one another.

"Sure would be nice if they were all that easy to win over," Elijah remarked.

"Probably won't be long before you regret saying that," Stephen said.

And it wasn't. In fact, it was only a couple stops later Elijah started eating his words.

"You can kiss my ass," a burly man on an ugly motorcycle spat. He and a skinny man on something Caprice called a scooter were glaring hard at the four riders from their spot near a run-down bar in a rough neighborhood.

"I don't kiss asses, I kick 'em," Elijah snapped back. Caprice was clearly fighting extremely hard to keep from laughing. The longer she was around Elijah, the more humor she seemed to find in the scathing remarks Elijah threw around.

Theocritus was far less amused. He watched the scene with very visible distaste, though it was hard to tell if it was aimed at the two strangers or at Elijah. Theocritus clearly didn't have a lot of patience for ridiculous and disrespectful interactions, and Elijah was an expert in both.

Meanwhile, Stephen was uncharacteristically detached from the entire thing. Normally during scenarios that involved Elijah becoming hilariously flustered, Stephen was right alongside Caprice in her struggle to keep a straight face. It seemed this time didn't hold the same entertainment value.

"I'd love to see you try it, cowboy," the burly stranger sneered at Elijah. "I already gave you our answer. We're not going. We've been doing just fine so far on our own, got it?"

"Oh, yeah, I can tell," Elijah scoffed. He waved a hand at their surroundings. "You're just livin' the high life out here, ain't ya? Should I call you two dukes, or should I call you counts? Moron."

"Maybe we should try some kinder convincing?" Caprice suggested to Elijah quietly. Before Elijah could disagree and detail exactly what kind of "convincing" he was going to try next, Stephen finally spoke up.

"Don't bother," Stephen said to Caprice, sounding bored. He didn't even turn his head from whatever it was he was looking at off to the right. "There's only one language those two understand."

"Oh, yeah?" the burly man asked, glaring at Stephen. "And what's that? You gonna try and charm us to wherever it is you want to have this talk?"

"I save my charm for people I can actually respect," Stephen replied. He finally turned to look at the two strangers, and the dark glower he gave them actually made Elijah and Caprice lean away slightly. Ever since learning a little about Stephen's background, Elijah had tried very unsuccessfully to imagine Stephen's role in a gang. It just didn't make sense in Elijah's head. The guy was so passive and good-humored that it was nearly impossible to picture him involved in crime at all. But seeing the wrath and malice in Stephen's eyes as he glared at the two cheap imitation badasses helped. A lot.

"So now you're disrespecting us?" the skinny guy asked incredulously. It marked the first time in the conversation he'd said anything other than a word of agreement directly following whatever his bigger partner said.

"Telling you I don't respect you isn't disrespect," Stephen informed him. "It's just honesty. Now, telling you that I think you're a pair of piss poor excuses for whatever it is you think is 'cool' would be disrespect."

Elijah's eyebrows went up and he looked back to the strangers to see their reactions to that. Caprice and Theocritus did the same, and found both of the men staring at Stephen, shocked. Elijah wasn't sure why. Surely they had been told they were losers in the past. It couldn't have been news or anything.

The big guy started to spout something that would be undoubtedly offensive, but Stephen never gave him the chance to get it out. Quick as a snake, Stephen whipped out his Heaven's rope and threw the loop over the man's head. Once it was around the man's neck, Stephen yanked the rope hard, pulling the man right off his motorcycle and to the ground.

"You stay right there if you don't want the same treatment," Stephen ordered the skinny rider, who was far too horrified to do much of anything anyway. Then Stephen got off Cleopatra and walked over to the big guy, who was presently trying to figure out exactly what the hell just happened. "Here we were, trying to be polite and give the two of you a chance to act like proper gentlemen," Stephen said, "and you have to force me to make a scene."

Once Stephen was over the man, he reached down and grabbed him by his shirt to heft him up into a sitting position. "I'm going to give you one more chance to consider our offer," Stephen said darkly. "And if you carry on like before, I'm going to make certain one of those monsters kills you a second time. You know, just to eliminate any chance of our plan failing because you're too stupid to even turn up for a meeting."

The man stared up at Stephen with wide eyes for a second and then opted to make the smart choice. "You...said it was in a wheat field, right?" he asked meekly.

"Yeah," Stephen said, releasing the man and taking his rope back. "Full of windmills. You can't miss it."

"Sure," the man said. He wasn't moving from his spot on the ground, and Elijah figured that was a good move on his end. "We'll swing by."

"Glad to hear it," Stephen replied. He looked both bikers over one more time before turning and walking back to Cleopatra. "Right, then," he said to his three partners, who were watching him with quite a bit of interest. Before she and the others started off, Caprice looked over at the two defeated riders and gave them a pleasant smile.

"Can't wait to see you there, gentlemen!" she called cheerfully. Elijah smirked and Theocritus actually chuckled.

The four riders left the still stunned men there in the street, and once they were a respectable distance away, Elijah looked over at Stephen.

"Didn't think you had it in you, Pritchett," Elijah said, fairly impressed.

"I had to deal with that all the time back home," Stephen said with a flippant shrug. It was almost surreal how quickly Stephen flipped back into his normal relaxed demeanor. "Blokes like that don't know how to respect anything unless it's accompanied by a kick in the chin."

"A trait many possess throughout the ages, it would seem," Theocritus remarked. "You would encounter men like them in my era as well."

"I thought people back in the day were supposed to have more honor and stuff," Elijah said, looking at Theocritus.

"Had you said that to me at the beginning of this competition, I would have told you that you are correct," Theocritus admitted. "People beyond my time seemed crude at first, but I have learned better since then. The fact they wear different garments and speak different words was merely a distraction from the reality that their minds and ways of living really aren't so different from those of my day. And the methods of enforcing discipline and respect have changed little." He looked at Stephen. "You would have made a formidable commander."

Stephen chuckled and said, "I don't know about all that. But I like to think I did all right before everything went south."

"You weren't just some member in that gang of yours, were you?" Elijah guessed. Stephen had sort of shown his hand during the beat-down, as far as Elijah was concerned. No lackey took control of a situation that easily. "You were the damn ringleader."

"Suppose that's one way of putting it," Stephen replied. "I got pretty tight with the man running things when I was around seventeen. He ended up passing things on to me after he took a bullet to the spine, which landed him in a wheelchair."

"How old were you when that happened?" Caprice asked. Stephen squinted as he thought back, trying to remember.

"Just hit thirty," he said finally. "Yeah. It was around a week after my birthday."

"How long were you around after that?" Elijah inquired. Stephen gave him an odd look.

"If you want to know I'm an old man, just come out and say it," Stephen joked. "Eighteen years, thank you."

"Shit, you don't look much older than thirty-five," Elijah said in surprise. "I know a buncha women back home who'd kill to have your secrets."

"You get a free fountain of youth when you take over," Stephen said sagely. Caprice laughed, and Elijah rolled his eyes, but Theocritus didn't seem to be listening anymore. He was frowning at something up ahead. The others followed his gaze, and Elijah squinted.

"The hell is that?" Elijah muttered.

# Chapter 26

Standing quite a distance down the road from the four riders was what looked like a shining, golden horse. It was staring straight at the riders, and it shifted its weight restlessly every few seconds.

"Is that one of the ponies?" Caprice asked. It certainly didn't look like any of the gruesome horses they'd been chasing.

"I do not think so," Theocritus replied cautiously. "But we shall find out."

Theocritus and Benedicta started towards the strange horse, and the others followed suit. They fanned out a bit as they approached, just in case the animal either tried to charge them or turned out to be bait for an ambush. Elijah had to admit the horse was incredibly lovely. It had a slender frame and a sleek golden coat which looked as if it had been brushed for days on end. As the riders got closer, the horse tossed its head prettily, sending its mane up and down in graceful billows, and it tapped a front hoof on the street.

Something was wrong, though. The closer they got, the more Delilah, Shu, and Benedicta tensed. Even Cleopatra seemed hesitant with the way her motor began grinding and even halting. Elijah frowned and exchanged glances with the other riders. He wasn't really sure what they should do. Turn tail and get out of there? Try to catch the thing? Somehow, neither of those responses felt like the correct one.

Despite the overwhelming suspicion, the group continued to creep closer to the strange horse. For some reason or another, they simply had to get a closer look. That right there should have been a warning, but by the time Elijah realized, it was too late.

Four black cracks suddenly opened in the ground; one beneath each horse and rider. Before anyone had time to react, they were all falling with cries of surprise. Elijah found himself and Delilah tumbling into a great, dark space of nothing at all. The minute the world around them vanished, Elijah was no longer able to see or hear Caprice, Stephen, Theocritus, or their respective steeds.

A sick fear gripped Elijah, but he simply clung to the flailing and panicking Delilah as the two of them continued to drop through space.

He wasn't all that afraid for himself and Delilah. Elijah was honestly more concerned for the others. Were they all going to the same place? Was this the work of the Angel? Did he find out about their plan? If that was the case, was this the first step to some sort of horrible punishment? Elijah could handle whatever he was about to be slapped with, but the other three didn't deserve it. As far as Elijah was concerned, Caprice, Stephen, and Theocritus had just been going along with him.

Another world suddenly sprang up around Elijah and Delilah, and the mustang landed clumsily on a smooth surface of what looked like hardened clay. Just like that, Elijah and Delilah were in an open and rather abstract structure made of the same reddish brown material beneath Delilah's hooves. Large, glassless windows in the walls gave a clear view to a vast desert, as well as the strains of pink and orange bleeding from the horizon. Smooth steps with no railings ascended to a level above which had large holes in the floor. The openings allowed Elijah to see there were walls with glassless windows on the second floor as well, but no roof. The sky overhead was deep cobalt, and the golden crescent moon hanging there provided plenty of light.

Was this the desert where they found Theocritus? Elijah couldn't be sure. The sand wasn't as red, the moon was in a different phase, and the sky was the wrong color, but then again, it could have simply been a different time of day and month. Did time even pass in strange worlds like that?

Elijah looked around the large chamber he and Delilah had landed in, but there wasn't much to see besides a large, rectangular pool in the floor, filled with sparkling blue water. It looked shallow enough to stand in, but Elijah wasn't keen to try it.

Just as Elijah was starting to wonder what the hell he was supposed to do, a calm male voice spoke.

"Sorry for the rough trip in," the voice said. "But now we can have a talk in private."

Elijah looked to his right and found a pleasant-looking man in a suit standing a couple of yards away, smiling at him. The man wasn't terribly tall or terribly short. He wasn't particularly good-looking or particularly ugly. He simply looked average; like the sort of man who would blend right into a crowd. The man gave Elijah a friendly wave and said, "I would have given you more notice, but time's growing short."

"Time looked pretty tall, last I saw," Elijah said, eyeing the man warily. "So he's got a ways to go before he gets short enough to worry about."

The man laughed, and Elijah looked down at Delilah, who looked back at him in turn. What the hell was this?

"So who the hell are you supposed to be?" Elijah asked the stranger.

"Call me the Go-Between," the man replied, still smiling.

"The hell kinda name is that?" Elijah scoffed. He wasn't planning on making nice with someone claiming responsibility for sucking him into another dimension.

"It's more of a title than a name," the Go-Between said kindly. "But that's not important. What's important is why I brought you here."

"Yeah, about that," Elijah said flatly. "This had better be pretty goddamn important. And you'd better tell me what happened to the others before I come down there and pound it outta you."

"There's no need for violence," the Go-Between assured. "When we're done here, you might even thank me for splitting the four of you up."

Elijah seriously doubted that, and the look on his face said it pretty loud and clear. When the Go-Between got no verbal reply, he carried on and said, "I couldn't help but notice how close you've become with those three riders you've been accompanying."

"First off, I wouldn't call us close," Elijah said irritably. "Second of all, how the hell have you been watchin'?"

"Word gets around, Mr. Blanco," the Go-Between said calmly. "Just as in the worlds of the living, there are eyes and ears everywhere, along with mouths to pass things along."

"Then I'll tell you what I used to tell folks back home," Elijah shot back. "Mind your own damn business."

"Now, now, hear me out first," the Go-Between requested, holding up his hands. "I simply thought you might like to know if you were, say, traveling with a group that isn't exactly trustworthy."

"None of us are trustworthy," Elijah said obstinately. "Sinners on their way to Hell, remember?"

"True, and that's why I know you'll believe me when I tell you there appears to be a plan in place to leave you behind," the Go-Between said.

Elijah hesitated. Truth be told, he had considered double-crossing the others at the most opportune moment to ensure he'd win a spot as a Horseman. Horseperson. Whatever the hell Caprice wanted them to be called. That fact alone made the concept of one or more of the other three riders doing the same completely feasible.

"How the hell could you possibly know that?" Elijah asked, glaring at the Go-Between. "Sounds like you're just spittin' rumors."

"You haven't spent every moment with them since partnering up," the Go-Between pointed out. "There have been instances you've separated, even if it was just so the four of you could mop up your target horses. And while they've been careful to make certain you couldn't hear, they haven't always ensured no one else would hear them either."

Elijah's jaw tightened and his eyes narrowed as he watched the Go-Between. What really pissed him off was that it all continued to sound entirely plausible. In fact, Elijah had even wondered in the past if something like this was brewing behind his back. Having it said aloud to him by a complete stranger was turning fleeting wonderings into hard suspicions, and that was the last thing Elijah needed.

"You got some kinda proof?" Elijah asked. "'Cause you could be just tryin' to screw with my game."

"I'm afraid I've got nothing besides the knowledge of what I've seen and heard, and my word as an honest Go-Between," the Go-Between said regretfully. "I know you've got no reason to trust me. But if you want my input, Mr. Blanco, I would caution that sometimes the people you actually do trust are far more dangerous than the ones you don't. They're the ones who can really damage you, after all."

Elijah said nothing to that. As infuriating as it was, what the Go-Between said was entirely true. After all, it was why Elijah had avoided friendships and partnerships during his living days.

"Let's say I trust you," Elijah said after a good, long pause. "What exactly are you expectin' me to do?"

"Oh, I'm not expecting you to do anything, Mr. Blanco," the Go-Between said in surprise. "I'm simply advising you of a situation. If it was me, I would do my best to distance myself from those three, but that's a decision for you to make. Not me."

"Consider me warned then," Elijah snapped. "Now show me the way outta here." He wasn't about to ponder his options with some stranger breathing down his neck.

"Not just yet," the Go-Between said, his face clouded with concern. "There's one more thing I wanted to address."

"Yeah, and what's that?" Elijah asked in exasperation.

"Well, it's about the people running the game you've been pulled into," the Go-Between explained. "Did they even give you a choice in this?"

"'Course they did," Elijah replied. Even though he was already horrendously doubtful the Angel and his group were on the riders' side, Elijah wasn't about to give the Go-Between the satisfaction of a lack of argument. "One of the first things that Angel did was ask us to choose between competin' and goin' to Hell."

"That hardly sounds like much of a choice to me," the Go-Between said with a frown. "I hope they've at least assured all of you that even if you don't win, you get something out of all this."

Delilah stamped a foot impatiently and tossed her head, as if urging her rider to end the conversation. But for some reason, Elijah found himself wanting to hear more of what the Go-Between had to say.

"So what are you suggestin'?" Elijah asked. "You want me to just cut and run?"

"Is it so different from what you've been planning to do along with those other riders?" the Go-Between asked in return. "Think about it. In the end, you might be better off making yourself scarce before you go and piss off Angels and Gods and so on."

"Why the hell do you even care?" Elijah demanded. "You seem awful concerned for a guy who's not even involved in this thing."

"I don't like injustice," the Go-Between said earnestly. "I've been around a long time. I've seen people get pulled into these sorts of things with extremely unpleasant results."

Elijah watched the Go-Between suspiciously. While the Go-Between was bringing up some good points, Elijah still didn't entirely trust him.

"What are you, anyway?" Elijah asked after a moment. "I ain't seen any dead humans who ain't riders, and you don't seem like an Embodied."

"Do you mind if we take a bit of a walk?" the Go-Between asked, once again answering a question with a question of his own. It was getting irritating. "That might help explain a few things."

Elijah sighed loudly in frustration and rubbed at his face. He was never going to get rid of this guy, was he? "Fine, but you better make this quick," Elijah said. "And I swear to God, if I think you're tryin' to waste my time, you're gonna regret ever tryin' to warn me about anything."

"Perfectly fair," the Go-Between said agreeably. He turned and started for the stairs that led to the second level of the building. "It won't take long!"

"It better not," Elijah muttered. He signaled Delilah to go after the Go-Between, but the horse refused to budge. She even looked back at Elijah, as if scornfully asking if he was serious. "Look, I don't like it any more than you do," Elijah told her irritably. "Let's just get this over with."

Delilah acted like she was sniffing the ground disinterestedly and Elijah fought the urge to kick her. He really didn't need her giving him shit on top of everything else.

"Look, either you take me, or I get off and drag you," Elijah announced. "Better yet, I'll leave your ass here. You can just wander on your own."

It was an empty threat, and both horse and rider knew it. But Delilah clearly didn't trust Elijah to be on his own without ending up in even worse trouble, because she very slowly and begrudgingly started after the Go-Between. Elijah glared at her, but he did give her a pat on the neck. Something that had Delilah snorting.

"Oh, shut up," Elijah said to his horse, dangerously close to sulking.

Upstairs, the Go-Between was standing by one of the ridiculously large windows, waiting patiently for the horse and rider and keeping his eyes locked on them as they approached. When Elijah and Delilah were close enough, the Go-Between turned to look out the window and asked, "Do you know what this place is?"

"No, but I'm sure you're gonna tell me," Elijah said flatly.

"It's one of the Transit Places," the Go-Between said, disregarding Elijah's attitude. "Transit Places are very fluid planes of existence. They are defined by the occupants rather than an origin of its creation."

"What's that supposed to mean?" Elijah asked, confused. "You can change the way it looks?"

"Not consciously," the Go-Between replied. "As you travel through a Transit Place, it begins to reflect your heart and mind. It reaches out in an attempt to help you learn about yourself. It can even assist in making tough decisions since it digs up things you have buried deep within. You might already have the answer in your head, but you can't hear it because you're too overwhelmed by distractions. The Transit Place can help with all that."

"So you want me to go out there and ride through a damn desert for God-knows-how-long," Elijah said with narrowed eyes. "What the hell makes you think I'm interested in self-discovery and opening my mind and all that crap?"

"You asked me to show you the way out," the Go-Between reminded Elijah with a shrug. "I'm afraid the only way out here is to go through."

"Then why the hell would you bring me here in the first place?!" Elijah demanded, completely aggravated at that point. "Couldn't you just pull me to the side somewhere?! Hand me a goddamn note?!"

"I can see you're angry," the Go-Between said diplomatically.

"Well, Christ, good deduction!" Elijah snapped.

"But I really do think you'll benefit from this," the Go-Between went on, as if Elijah hadn't said anything at all. "And I really do think you should have some time to think before you go back to those three you've been riding with for so long."

Elijah simply glared at the Go-Between for a while. He was about two kind suggestions away from dropping off Delilah and kicking the Go-Between right in the stomach. When would people learn he wasn't interested in anyone's help or advice unless he asked for it? It wasn't like people actually cared what happened to him anyway, so why the hell were some pretending they did?

"Listen, asshole," Elijah said darkly, "you've come in here and said a lotta pretty things so far, but I ain't seen you do much of anything to prove that you're anything but a gossip and a busybody. So I'm gonna take off, and you're gonna do the same, but you're not goin' the same way I am. Got it? We're done. And while we're at it, you better leave those three idiots and their load-bearin' partners alone too, or I'll find you and kick your ass."

"That's perfectly fair," the Go-Between said agreeably. God, Elijah wanted to hit him. "Thank you for your time, Mr. Blanco. Good luck with everything."

And just like that, the Go-Between vanished into thin air. Elijah looked around to make sure the guy was really gone, then looked out the window at the desert beyond. It was strangely inviting in a serene sort of way, like it was waiting for someone to explore it.

It was about to get its wish, Elijah supposed. Because as things were, he and Delilah didn't have much choice but to go try to find the way out.

"Well," Elijah said slowly. "Guess we better get movin'." Delilah snorted and tossed her head.

# Chapter 27

Out in the desert, it was quiet and empty, but not exactly bleak. It was actually sort of elegant in its own way. After riding for a while, Elijah decided the desert most likely wasn't the same one the horse named Here called home. The sand and the moon simply looked too different. Apparently, Elijah thought, whoever made all the different dimensions had a thing for deserts. Either that or Elijah was being given a very limited view into everything that existed.

It was definitely the latter, but that wasn't exactly Elijah's main concern right then.

The further Elijah and Delilah went, the more Elijah's thoughts began to gnaw at him. The things the Go-Between had said were playing over and over again in Elijah's mind. And with nothing to look at besides smooth dunes and a strangely-colored sky, Elijah's train of thought was allowed to race uninterrupted down some pretty unpleasant tracks.

There were a lot of good reasons Elijah had journeyed alone for so long. Life had taught him some pretty valuable lessons about people and being around them. Hell, not five days after he'd left home as a teenager and struck out on his own, someone who was supposed to have been a friend of the family had robbed him. If that didn't set the stage for a lifetime of disappointment, Elijah wasn't sure what did.

So there he was, nearly two decades later; pushing people away and not regretting it. But even with all of that justification, Elijah kept grimly thinking back to when he had stolen Caprice's pony. The way she'd looked at him was a fairly common sight for Elijah. A lot of people had looked at him that way over the years. But somehow Caprice's eyes had been harder to look at when she realized what Elijah had done to her. They were the eyes of someone who had really trusted him, and for all her trouble, had just watched that trust get thrown off a cliff.

Though...that was just plain odd to Elijah. Had Caprice really trusted him that much so quickly? Was she stupid or something?

Elijah supposed in the end it didn't really matter. Either way, he had screwed Caprice over pretty hard, and even though he made it up to her and they hadn't talked about it since, Elijah had to wonder if Caprice was still holding a grudge. Jeopardizing a person's chance to see their lover again seemed like a pretty good way of ensuring you'd get burned later, after all.

Delilah snorted suddenly, disrupting Elijah's thoughts. Her head was lifted high as she walked, and her ears were pricked forward attentively. Elijah blinked and looked around to see what had the horse so interested, and got a bit of a shock.

The world around him and Delilah had begun to change.

Large, black, rectangular blocks now stood to the left and right of Elijah and Delilah, going up at least fifteen feet. There were tons of them, stuck in the ground intermittently like fence posts in the direction the horse and rider were headed. The lines of the blocks went as far as Elijah could see both ahead and behind. He hadn't heard a thing, and he hadn't been riding for all that long. The things must have just sprouted up out of nowhere while he wasn't paying attention.

"The hell?" Elijah muttered. He reined Delilah in to a halt, and the two of them took a moment to look around. There was still no sign of life. Everything was as still and silent as before. It was only sand, sky, a moon which hadn't moved at all, and the new decorations. Elijah dismounted and took Delilah's reins, leading her over to one of the blocks. There were no markings on it. Elijah even wandered all the way around the thing just to make sure, but there was nothing.

After a brief investigation yielding nothing interesting, Elijah climbed back into the saddle and signaled for Delilah to walk on in the same direction they had been traveling before.

Although the blocks were strange and extremely intriguing, after another long while of nothing new happening, Elijah slipped back into his thinking from earlier. Having established there really was a good chance Caprice was either planning or simply willing to turn on him, Elijah turned his thoughts to Stephen. Elijah had quite honestly never considered Stephen to be a person who would double-cross anyone, but then again, Elijah had never considered Stephen to be the sort of person who would rough up and threaten a couple of strangers either.

There was also the fact Caprice and Stephen had most likely traveled around together at some point before ending up with Elijah and Delilah. Elijah had never explicitly asked, but the two did seem awful friendly with one another. That laid groundwork for Stephen having more loyalty towards Caprice than anyone else, and if Caprice had a bone to pick with Elijah, it wasn't unthinkable that Stephen would support her. After all, Stephen had made it extremely clear he was aware of Elijah's reputation amongst other riders when he first started tagging along with Elijah and Caprice.

As a result, Elijah had to wonder if Caprice and Stephen had agreed to keep Elijah around only until they were sure they had squeezed every ounce of usefulness out of him. It wasn't like people hadn't done that before. Elijah seemed to be a prime target for that sort of crap.

Movement in the corner of Elijah's eye suddenly caught his attention, and he turned his head to see what it was. When he looked, nothing was moving, but things were suddenly different again. This time, fences of black iron had appeared between the black blocks providing a makeshift path. The bars went all the way up to the tops of the blocks and were capped off with sharp points. Elijah and Delilah were suddenly walled in. They could still go forward or turn around and go back, but Elijah had to hope the way out wouldn't suddenly appear off to the side.

"What the hell is goin' on?" Elijah demanded. Delilah snorted and tossed her head as if expressing the same frustration. Elijah brought the mustang to a halt and thought for a second.

"Okay, so that asshole said this place reflects what you've got inside your head," Elijah contemplated aloud. Sometimes it was easier to think if he talked it out with Delilah. "So, what, I'm boxin' myself in right now? This is stupid. If I think real hard, will all this shit disappear?"

He gave it a shot.

Nothing happened.

"Damn it!"

Delilah huffed and lowered her head to sniff at the sand beneath her feet. Elijah rubbed at his face and took one more look around before giving up and nudging Delilah forward again. Standing around wasn't going to solve anything.

Elijah tried very hard to stay alert so he could catch any further changes as they happened. However, that was unbelievably difficult to do. It was like his thoughts were louder than ever in that desert. No matter what tactic he used to keep his focus on the world around him, Elijah always found himself getting lost in his contemplations once again. Eventually his mind gave up on attentiveness, and he was swallowed by doubts and wonderings. This time his brain kept circling around the puzzle that was Theocritus.

At first glance, Elijah would say Theocritus didn't have any favorites in their little group, but the soldier was such a hard man to read. When it came down to it, all Elijah had to go by was what he knew about Theocritus's personality and how it differed in his interactions with the three of them.

As far as Elijah could tell, Caprice was the only one who had managed to soften Theocritus up at all. She had an undeniable way with people, and the way she and Theocritus spoke to one another was proof of that. Maybe it was because she was careful to never come off as an opponent. Maybe she was simply kind enough that she tugged at Theocritus's heartstrings the way a sister would. Elijah wasn't sure.

Stephen and Theocritus's relationship was obviously different from that sort of dynamic, but it was still a friendly one. There was a lot of mutual respect there, which had only grown as the two learned more about one another. Although they were from extremely different times and cultures, at the end of the day, Elijah supposed they really weren't so different. After all, they were both soldiers in their own rights. They were both leaders and commanders. And even with those facts aside, Stephen had a charm and humor that made it difficult to dislike him.

With all those thoughts in mind, Elijah began thinking back on his interactions with Theocritus. It wasn't that they had all been negative, but Elijah couldn't help but remember moments where Theocritus looked at him with no small amount of disapproval. And the two of them didn't exactly get off to a very good start in Here's desert.

As Elijah reflected back on his first conversation with Theocritus, he actually winced a little. Admittedly, there might have been a couple of times Elijah could've handled things a bit better.

Arguments with Caprice and Stephen came to mind. Maybe those could have been avoided or even just shortened.

Though, the more he thought, the more irritated Elijah became. It wasn't like anyone held a gun to the others' heads and forced them to keep tagging along with him. If they felt like he was such a pain in the ass or a weight around their necks, why didn't they just take off?

The light from the moon in the sky above suddenly dimmed, and Elijah looked up and saw a tangle of iron bars had stretched overhead from the fences around him and Delilah, making a kind of roof. He and Delilah were officially caged in. It got worse when he realized Delilah had stopped to stare at a thick, black wall completely blocking her path a few yards ahead.

"Are you serious?" Elijah asked no one in particular, exasperated. He turned to look behind them and found they were walled in that way as well. "Son of a bitch."

Elijah dismounted once again, though this time he didn't bother holding onto Delilah's reins. It wasn't like she could go very far. He walked over to the wall in their path and pushed his hands against it. It definitely wouldn't be moving anytime soon. Elijah sighed and scratched his head as he tried to think. It all clearly meant something, and since death had been one puzzle after another so far, Elijah knew it was something he'd have to figure out instead of trying to just force his way through.

"All right," he said, putting his hands on his hips. "So when we first started walkin', none of this shit was out here. It was just desert." Delilah bobbed her head, which Elijah took as a nod of affirmation. He looked at her and squinted thoughtfully. "We didn't actually do anything, but I got to thinkin', and that guy did say your mind changes this place."

Elijah turned to look at the wall again and fell silent for a bit as he continued putting two and two together. "The more I thought about the other three, the more stuff got in our way," he said slowly. "So is this place tryin' to tell me I'm bein' caged in by those idiots?"

Elijah looked at his horse, but got no reply. Delilah looked doubtful somehow, but then again, she often looked doubtful. Elijah frowned at her, and then began glaring at the obstacles around them. Helpful advice was one thing, but this was starting to feel like he was being told what to do, and he didn't like it. For all he knew, the Go-Between was still at work, this time refusing to let them go anywhere unless Elijah made the choice other people wanted him to make.

"So, what?" Elijah snapped at the walls. "You want me to decide to just go on alone? To hell with the others, just worry about myself?" He snorted. "Listen, I didn't join up with those morons for the company. In case you haven't noticed, they're actually pretty damn useful. This stupid competition ain't exactly the easiest thing in the world if you go solo. I stuck with 'em for me, y'hear? Nobody else."

There was no reply, of course. And there was a nagging voice in the back of Elijah's head asking if he even really needed the other three at that point. They were well on their way to winning, if that was what they wanted.

Come to think of it, was winning the race for the Apocalypse really what Elijah wanted? Did he really want to triumph in what appeared to be a game with loaded dice, only to be at the beck and call of an incredibly shady Heaven?

Elijah pinched the bridge of his nose. It felt like his brain was so overloaded with thoughts and doubts that it was in danger of overheating. Right then, all he really wanted was a damn break. He was starting to understand why Theocritus had been so grim about dying only to get thrown into another mess. Was giving Elijah a shitty life not enough for whoever made him? They had to give him a shitty death, too?

Moping wasn't getting him anywhere, so Elijah took to looking around again, trying to stay on one train of thought. It was getting harder and harder to do so, but he had to try.

Delilah could sense her human partner's agitation, and she began to shift and fidget restlessly. They needed to get out of there for both their sakes. In the interest of doing just that, Delilah snorted to get Elijah's attention, and then began pawing at the air in front of her with her front right hoof.

"The hell you doin'?" Elijah asked with a puzzled look. Delilah whinnied and repeated the motion. Elijah watched her, trying to decipher what she was trying to do. It was a bit like she was digging midair. When nothing registered, Delilah gave a frustrated squeal and paced away a little. Once she placed herself, she struck the air with her front hoof again, and then hopped forward like she was leaping through the spot she had just touched.

"You wanna bust through?" Elijah guessed. "All right, smartass, give me your chisel and hammer."

That was when Elijah suddenly had a flashback to Nigel showing him and the others how to tear through dimensions. Elijah stared at Delilah for a second and then slapped a hand over his face. God, he was such an idiot.

Of course, Elijah had never actually tried creating his own portal, so there was still a good chance they'd continue being stuck there. He figured giving it a shot was the only way of finding out if that was the case.

So he did, but simply grabbing at the air didn't produce any results, so Elijah had to try and think it through. "Mind over matter" had been Nigel's repeated guidance, so Elijah was obliged to think outside the box.

Elijah thought back to everything he'd seen and been through so far. He discovered that if he focused on being aware of things that weren't right in front of his eyes, he could sense a lot going on around him. It was almost like standing in the middle of a busy street with a blindfold over his eyes and cotton in his ears. His way out was just beyond a veil. The problem was that he wasn't sure how to pull the veil aside and step through.

After a moment of struggling with no real progress to show for it, Elijah finally stopped and decided to try a different approach. He sat down on the sand, closed his eyes, and lifted his hands like he was getting ready to grab something as it went by. Part of him was screaming about how ridiculous he must have looked, but since no one except Delilah was around, and since he didn't want to be stuck in that damn desert forever, he ignored everything except what he was sensing. Regardless of what he thought of the other three riders, Elijah wasn't going to spend eternity stranded in a cage. He would get out of there and figure things out later, no matter what he had to do or how stupid he ended up looking while doing it.

As Elijah focused, he became more and more aware of just how many possible exits there were at his disposal. He caught glimpses of people sitting around some sort of board with writing on it, a woman praying in a church, a boy drawing alone in his room, and all sorts of other things. There were whispers of chants, wails of desperation, somber hymns, casual talking to no one, and even a little girl bossing around an imaginary friend.

Was this really all it took for the dead to come back and visit the living? It was a hell of a lot more convenient than the Hub and Doorfields.

Suddenly, something in particular caught Elijah's attention. It was the singing of a woman. She had a voice purer and lovelier than anything Elijah had ever heard before, with rich and clear tones that were nothing short of hypnotic. Curious, he focused on that voice and began to search for the path to it. All at once, he could sense something right in front of him, and he grabbed at it with a hand and pulled hard.

With that, Elijah opened his eyes to see a jagged entrance into another world. Delilah whinnied and pranced in place, clearly looking forward to getting out and back on the road. Elijah grinned in spite of himself and stood up to hurry over to Delilah and get up onto her back.

All right, girl," he said to the horse. "Get us the hell outta here."

Delilah tossed her head and went barreling for the opening, leaping through with an eager kick of her hind legs.

# Chapter 28

Delilah clattered into the center of a nighttime garden brimming with strange plants. It was a rather clumsy entrance, with Delilah knocking over a decorative statuette and crashing through a bush. Elijah wasn't entirely sure how she'd managed to make physical contact with things so easily, but it wasn't like knowing the reason would undo all the damage she had just done.

As if that wasn't bad enough, it turned out there were witnesses. Most of them were tiny hummingbirds and large butterflies, but there was also a woman. She sat on the ground, clothed in a revealing outfit of bright orange, blue, and pink. Although, to be honest, Elijah wasn't sure undergarments and an open, flowing robe constituted an actual outfit.

The woman had a shocking amount of brown hair with locks of blonde here and there. It wasn't only that her hair was long, though it definitely was. The woman had so much of it growing from her head that it looked as though she had gathered a few separate wigs to make one rather impressive one.

But it was the woman's eyes that really got Elijah's attention. She stared up at him and Delilah with wide, startled eyes that glowed a brilliant pink, the color gently wafting into the air around her face.

She was Ervonian. And she could definitely see the horse and rider.

"Uh, hey," Elijah greeted awkwardly.

"Hello," the woman said simply, still stunned. She had to be the one Elijah had heard singing. Her speaking voice was just as pleasing to listen to as her singing

Elijah hesitated and looked around before looking back to the woman again. "Sorry about the mess," he said honestly.

"Oh," the woman said. She blinked and gave Elijah a chuckle and a wave. "Don't worry about that." She looked Elijah and Delilah over carefully and said, "You're a bit different, aren't you?"

"Nah, just dead," Elijah replied with a shrug. The woman pressed her lips together and slowly shook her head with a drawn-out hum.

Elijah couldn't tell if she was trying to wrap her head around that, or if she was actually disagreeing with what he just said.

Once she was done thinking, the woman asked, "What are your names?"

"The lady here is Delilah," Elijah said, patting his horse's neck. "I'm Elijah Blanco."

"What poetic names," the woman complimented with a grin. "I'm happy to meet both of you."

"Yeah, you too," Elijah said. There was something about the woman that made her disarmingly charming. Maybe it was her loveliness. Maybe it was her lilting voice. Maybe it was the crazy hair and lack of modesty. Hell, Elijah couldn't tell. "You got a name?"

"I do," the woman laughed. "Veona Ervine." Two birds landed on top of her head, but she didn't seem to notice. With all that hair, Elijah wasn't really surprised. "Have you seen a mirror lately, Mr. Blanco?" Veona asked.

"Huh?" Elijah said, confused. Then he remembered how he and the others had looked in the reflection of the shop window back on Earth. "Oh. We look like that to you, huh? All rotted and shit?"

"I wouldn't use the word 'rotted'," Veona said thoughtfully. She continued examining Elijah and Delilah, tapping a finger against her lips. "To say you're rotting is to imply that you're decaying, which in turn implies that you're departing. I'd say you're just the opposite. You're not departing. You're arriving."

"What's that supposed to mean?" Elijah asked. He was still at a loss, but for some reason Veona wasn't pissing him off like most people would. He'd chalk it up to relief that came from getting out of that stupid cage in the desert.

Veona stood up, revealing she was taller than she had first looked. She must have been at least six feet tall. Her hair and robe swept around her as she moved closer to the horse and rider, and she absent-mindedly swept the little birds and butterflies out of her path as she walked.

"It means there's more to you than just bones and dead lights," Veona said. She looked awe-struck as she got a closer look at Elijah and Delilah, and an eager smile spread over her face. "Aren't you both lovely?" she whispered. Then she whirled around with a laugh and glided over to a nearby fountain that flowed with mist instead of liquid. Elijah was honestly too baffled to really react, so he chose to just watch the woman and see if he could figure out what she was doing.

"Do you know what it is I see, Mr. Blanco?" Veona asked brightly, taking a seat on the edge of the fountain's pool. She beckoned him and Delilah closer with a wave of her hand as she waited for him to answer her.

"Well, I'd guess you see the dead, but your eyes ain't the right color," Elijah replied, nudging Delilah on. "The guy I met who was able to see us had kinda bluish green eyes."

"I'm not Gorvon, that's right," Veona chuckled. She reached out kindly as Delilah walked closer, allowing the horse to sniff her hands. "I'm one of what we call the Arvon. I see the streams of life."

"Life?" Elijah echoed with a blink. He looked down at himself and Delilah, and then gave Veona an odd look. "Pretty sure I ain't alive, lady."

Veona laughed, throwing her head back and slapping a hand against her breast. She was either naturally joyful or she was deep into opiates. Elijah wasn't sure which it was.

"Life and being alive aren't mutually exclusive," Veona said, still giggling as she waved her hands dismissively. "You can find new life after you stop being alive. Did you know that?"

"Not really," Elijah admitted. "I thought dead meant dead."

"Oh, it does," Veona insisted. She turned and began swirling the mist in the pool next to her with her hands. "But that doesn't exclude you from being rebirthed or reimagined."

"Oh," Elijah said. Then after a pause said, "Wait, I don't get it."

"Here, think of it like this," Veona said, spinning around to face Elijah again. She held her hands up in front of her face, pointing at him as she spoke. "Say you have some clay, and you make it into a bowl. Then imagine you decide to change it into a plate. When you reshape that clay, does the clay itself actually change?"

"No," Elijah replied slowly. "It just has a different shape."

Veona grinned and dropped her hands down into her lap. "Very good," she said. With that, she twirled back around on her seat to face the mist once again.

"Now then," the Ervonian said cheerfully. She dipped her hands into the shallow pool and scooped up the vapor like it was water, then quickly stood up and turned, tossing the mist towards Elijah and Delilah.

Elijah's instinctive reaction to recoil from things being hurled at him had all but vanished thanks to living so long as a dead man. But when the mist that Veona threw slammed Elijah with a cold and then tingling sensation, he realized that trying to move out of the way probably would have been a great idea. At least he had the consolation of knowing he wasn't the only one caught completely off-guard. When the mist hit her, Delilah suddenly started and shied away.

"The hell was that?!" Elijah asked, feeling a little betrayed. Things had been going so well for a whole five minutes. Why couldn't he meet a kind and attractive woman who *didn't* spontaneously throw something at him while he was on his horse?

"Shh," Veona said quietly, holding up an index finger. Her eyes were locked on the mist that was streaming down the horse and rider, watching as it pooled and swirled. She tilted her head curiously and breathed, "Oh, you *are* different." Veona blinked and looked up at Elijah's face. "Not just different. *New*."

"What?" Elijah blurted out, just staring at Veona. "New?"

"Yes," Veona replied, acting somewhat enchanted. "But I can see that you're also old. And since you know of the Gorvon, chances are very high that you've met..."

A smile slowly spread across Veona's face as she lit up in realization. "Our Negotiator," Veona said in a low and somewhat ominous tone. Then Veona laughed loudly and clapped her hands together, attracting several birds and butterflies that began fluttering around her. "How fun!" she said enthusiastically. "We get an excuse to go and ruffle his feathers! I love him when he's fussy."

Without even waiting for Elijah to reply, Veona spun around and began making her way down a glassy path on the ground. "Come along!" she called as she went. "We need to get you set on the right path again!"

Neither Elijah nor Delilah moved at first, still not sure exactly what the hell just happened. Elijah was beginning to seriously question his choice of paths out of that desert. He considered sneaking away and figuring out where he'd go from there, but he was curious about this other person Veona wanted to see. Elijah guessed it could be Nigel, but he had no way of knowing that for sure. Caprice had mentioned that Nigel was just one person out of a group, after all.

So Elijah sighed and nudged Delilah to go after the humming Veona and her entourage of little flying animals. He just hoped to God she wouldn't throw anything else at him.

Veona led Elijah and Delilah out of the garden, which turned out to be impressively large, and through a strange forest of crystalline structures. Like the city architecture, the structures didn't look so much like things that had been built as they did things that had actually grown up out of the ground on their own. The odd branches of thick, glassy material curled and spiraled like twisted trees with no leaves, and some of them reached so high Elijah couldn't even see the tops of them. Some were sharp and angled, and others were curved and smooth, but they were all undeniably pretty.

Once they were through the strange trees of crystal, Veona, Delilah, and Elijah ended up on one of Ervonia's city streets, but in an area much quieter than those Elijah had seen before.

"Where are we goin', exactly?" Elijah asked, looking around.

"You just keep riding, Mr. Blanco," Veona chuckled. "Leave the worrying to the world. It does that plenty enough for everyone."

Elijah wasn't even going to bother trying to argue that one. He'd learned a long time ago that it was sometimes just easier to let the weirder replies go, and wait and see what happened next. The three of them went on in silence for a while, and Elijah took the opportunity to examine the space around him.

There were small homes along the street, made of the same glass that sprang from the ground as most everything else in that city. But it didn't look like any of them were occupied. There were no lights. There were none of the hovering vehicles Elijah had seen elsewhere. Really, there was no indication of life being present at all. In fact, when Elijah looked more carefully at one of the little buildings, he could see signs that the normally sharp edges had been worn down, and that there were cracks and dents in the material. Whether it was deliberate damage or just the work of time, Elijah couldn't tell.

"What happened here?" Elijah asked with a small frown. "Everybody find a better part of town?"

"Some with a cruel sense of humor might say so," Veona replied, looking around. "Suffice it to say that no one lives here anymore. But one person comes to stay sometimes. Maybe he hopes he'll speak to one of his own again."

"Too bad," Elijah murmured as he continued taking in the scenery. "Looks like it was nice."

Veona smiled serenely as she nodded. "It was," she assured. "Maybe one day you'll see it as it used to be."

Elijah said nothing to that. Part of him wasn't sure he wanted to see anything since it sounded like there was a risk of witnessing something really horrifying. But the idea of dimension-hopping to see places at different times was sort of an interesting one. Elijah was still honestly toying with the notion of forgetting about the competition altogether and doing something else, so he was taking alternate options to consider as they came to him. Hell, at least maybe a break would help him clear his head.

Elijah's train of thought was cut off there by Veona's suddenly veering off the path to walk for a little house standing a bit further from the street than the others. It was a very unassuming structure that looked like it was trying to just blend in with its surroundings. Veona went right up to the front door, though her pace slowed to a cautious creep as she got close. She reached out with slender hands and gently touched the surface of the door, like she was listening with her fingertips.

"Mm-hm," Veona hummed with a smile. She turned to look at Elijah and invited him over with a crook of her finger. Elijah dismounted quietly, and slowly made his way over to where Veona was standing, with Delilah stepping carefully behind him.

Once Elijah was what Veona considered close enough, she turned back to the door and very slowly opened it to peek inside. Elijah leaned to one side so he could see past Veona and into the house. What he saw had him raising an eyebrow.

The entrance to the little house opened into a modest sitting room furnished simply with a couch, a small table, and an armchair which had definitely seen better days. Sitting in that armchair, fast asleep, was Nigel Cairnahm.

# Chapter 29

"The hell is Cairnahm doin' here?" Elijah whispered to Veona. It seemed a bit odd for Nigel to go take a nap in an abandoned neighborhood. Though, of course, Elijah had to admit it was hardly the oddest thing he'd seen lately.

"Sleeping, it looks like," Veona whispered back. Elijah rolled his eyes. Good, someone else who was comfortable stating the obvious. Before he had the chance to say something pithy, Veona slid into the house and approached Nigel with a finger pressed to her lips. She stopped just in front of Nigel and watched him in silence for a moment. Then she climbed onto the armchair, straddling Nigel's lap.

"Nigel!" Veona sang happily. She took Nigel's face in her hands as she said it and gently squeezed his cheeks. The way Nigel reacted, one would have thought a gun had gone off next to his head. He jolted and tried to wrench away from her touch, damn near flipping the chair backwards in the process. Veona fumbled and fell off Nigel's lap and onto the floor, landing on her rear while laughing hysterically.

"What the hell is the matter with you?!" Nigel demanded from the chair, staring at Veona with wide eyes. "If you want to kill me, just stick a knife in my heart, woman!"

"That wouldn't work!" Veona protested, staying where she was. That was when Nigel noticed Elijah and did one hell of a double-take.

"And now you're meddling with the dead!" Nigel said to Veona, thoroughly irritated. "Precisely how much have you had to drink today? I thought we agreed—"

"Nigel, he's not all dead," Veona interjected. Nigel stared at her some more, and Veona swept a hand over her head in a grand gesture. "He's a mystical being, flung far into the designs of Fate," she said in a deep and somber voice.

There was a pause, during which no one moved or spoke. Then Nigel dropped his head into his hands.

"Please tell me this is some sort of hallucination," Nigel groaned. Veona grinned and rocked forward so she could reach up and play with Nigel's hair.

"I *am* meant to be your dream girl," Veona said with a laugh.

Elijah had no idea what to think as he watched the odd little scene play out. But he had to admit it was sort of fun watching Nigel get flustered by Veona. Elijah could see what she had meant back in the garden about Nigel being an entertaining person to annoy.

Nigel lifted his head then and looked over at Elijah with a frown. "What are you doing here?" he asked. "Are you the only one?"

"Yeah," Elijah said flatly. "Well, Delilah's here too, but that's it. We got split up."

"Split up?" Nigel echoed in confusion. He and Veona looked at one another, and then looked back to Elijah. "What do you mean?" Nigel asked. "What split you up?"

"Look, that don't matter right now," Elijah insisted. He really didn't feel like going into what happened. It would force him to think about the others some more, and that wasn't exactly high on his to-do list right then.

"Oh, no?" Nigel asked, his frown deepening. "Then I suppose I'm expected to believe that you simply popped in for a visit?"

"Hey, she brought me here," Elijah said, pointing an accusatory finger at Veona. She looked a bit surprised at that and put a hand to her chest in disbelief.

"I brought you because you came," Veona said incredulously. "And because I saw questions in your eyes."

Nigel watched Veona for a second, like he was making sure she was finished. When she didn't say anything else, he looked at Elijah and said, "You see? That's what happens when you have questions in your eyes. Whatever the hell that's supposed to mean."

"Hey, I just needed a way outta that damn desert," Elijah told Veona. "I heard you singin' and figured this would be a good way out."

"Oh, he liked my singing," Veona said delightedly to Nigel.

"Everyone likes your singing," Nigel replied, keeping his eyes on Elijah.

"Do they?" Veona asked in surprise. Elijah put a hand over his eyes and took a second to remind himself to keep pretending this was normal.

"Anyway," he said firmly, dropping his hand. "The point is, I ain't lookin' for help from either one of you."

"Sometimes the help you need comes without any looking," Veona said. She dropped down onto her back on the floor and stared up at the ceiling with her fingers against her lips. "Why would She lead him to both of us?" she murmured around her hands.

"We aren't meant to be solving puzzles," Nigel warned Veona lowly. She scoffed and lifted her arms to wave them gracefully through the air.

"The puzzles are woven all around us, Nigel," Veona insisted. "None of us would exist if we weren't meant to have an impact on the world."

Nigel made a face, but he sat back in his chair and interlaced his fingers, apparently going to allow Veona to have her way. He did, however, mutter, "That's your argument for everything."

Veona ignored Nigel and sat up to solemnly look Elijah in the eye. "Tell me of the others," she requested. "Your companions."

"What do you wanna know?" Elijah asked with a sigh. It was pretty clear at that point that he wasn't getting away from the subject, so it was easier to simply give in.

"What do you want me to know?" Veona countered with a tilt of her head. Elijah gave her a flat look. He really hated all that cryptic shit. Why couldn't people just say what they wanted out of him?

"How 'bout the fact they ain't really my companions?" Elijah asked a bit snidely. "We were just ridin' together 'cause it got convenient."

He paused there to allow a chance for a reply, but he didn't get one. Both Veona and Nigel simply watched Elijah, waiting for him to continue. So Elijah decided to just give them what he assumed they wanted: his opinion.

"Well, let's see," Elijah said. "Guess I should just go down the list, huh?" The question was asked rather sarcastically, but his audience continued staring at him expectantly. Figuring he should just go ahead and take that as a yes, Elijah said, "I started ridin' with Caprice as an agreement. She didn't take too kindly to gettin' cheated. She's a pain in the ass, but she's got a way with people, and she's not as dumb as a lotta folks out there."

A corner of Nigel's mouth twitched into a slight smirk at that description, but it was very brief. Nigel probably knew all too well just how much of a handful Caprice could be, Elijah thought. After all, it had been pretty obvious that Nigel and Caprice were close and likely had been for quite some time. Elijah knew for a fact that no one knew a person's flaws better than a friend.

"We picked up Pritchett sometime later," Elijah went on. "Wasn't real sure what to think of that machine of his, but it never got in the way. Might be just 'cause he knows how to handle it, though. The guy's sharp, even if he does find some pretty weird shit to be just interesting or funny." Even when he was still alive, Elijah had known to be careful with people who weren't emotionally affected by dark or grim situations. They made great allies, and really horrifying opponents.

As Elijah spoke, Veona began to smile fondly. He wasn't really sure why, and he wasn't about to waste time trying to figure out what was going on in that head of hers.

"And then we joined up with a Roman, 'cause hell, why not?" Elijah said, waving a hand around. "We found him sittin' in a desert, starin' up at some sand runnin' up into the sky. I'm just glad he got over whatever the hell was buggin' him back then, 'cause I doubt he woulda been useful if he didn't."

"But he was?" Veona prompted. "Useful, I mean."

"Outta the four of us, I'd say he's the best at all this shit," Elijah replied plainly. "No matter what we run into, he acts like it's just another notch in his belt and looks for a way to beat it."

Veona chuckled and began to rock back and forth slowly, as if keeping the beat of some music Elijah couldn't hear. "You'd better find them again soon," she advised. "It seems like you still have work to do."

"What do you mean?" Elijah asked with a frown. He wasn't sure how anything he'd just said gave that impression.

"You aren't complete yet," Veona explained. "But when you speak of them, you flicker into wholeness."

Elijah stared at Veona for a second and then looked at Nigel, who raised his hands.

"Don't ask me," Nigel said defensively. "I rarely know what she's talking about."

"You don't need to worry about all that," Veona assured Elijah, blatantly ignoring Nigel. "But you do need to worry about you. And them."

Nigel looked thoughtful then, and he asked Elijah, "Out of curiosity, how much have your circumstances changed since the four of you started riding together? I recall you sought me out to assist in learning more about some new developments."

"How much?" Elijah asked rhetorically. "Completely. The whole damn game turned on its head after we met Theocritus, and it's only been gettin' weirder."

"Intriguing," Nigel murmured. He leaned forward a bit in his chair. "Did the four of you decide to part ways, or did someone decide that for you?"

"Some asshole decided we needed some time apart," Elijah said, getting irritated all over again just thinking about it. "Started tellin' me I should think twice 'bout ridin' with 'em."

"Did he now?" Nigel said slowly. "Hm."

Elijah started to ask what that reaction was about, but then he started thinking. His brain raced through the things that had happened ever since he became part of a group of four, from the turning of the key inside the strange pillar, to learning they were the only ones who had managed to break apart the giant horse clusters.

"Son of a bitch," he blurted out as realization dawned on him. "They're tryin' to keep us from blowin' this whole thing up."

Veona grinned broadly at that statement and brought her hands up in front of her face, pointing her index fingers at Elijah. "That's why you came," she said. "You needed to hear that." Then she looked back at Nigel and tutted at him. "I thought you said we aren't meant to be solving puzzles," she said reproachfully. "Hypocrite."

"Hippie," Nigel retorted as he let his gaze trail idly around the room.

While Nigel and Veona bantered, Elijah's jaw clenched. It was sinking in that he had been played by some jerk in a suit. Once he was good and mad, Elijah turned and stormed for the front door to return to Delilah. He didn't even notice the way the area around him began to light up with a sickly pale green glow. The Ervonians did, however, and both Nigel and Veona watched Elijah curiously as he walked away.

"You see?" Veona asked Nigel without looking away from the rider.

"Hm," was the only reply Nigel offered as he rose from his chair. He extended a hand to Veona, who took it and pulled herself up to her feet. The two of them followed Elijah outside, and Nigel asked, "So what do you plan to do now?"

"Simple," Elijah said as he swung himself up onto Delilah's back. "I'm gonna find those other three morons, and we're gonna make Heaven's life a livin' Hell."

Veona laughed, and Nigel actually smirked at that. "I take it you're off, then," Nigel commented.

"Yeah," Elijah replied, picking up Delilah's reins. Though he paused there, and then asked, "Think you can do somethin' for me, first?" Veona and Nigel both looked surprised.

"I think so, but I won't know until you tell us what it is you want us to do," Nigel said with a shrug. Veona rolled her eyes at the reply, amused.

"You familiar with the Bible?" Elijah asked.

"One of the human Holy Books," Veona mused, swaying in place and playing with her hair. "I read it a few times."

"I read it often," Nigel said dourly. There was clearly a story there, but Elijah didn't have the time to ask, and he doubted Nigel would share much anyway.

"You remember the part about the Horsemen of the Apocalypse?" Elijah pressed. "What's it say about them?"

"End-bringers," Veona said, though it was more to herself rather than Elijah. "Blessed with curses."

Elijah watched Veona for a second and then looked to Nigel for a reply in English. This time it was Nigel's turn to roll his eyes.

"There are four," Nigel said in answer to Elijah's question. "One rides a white horse, one a red horse, one a black horse, and one a pale horse."

"It don't say nothin' about a competition, right?" Elijah asked firmly. "Just says they're brought out by God or whoever and sent to Earth."

"Well, yes," Nigel said, growing visibly confused. "Why? Is that what this is?"

"Don't worry 'bout all that," Elijah insisted. "I just wanna know one thing."

"What is it?" Veona asked.

"Does it ever say what happens to 'em when everything's said and done?" Elijah asked. "After all the Apocalypse shit blows over and everybody's been sorted out?"

Veona's brow furrowed and she looked at Nigel, who glanced at her briefly before solemnly telling Elijah, "No. It doesn't."

"That's what I thought," Elijah muttered. He leaned over a bit more towards Veona and Nigel, and lowered his voice to say, "Listen, I think I know how to square things with the people makin' us do all this, but I'm gonna need your help."

Veona perked up eagerly, obviously happy to assist. Nigel, on the other hand, stiffened with a displeased expression. Yeah, he was going to need to be won over, Elijah could tell.

"I know, I know," Elijah said to Nigel before he could speak. "You don't like the idea of foolin' around with the grand scheme of things, but let's face it: you kinda already have."

Nigel frowned, and Elijah honestly thought the man was going to refuse to meddle any further, but then Nigel sighed and his posture relaxed slightly.

"What do you need?" Nigel asked.

"I need to track down some corrals holdin' a buncha real pissed-off ponies and horses," Elijah replied. Nigel lifted an eyebrow, and Veona dropped her head to one side curiously.

It wasn't much of a plan yet, but Elijah explained what it was he was trying to do, and Veona and Nigel were able to help that plan grow a little. A lot of it involved things Elijah didn't completely understand, but the Ervonians assured him that they would take care of those details.

Once it was all said and done, Veona walked over to stand next to Delilah, and reached up towards Elijah's face with a smile.

"Come on," she urged, waving him down so she could touch him. "Let me bless you. Every life should have favorable rolls of Fate's dice, even if they're in the realm of Death."

"It's not like you can touch me," Elijah reminded Veona with an odd look.

"Oh, no?" Veona said playfully. "That's a very confident thing to say."

Even though Veona's tone was light, her statement still seemed like something of a challenge, and Elijah wasn't about to pass it up. He leaned down in the saddle enough for Veona to be able to touch his cheeks, and his eyebrows shot up in surprise when he actually felt her hands there.

"May your ride take you where you need to be, Elijah Blanco," Veona murmured, her voice deep and hypnotic. For just a brief moment, Elijah felt warm and alive again, but then it passed, leaving just the sensation of Veona's skin on his face. Once that was done, Veona released Elijah and took a step back. "Peace find you," she lilted.

Elijah slowly pulled away to sit back up and looked between Veona and Nigel. "Guess I owe both of you, huh?" he asked.

"You owe me *still*," Nigel reminded him. "Do you know how much cleaning up there was after your little escapades the last time I saw you?"

"Yeah, yeah," Elijah said flippantly. He turned Delilah and nudged her on, waving a hand to the Ervonians. "If I don't see you again anytime soon, I guess I'll see you on judgment day," he remarked.

"I suppose you will," Nigel said with a chuckle. He lifted a hand in farewell and said, "Peace find you."

"Yeah, same to you two," Elijah said with a nod. He signaled to Delilah to pick up the pace, and the mustang took off without hesitation. They had a lot of work to do, and a lot of people to get on board to help do it.

# Chapter 30

The first challenge Elijah faced was reuniting with Caprice, Stephen, and Theocritus. He started by searching Ervonia, hoping things would be easy for once and that he would find them all in one place. But true to Elijah's luck, the other three were nowhere to be found, and Elijah was forced to guide Delilah back to the Hub. They would just have to start going dimension by dimension.

When Elijah and Delilah entered the Hub, Elijah was surprised to find it empty and silent. He couldn't remember a time he'd been in the Hub without seeing at least a few riders with their steeds, either loitering for a little break or passing through on their way to another world. The stillness made the corridor of portals eerie and foreboding, which struck Elijah as a little strange. He'd always imagined the Hub would be a pretty nice place to find some peace and quiet. But with no one there, Elijah found himself constantly looking around in an attempt to figure out why he felt like someone was watching him.

Theocritus had probably been right about eyes always being fixed on that place. For all Elijah knew, the Angel was there right then, hidden somehow.

Just in case he *was* being watched, Elijah played it cool as he steered Delilah for a random portal. He was just passing through. Nothing to see. No reason for anyone to be interested. Just another traveling rider.

Right before Delilah could cross the threshold of Elijah's chosen doorway, someone else entered the Hub. A woman in strange and intricate armor strode in through the vortex to Elijah and Delilah's right, leading her tall and antsy horse in along with her. The woman caught sight of Elijah and Delilah, and came to an abrupt halt to give them a hard stare.

"Well," the woman said, "I didn't expect to find you here."

Elijah stole a glance back over his shoulder to see if the woman was talking to someone else. When he was sure she was addressing him, Elijah said, "I really hate it when people act like they know me without saying who the hell they're supposed to be."

"A lot of people know who you are," the woman informed Elijah calmly. "But if it makes you feel better to know my name, fine. I'm Una."

"I'm happy for you," Elijah said dismissively. "Now why are people talkin' about me? They all still that pissed 'bout all the cheatin'? 'Cause I'm gonna be straight with you: it's about damn time y'all just let that shit go."

"Some people are still that pissed, yes, but that's not what you've been famous for lately," Una replied. "Word's gotten around about how you've handled those herds. And also about how you've been trying to round everyone up for a meeting."

"It ain't just me doin' all that," Elijah said with a roll of his eyes. Bunch of goddamn gossips.

"Oh, we know, don't worry," Una said. "People have been talking about Stephen, Theocritus, and Caprice, too. You four have been busy."

"Busy tryin' to figure all this shit out while the rest of you just keep on stickin' to this game you think you have to play," Elijah shot back. But before he could get more offensive, a voice in the back of his head reminded him that he had three wayward riders to find, and Una could be a lot of help. "You met any of the others in our little group yet?" he asked, his voice a bit flat. At least it was a step up from hostile.

"Yes, I have," Una confirmed with a nod. Elijah stared at her expectantly as he waited for an answer, but all he got was silence.

"...And?" Elijah prompted. Una shrugged and began to lead her horse away.

"As I understand it, you don't like it when people discuss things that aren't their business," Una said airily as she walked.

"Oh, for—" Elijah slapped a hand over his eyes and counted to three in an attempt to curb his frustration. It only worked a little. "Come on, don't be like that," he said, dropping his hand from his face. Una didn't turn, so Elijah was forced to suck it up and say, "Look, I'm sorry, all right? Just gimme some kinda hint or somethin'. It's for the good of everybody in this mess."

Una stopped and looked back at Elijah. She didn't seem terribly convinced, but she said, "I might have seen one of them in there." She pointed back to the portal she had just exited. "It was a while ago, however."

"Hey, it's a start," Elijah said with a shrug. "Thanks." He redirected Delilah for the other gateway, but before they could go through, Una called over to him.

"Is it true?" she asked. Elijah looked back at her, puzzled.

"Is what true?" he asked in return, reining Delilah back to a halt.

"That the four of you know a way to get us out of this competition," Una explained. Elijah watched her carefully for a moment before replying.

"I think so," he said. "But it's gonna mean gettin' most everybody on board with it. And that ain't exactly a walk in the park."

"Do you need help?" Una asked. Elijah hadn't really expected that. Una hadn't been the most receptive person to his plight a moment ago. Maybe he needed to start apologizing to people more often.

"Yeah, actually," Elijah said after shaking off his surprise. "I need to get everybody to Doorfields. You know what that is?"

"The field of windmills," Una said with a nod. "Yes, I know."

"Good, then have everybody you meet head that way," Elijah instructed. "I'll be goin' there myself once I find the three I've been travelin' around with."

"See you there, then," Una said agreeably. She resumed leading her horse away and called over her shoulder, "Good luck."

"Yeah, you too," Elijah said, nudging Delilah on.

The world beyond the portal Elijah and Delilah entered was one they knew fairly well. Elijah had admittedly found excuses to go back there for a breather more than once. It was an extremely peaceful world that seemed to be mostly covered in ocean. There were small islands here and there, but none were inhabited by people. The only towns were the ones found floating on the water. They were all comprised of massive lily-pad-like plants folded into huts of various sizes, and carefully tethered together. The floating villages were generally located in lagoons, but there were a few that were out in open waters. Elijah imagined it was a real challenge to keep them from breaking apart and drifting away in bad weather, but he'd never seen any evidence of damage.

Elijah wasn't the only one who liked to visit. The watery planet was a fairly popular location for quite a number of male riders, though for reasons that were very different from Elijah's. They were more interested in the citizens of the floating towns than the landscape. Elijah honestly found it a little strange, but then he'd never really understood why a lot of guys acted the way they did around beautiful women. Even women who were as lovely as the inhabitants of the lily-pad towns.

All the women living on the ocean-covered planet had smooth, black hair of varying lengths that some wound into braids, while others let hang free. Their facial features were delicate, with sweet smiles and elegant brown eyes. Their body shapes came in all forms, ranging from petite to wider and curvier figures, and there wasn't a single one of them Elijah would consider unattractive. He might not have been as interested in women as most other men he ran into, but he could appreciate a pretty face and shape.

While none of the women were shy about showing off their torsos and arms, there was a common trend in their clothing of keeping their throats and legs covered with heavy silk fabrics. Elijah had heard stories that the women were actually mermaids who had to cover up their scaly legs and gills, and he found that pretty believable. They certainly took to the water like fish.

The odd thing was the fact there were absolutely no men to be found. Elijah wasn't sure if they lived separately from the women, if they had all died out, or if there had never been any men in the first place. He wasn't sure how it would be possible for the women to exist without the contribution of a male or two at some point, but Elijah's mind had been opened up to some pretty damn strange possibilities since his death.

The floating lily-pad town Delilah and Elijah landed in this time around was one of the larger communities they had visited in the past. It wasn't the biggest, but it was unique in that the central structure of the community was a massive, white flower. All the other residences and shops Elijah had ever seen were made from the green lily-pads.

"Least we know where we are," Elijah muttered to Delilah. The mare bobbed her head and started carefully picking her way down the floating walkway she had landed on. She knew she didn't have to be careful to stay out of the water, but following paths was like a game for the mustang at that point. Elijah just let Delilah do as she pleased and carefully scanned their surroundings.

None of the inhabitants seemed to notice the horse and rider, which was a relief. Dealing with fleeing and screaming citizens started to wear on a person after a while.

After a thorough search that yielded no results except disappointment, Elijah had Delilah veer off the pathway and set a quick pace across the water. It was a shame they couldn't have done that while they were alive, Elijah thought. The ocean wasn't so daunting when you could just walk or ride right over it.

They rode on in no particular direction until Elijah caught sight of a lone demon horse tearing its way down the watery plain. The horse itself was made up of angry, stormy seawater, so it was a bit of a trick to tell where the ocean ended and the horse began. Elijah didn't even have to direct Delilah to give chase. She was all too eager to get back into the game.

As they got closer to the horse, Elijah spotted something else chasing the thing as well. It was definitely a horse and rider, but he couldn't quite make out who they were until they got closer.

"Well, if it ain't our Roman soldier," Elijah said to Delilah. He waved one hand to Theocritus, who ignored him in favor of focusing on Benedicta as she closed in on the monster horse. Delilah moved to help Benedicta by trying to head off the creature and slow it down, and succeeded in throwing their target into a rage. It shrieked and snapped for Delilah's throat, but the mustang was too quick. Theocritus took advantage of the distraction and tossed his rope over the hell horse's head, holding onto it until the horse finally disappeared.

Once the monster was gone, both Delilah and Benedicta came to a halt and gently touched noses in greeting. Theocritus, however, didn't seem to share Benedicta's pleasant sentiments towards the reunion.

"Good to see you again," Elijah said to Theocritus in an attempt to break the ice. Judging from the hard stare he was getting, it didn't work too well.

"I must confess," Theocritus said after a pause, "I did not expect to see you again like this. It's been said you've been quite busy."

"Yeah?" Elijah asked, watching the soldier carefully. "Who was sayin' that?"

"Others," Theocritus replied flatly. Elijah squinted at Theocritus and then leaned forward to cross his forearms over the horn of Delilah's saddle.

"Lemme guess," Elijah said dryly. "Some little jackass in a fancy suit."

Theocritus didn't say anything, but Elijah could see on the man's face that he was right. So Elijah just nodded slowly and said, "And I just bet he was talkin' shit 'bout the others too. Right?"

"He did the same with you," Theocritus guessed with a hard edge to his voice. At least he was able to immediately see just how suspicious that was. That made Elijah's job a little easier.

"Sure did," Elijah said. "I dunno 'bout you, but I personally get real agitated when people try to cut in with their opinion like it counts for somethin'."

"He had some very valid points," Theocritus pointed out.

"That's true," Elijah said. "He did." He sat up in the saddle again and looked at Theocritus evenly. "But don't you think that if I wanted to screw you over, I never woulda bothered lookin' you up again? It ain't like I really need you to win this damn competition at this point, right?"

Theocritus remained silent yet again, and Elijah turned to look out over the water around them. He couldn't think of a single time in his life he'd bothered trying to win people's trust, so he didn't exactly have much to work off of at the moment. But everything depended on the help of the three who had stuck with him for so long in the afterlife. That meant giving it a try.

"All right, listen," Elijah said after a pause. He looked back to Theocritus with a frown. "We don't have a lotta reason to trust each other, right? That guy kinda proved it, honestly. Guess I can give him that much. But if you think about it, we got a lot less reason to trust the people behind this game."

"That much has been made clear," Theocritus agreed direly.

"So I say we go with the folks that we don't trust the least," Elijah concluded. Theocritus briefly looked confused as he tried to unravel

Elijah's wording, but once he was sure he understood what Elijah meant, Theocritus nodded.

"At the very least, no one of the four of us has much of an advantage over the other three at this point in time," Theocritus mused.

"Right," Elijah said. "Which is good, 'cause I think we need to step things up and end this competition once and for all. I don't think simply refusin' to play anymore is gonna give us what we want."

"What are you suggesting?" Theocritus asked. "That we fight the forces of Heaven?"

"Sorta," Elijah replied calmly. He signaled for Delilah to walk on, and jerked his head to beckon Theocritus to follow. "Come on. Nigel and a friend of his helped me come up with an idea. I wanna know what you think about it."

# Chapter 31

Theocritus and Elijah rode on, and Elijah explained to Theocritus everything he had discussed with the Ervonians. It was clear Theocritus wasn't completely sold on the concept at first, but the more details that Elijah brought to his attention, the more open to it Theocritus became. Elijah would have been surprised if Theocritus had objected, honestly. After all, the soldier had been crazy enough to agree to Elijah's first idea.

Once Elijah was finished, Theocritus asked, "So what do we do now? This new strategy still requires us to assemble everyone in Doorfields to inform them. And our company is short two people and two steeds."

"I'll get Pritchett and DeGaglia," Elijah informed him. "You let me worry about that. For right now, you worry 'bout gettin' others to turn up at Doorfields, just like before we all got split up. When I get the other two on board, I'll have 'em go off in different directions so we can cover more ground. We might not be runnin' with Time anymore, but I've got this weird feelin' that we need to get a move on things."

"Then Benedicta and I shall meet you in Doorfields," Theocritus said with a nod. "Whenever that may be."

"It'll be a shorter wait than eternity," Elijah promised. Then he signaled to Delilah, who took off at a dead run back for the Hub.

One down, two to go. Elijah just hoped his luck would hold out and that Caprice and Stephen would be as relatively simple to find as Theocritus.

Naturally, his luck *didn't* hold out, and they *weren't* as relatively simple to find, which resulted in Elijah's wondering why he still bothered putting any hope in his luck anymore. He really felt like a guy should have learned by then.

Elijah and Delilah searched at least five worlds with nothing but dead ends to show for it. Elijah was dangerously close to throwing his hands up and giving up out of spite, at least temporarily, but then he ran into a pair of familiar faces. It was the woman and camel he had met with the others. Senet? He was pretty sure her name was Senet. So he tried calling out to her with that.

When the woman turned and said, "Oh, hello again," Elijah silently congratulated himself. He wished Caprice was around so he could point out to her that he was capable of remembering people's names if he cared enough.

"Hey," Elijah said with a wave of his hand. "Listen, I don't suppose—"

"You need help finding the others, right?" Senet guessed before Elijah could get even one word out.

"Uh, yeah," Elijah said in surprise. "But how'd you know that?"

"I saw your friend on the motorcycle some time back," Senet explained. "He was alone and apparently meant to stay that way for a while." She was eyeing Elijah carefully as she spoke, as if trying to look through him and see something. Elijah fought hard to hide the fact that it was making him uncomfortable and a little suspicious, but he wasn't convinced he was doing a good job of it.

"No kiddin'," Elijah said slowly. "He happen to say where he was headed? Kinda need his help with somethin'."

Senet frowned slightly and Elijah finally decided he was fed up with the run-around. "What?" he demanded. "Spit it out."

"Did the four of you have some sort of lovers' quarrel?" Senet asked. Elijah stared at her. There was a pretty lengthy silence as he tried to figure out if he'd heard right.

"The hell are you talkin' about?" he asked, flabbergasted. "Are you serious?"

"The four of you seemed rather close," Senet said. She sounded disturbingly convinced.

"I don't—what?!" Elijah barked. He slapped a hand over his eyes and clenched his teeth while he counted to ten. Counting to three wasn't going to cut it that time. Elijah made it to "two" before dropping his hand and shooting Senet a filthy look. "Even if we were, that ain't your damn business. He say where he was goin' or not?"

"He went to the Ancient Amazon rainforest," Senet replied. She seemed quite eager to assist after that little outburst. It suddenly hit Elijah that he'd probably just encouraged a whole lot of rumors, but what-the-hell-ever. At least she was being helpful. "Stay by the river's edge. You'll find him."

Elijah glared at Senet for a few seconds, still incredibly unhappy with the way the conversation had gone. But he had to admit he would still be stuck without her, so he did the decent thing and told her, "Thanks a lot. I owe you one."

"It's my pleasure," Senet said with a pleasant wave. She grinned as she said it, marking the first time Elijah had actually seen her smile. That made things even worse somehow.

Elijah and Delilah were off once again, and Elijah was glad their destination was a scenic one. The rainforests he had explored after crossing over completely fascinated him, so he was all too happy to go and ride through one again. It was a hell of a good thing he liked the rainforests too, because it turned out that the "river" Senet had directed him to follow was goddamn huge.

When Elijah and Delilah finally found Stephen and Cleopatra, they were at the top of a cliff overlooking an extremely impressive waterfall. Stephen didn't react besides glancing over briefly when Elijah and Delilah turned up. He just went back to watching the waterfall with a thoughtful look on his face.

Before Elijah said anything, he watched Delilah nose one of Cleopatra's handlebars gently, like she was greeting another horse. That was odd, but Elijah let it go and turned his attention back to Stephen.

"You takin' a vacation, Pritchett?" Elijah asked casually.

"Good spot for one," Stephen remarked, keeping his eyes on the falls. "You taking one as well?"

"No time for it now," Elijah said. "We got more work to do."

Stephen gave Elijah a flat look, and Elijah wondered why he couldn't have even one thing go smoothly with no questions asked.

"So I'm guessin' that Go-Between guy said shit to you too," Elijah sighed, throwing his hand up. "If you think you're special 'cause you had him in your ear, think again. He was tryin' to convince me and Theocritus to take off, too."

"So where's Theocritus?" Stephen asked.

"Well, I'm hopin' he's roundin' people up to meet in Doorfields like he said he was," Elijah replied. "Guess there's a chance he was all talk, but you gotta trust at some point, right?"

"Suppose," Stephen agreed, but he still sounded somewhat unsure. In a rare moment of discretion, Elijah decided to be less heavy-handed for once. Stephen seemed like the type who simply needed to warm back up to a person after a rift.

"So what're you doin' out here, anyway?" Elijah asked, gesturing towards the waterfall. "Why this place?"

"Originally I came here on a whim," Stephen admitted. "But then I noticed something, and I popped over to a few different places and times before coming back here."

"What'd you notice?" Elijah asked with a frown. Stephen finally turned to face Elijah properly and reached up to pat Delilah's neck idly as he spoke.

"Ever since those horses were released, we've been seen by the living, right?" Stephen said. "But not *all* the living have been able to see us. Have you noticed? You go to planets not inhabited by humans, it's like you're not even there. The only exception has been Nigel, and that's only because he can see the dead. And Maral's got all sorts of tricks up her sleeves, so she doesn't really count, either."

"What about that planet where we tore that first horse clump apart?" Elijah pointed out. "There was other kindsa folks there, and they were runnin' and screamin' too."

"That's the *really* strange part," Stephen said earnestly. "I went back there and did a little testing. I found out that the only time someone who wasn't human reacted to me and Cleopatra was if there was a human standing right there with them."

Elijah thought about all of that with a growing frown. He had to admit, that *was* strange. And the more Elijah thought about it, the more he wondered who was seeing what. Given their reactions, he was pretty sure that the living humans saw the riders the way Elijah had seen them in the window's reflection back in San Antonio. Nigel and Maral, on the other hand, acted like the riders were nothing special to look at. For all Elijah knew, Ervonians were just extremely deadened to strange and frightening anymore. But then there was Veona's reaction to seeing Elijah and Delilah for the first time. What did they look like to her? What did she see that made him and Delilah so captivating? Those monstrous figures or something else entirely?

The more Elijah thought, the more questions he had. He was starting to regret not asking more questions of Nigel and Veona when he had the chance.

"All that still don't explain why you came back to this place in particular," Elijah pointed out, trying to put his thoughts on the back burner for the time being.

"I'll show you why," Stephen said. He turned and went to get on Cleopatra. "Don't worry, it's good and strange."

"Oh, whew, you had me scared there for a minute," Elijah said dryly.

Stephen and Cleopatra led Elijah and Delilah down from the cliff and into the thick jungle. They journeyed on until they came across a small village of simple huts with a handful of normal humans going about their day. Elijah wasn't sure what the hell Stephen was thinking, riding right into the place when there were people outside who could see them. Surely the riders were going to cause a panic.

Turned out Elijah was dead wrong about that.

When the villagers spotted the riders, they immediately stopped what they were doing. But rather than screaming and running, they turned to greet Stephen and Elijah with respectful bows. Their eyes were wide with awe and a little fear, but they stood their ground. Elijah looked at Stephen in surprise, and the biker smirked.

"See?" Stephen said. "Funny how strange it is to meet breathing humans who aren't afraid of us, isn't it? And for the record, they can understand us. Turns out Death does the translating for us when we talk to the living just like he does when we talk to the other dead."

"Huh," Elijah said, turning his head to look at the villagers again. After an awkward silence, Elijah lifted a hand and said, "Howdy."

"Hello," a few of the villagers said.

One of the older men of the small, living tribe stepped forward and examined Elijah and Delilah carefully.

"It is an honor to meet another one of you," the man said respectfully.

"You almost make it sound like you've been waitin' for us," Elijah remarked. He was still so confused, but he was trying to be patient and let the others explain things at their pace.

"We have," the man confirmed with a nod. "The Great Ones have told us of your coming. They said you would come to many times, to one day bring about the end of all times."

Elijah's eyebrows shot up at that. Now that was interesting. "Who are these Great Ones of yours?" he asked curiously.

"They came from the heavens," the man said, gesturing up to the sky. "They taught us many things, and helped us map more than just the land around us and the stars overhead."

"What else you mappin'?" Elijah pressed. The man somberly put a finger to his lips and shook his head. "Trade secrets, huh?" Elijah asked.

"I've been talking to them a bit," Stephen told Elijah. "Apparently they aren't supposed to be telling us much of what these Great Ones told them, but they did say they aren't the only people who have been prepared like this."

"Prepared for what, exactly?" Elijah asked with a frown. He looked back to the man he'd been speaking to. "Or can you even tell us?"

"I can tell you that Ends are not as simple as some would say," the man replied simply. Elijah set his jaw and looked over at Stephen.

"Y'know," Elijah said in a sour tone, "that just kinda confirms what I've been thinkin'."

"What's that?" Stephen asked with a raised eyebrow.

"That there's a lot more planned for us than anybody's sayin'," Elijah replied. "And I dunno about you, but I'd prefer it if they were all a little more upfront about the whole thing."

"So would I," Stephen agreed. "And that's why we decided to change things up, isn't it?"

That was a promising sign. Stephen hadn't been openly cold or hostile about Elijah showing up and implying the plan was still on, so it had been difficult to read him. But the casual way Stephen spoke about going on like they had been before told Elijah that Stephen wouldn't be that hard of a sell after all.

"Well, after some recent circumstances, I don't think just refusin' to move is gonna be enough," Elijah said. "They keep uppin' the ante in this thing. I think it's time we show 'em we ain't afraid to play our hands."

"Sounds all right, but how can we expect to have any sort of upper hand?" Stephen asked with a frown. "This isn't just a gang of people, remember. We're talking about angels and God-only-knows what else."

"Guess we need some nightmares on our side," Elijah agreed. Stephen lifted an eyebrow at that, and Elijah motioned for the biker to follow him. "C'mon," Elijah said. "I'll tell you what I've got in mind."

Before actually departing, however, Elijah looked at the villagers once more. "Nice meetin' you, I guess," he said with a nod of his head. "Wish we could talk more."

"We will, once all has been completed," assured the man who had spoken before. "Be blessed."

That was a little ominous. But the guy seemed well-meaning enough, so Elijah said, "Yeah, you too."

# Chapter 32

Elijah and Stephen left the tiny village to start back for the Hub, and Elijah gave Stephen a rundown of his new and improved rebellion plan.

"Certainly kept busy, didn't you?" Stephen asked once Elijah was through.

"Yeah, well," Elijah said with a shrug. "No rest for the wicked, right?"

Stephen snorted and shook his head. "Can't say it's the sanest idea, but I can say it's the best one we have." He looked at Elijah curiously and asked, "Have the others agreed as well?"

"Theocritus, yeah," Elijah replied. "Haven't even seen DeGaglia yet. She's next on the list."

"You might want to be careful with her," Stephen advised. "Hell hath no fury and all that."

"It ain't like she's actually been scorned," Elijah pointed out with a scoff. "And she's gonna realize that." For God's sake, the Go-Between had spoken to Elijah, Theocritus, and Stephen, and the three of them had been able to see pretty quickly how full of shit the Go-Between was. Sure, it took the input of someone else to get them to realize it, but it hadn't been a huge fight or anything.

"I'm fairly certain it goes for women who *think* they've been scorned, as well as those who actually *have*," Stephen said. He wore the look of a man who was speaking from experience, but Elijah didn't care. One of the biggest mistakes anyone could make was generalizing a person. That was how people got shot or dumped, from what Elijah had witnessed.

"She's not an idiot," Elijah said firmly. "Give her some damn credit."

"You're the one I'm not giving any credit," Stephen informed Elijah. "Your bedside manner isn't what I would call dazzling." Stephen thought about it for a second before amending, "But if anyone could see through that, I suppose it would be Caprice."

"Yeah, exactly," Elijah said, insulted. "So shut up."

Stephen looked amused, and Elijah had to wonder if that entire conversation had only taken place so Stephen could screw with him. Elijah supposed he sort of deserved it, but it was still annoying.

The two men parted ways in the Hub. As agreed, Stephen set off to do his part in rounding up more riders. It was progressively becoming easier to do since so many other contestants had agreed to spread the word as well. Elijah had never really been one to put a lot of stock in working with others, but the help was actually turning out to be pretty nice.

Once he was on his own again, Elijah continued his search for Caprice. She was surprisingly elusive for someone who did her best to stand out. Elijah had to do a lot of inquiring and exploring before finally tracking down the former singer and her mechanical horse to a frozen tundra on the Earth of Caprice's own time. Elijah had been worried he wouldn't be able to spot Caprice and Shu with so much white everywhere, but the sparkling little prisms of light on Caprice's clothes put that fear to bed.

"Hey!" Elijah called over to the rider and her horse. "I've been lookin' for you, lady!"

Caprice looked over her shoulder towards Elijah, but he couldn't see her expression, thanks to that damn hat. She didn't say anything, allowing the howling wind to fill the silence.

"What, no 'hello' or nothin'?" Elijah asked. "I'm—"

Before Elijah could describe his feelings, Caprice suddenly snatched her rope off its loop on her hip, and whipped the rope fiercely in Elijah's direction. Elijah wrenched away in surprise, and Delilah quickly moved over to get out of harm's way. Caprice's rope sailed past Elijah's neck, and he turned to watch it go.

That was when he saw the hell horse of bloodied ice, which had been closing in on him and Delilah. It had managed to get disturbingly close without a sound, but before it could make any contact, Caprice's rope lashed around the monster's throat. The horse skidded to a stop and reared, but when it opened its mouth to scream in rage, Elijah didn't hear anything but the keening snowstorm around them.

It all happened in the blink of an eye, and then the horse was gone. Stunned, both Elijah and Delilah stared after it for a second, and then Elijah turned to stare at Caprice instead.

"Shit, I thought you were gonna lasso me with that thing for a second," he said with wide eyes. "Again."

Caprice continued looking at Elijah without a word, and it was starting to make Elijah edgy. Was she pissed? Why wasn't she saying anything?

"Look," Elijah said cautiously after an awkward silence. "Now, I know that guy probably hauled you off and told you a lotta bullshit about why you shouldn't trust the rest of us. And maybe he's right. But we've got bigger fish to fry in this thing, right?"

There was no reply. Caprice's posture didn't even change.

Delilah didn't seem to notice any sort of tension in the encounter. She even stretched her neck out and offered her nose out to Shu for a sniff. Shu bobbed his head passively and reached out his nose to touch it to Delilah's gently, and then both horses went back to standing at rest. At least they were still partners, Elijah thought.

"What do you want me to say?" Elijah asked Caprice, starting to get agitated. "That I'm sorry for shit I didn't do, or only thought about doin'? Look, nobody's run off on ya or anything! Hell, I just saw the other two!"

Still nothing.

Elijah threw up his hands and said, "What, you don't trust me?!"

That was when Caprice's lips suddenly curled into a pleased grin, and she laughed as she said, "Of course I trust you, but that was fun."

Elijah actually jolted in surprise at that response. He gaped at Caprice before glaring at her. "You didn't have a problem with me and you just sat there and let me think you did?!"

"Why did you assume I'd have a problem with you?" Caprice shot back. "Just because a little man in a suit started reciting gossip about you three?" She lifted a hand to wave a finger with feigned scorn. "Shame on you, Elijah Blanco. You've got to have more faith in your friends."

"Is that what we are now?" Elijah asked flatly. Caprice laughed again. Elijah rolled his eyes and said, "Just come on. We've been workin' on some developments I think you're gonna like."

Caprice eagerly went along with Elijah, and while they rode on, Elijah told Caprice about Veona and Nigel, and the things they had come up with together. Caprice had a few questions here and there, but she mostly just listened and thought. When Elijah was finished, Caprice hummed to herself and then said, "You realize that we're going to owe Nigel a lot of drinks for all of this."

"Oh, trust me, he made sure to remind me that I owe him," Elijah said sullenly.

"You know, I've heard Nigel talk about her, but I've never met Veona," Caprice said in a reflective tone. "Did they tell you what they are to each other?"

"No, but I was wonderin' about that," Elijah said. He looked at Caprice, honestly interested, and asked, "They brother and sister?"

"No, they're husband and wife," Caprice said nonchalantly. Elijah stared at her.

"Wait, what?" he said, confused. "I thought he was married to a guy."

"Well, he and Veona aren't husband and wife like *that*," Caprice explained. "It's more of a religious sort of thing. They're living incarnations of Death and Birth, so they share a special bond with one another."

There was a lengthy pause before Elijah said, "Somehow I understand less after you explainin' it. How the hell does that work?"

"Ervonia is a funny place," Caprice replied. "Maybe one day they'll explain it better for you."

"I seriously doubt that Veona can explain anything without soundin' like she's been hittin' the whiskey," Elijah muttered. Caprice grinned, and Elijah took a second to look at the blizzard around them. "So why this place?" he asked. "Seems awful bleak."

"I like the ice and snow," Caprice replied with a fond smile. "It reminds me of being alive."

"Yeah?" Elijah asked, looking at Caprice. A memory suddenly popped up in his head, and he asked, "That why Maral called you Songbird of Ice?"

"Partially," Caprice said, her smile becoming secretive. "There's another reason, but... I'll tell you when all of this is over."

"Assumin' we make it outta eternal damnation," Elijah said dryly. Caprice chuckled, but her humor only lasted a moment before she was becoming somewhat somber. She watched Elijah carefully and tilted her head.

"Did you believe whatever that Go-Between said to you?" she asked. There was no sense of accusation in her tone, so Elijah didn't immediately become defensive, but he would stay prepared to do so. For the time being, Elijah decided honesty would be the best approach.

"I thought he mighta been onto somethin'," Elijah admitted. He glanced over at Caprice before looking out ahead of him again and shrugged. "After all, you had pretty good reasons to still be pissed."

"Yeah, for a few minutes," Caprice pointed out. "But you helped make it better, right? I have no reason to be pissed now."

"Sure you do," Elijah said, making a face. "I screwed you over. Pretty sure that don't just disappear."

Caprice looked surprised and said, "Do you think you only get one chance, and that if you blow it, people get to hate you forever? Elijah, I forgave you a long time ago. You're an asshole, but you're not as bad as you seem to think you are."

Now *that* was a strange thing to hear someone say. Elijah looked at Caprice in surprise. He couldn't recall anyone ever saying they'd forgiven him. It wasn't like he'd made a lot of apologies in his time, so he didn't exactly expect forgiveness for anything.

"So you're really not pissed about that pony?" Elijah asked slowly, still not believing what he was hearing. "You can forgive a person just like that and be over it?"

"Well, I was still mad for a while, but a thing or two has happened since then," Caprice said with a chuckle. "I think I can let you off the hook." She tilted her head then and her smile became a little sad. "You really aren't used to people thinking you're not all bad, are you?" she asked gently.

Elijah frowned and said nothing. He really hoped it was a rhetorical question, because it sounded like the beginning of a conversation about feelings and crap, and he really wasn't keen on engaging in *that*.

Thankfully, it was apparently rhetorical, because Caprice said, "Good thing you've got me and the others now, then. It's like a new age."

Elijah rolled his eyes and shook his head, and Caprice smirked at him. Though he would never, ever admit it out loud, he was extremely relieved to have Caprice back and assuring him nothing had changed. He couldn't believe the thought was crossing his mind, but he was actually glad to hear her teasing him again, too.

The Go-Between must have done something horrible to his brain. It was the only explanation.

"Anyway," Elijah said, as if Caprice hadn't said a thing. "We need to get back to tellin' folks to meet us in Doorfields. And I know you weren't crazy about it before, but since things are heatin' up, I think it's better if we all spread out and meet back up once we think we've got everybody."

"All right, but don't try and take on any of those horse clusters by yourself while we're split up," Caprice warned. "Trust me, I've tried it."

"Didn't work out so good, huh?" Elijah asked.

"Let's just say I'm glad the dead don't get bruises," Caprice said somberly. Elijah snorted. Whatever happened must have been pretty entertaining to watch.

"You got anything else to say before I leave your ass and get to work?" Elijah asked in a complacent tone. "Daylight's burnin' somewhere."

Caprice hummed to herself as she thought, and then shook her head. "I don't think so," she said pleasantly. "Just try not to take forever."

"Back at ya," Elijah said. "I don't plan on spendin' my eternity doin' this."

Caprice smirked and gave Shu a signal to pick up the pace. "See you in Doorfields, Mr. Blanco!" she called over her shoulder.

"Yeah, yeah," Elijah replied, tossing Caprice a wave. As she rode away, it suddenly occurred to Elijah there was actually a possibility everything would work out, and that he and the others would succeed and come out on top. There was a real chance they would no longer be slaves to the whims of higher powers playing them like chess pieces.

Then Elijah remembered that their chances of winning relied on a couple of glowing-eyed aliens and a group of liars and criminals.

Well, it was good to have hope in the face of unsettling odds.

# Chapter 33

When Elijah was young, his mother used to complain about trying to keep him and his siblings in a contained area. It was one of the very few things he remembered about his mother with any real frequency. In particular, he remembered her yelling, "It's like herding cats! How am I supposed to keep up with all of you?!"

The cat-herding analogy had stuck with Elijah over the years. He never used it in conversation, but it often popped into his head when he was struggling to keep things in line. However, in light of recent circumstances, Elijah was rethinking using it as his go-to mental comparison. The reason being he had a feeling that herding cats would have taken a lot less effort than getting all of the dead riders to agree to show up in Doorfields.

At least despite the sheer magnitude of the task, and how difficult some riders made it, there was clear evidence that progress was being made. As more and more riders agreed to move to Doorfields, the realms became extremely quiet. No riders passed through. Encounters with the demonic horses became few and far between. In some sort of cosmic irony, the universe as Elijah now knew it was becoming a ghost town.

Before Elijah knew it, he and Delilah were traversing empty dimensions. He decided to take that as a sign it was time to see how many he and the others had managed to round up. So Elijah and Delilah headed back for the field of wheat and windmills. What they found there was enough to give Elijah another little glimmer of hope that Fate was on his side after all.

It looked as though every single rider and their varied steeds had gathered in Doorfields. Some squabbled and argued, while others swapped tales of their adventures, and still others simply ignored everyone around them and waited for whatever was supposed to happen. Storm clouds continued to roll and flash overhead, accompanied by a wind that howled around the windmills and flattened the wheat against the ground. Fortunately, the thunder had gone silent for the time being, which was going to make it a hell of a lot easier to be heard.

It didn't take long for some of the riders to notice Elijah's presence, and when they did, one of them shouted, "Finally! So are we gonna find out what the hell this is about, or what?"

"Oh, quit actin' like we're takin' you away from somethin' important," Elijah said with a scowl. "You're gonna thank us once this is over with."

"Yeah, we'll see about that," the rider shot back. Elijah ignored him and continued guiding Delilah through the crowd in search of their three comrades. He found Stephen first, who waved him over and then led Elijah to where Theocritus and Caprice were loitering on their horses.

"Well, this is quite the reunion, isn't it?" Caprice remarked as she looked around.

"They have all grown restless," Theocritus advised Elijah. "I think it would be best to address them now."

"Lemme guess," Elijah said a bit dourly. "You want me to do the talkin'."

"This is your plan," Stephen pointed out. "You know it better than any of us."

Elijah sighed with exaggerated irritation, and turned Delilah so he could look at the crowd of riders.

"All right, listen up!" Elijah barked over the voices of the crowd. "We all wanna get this shit over with, so don't make me drag this out!"

The riders began to quiet down and turned their attention on Elijah, though some sneered and told others nearby how stupid the whole thing was. Elijah was tempted to start punching people one-by-one, but he took the high road and said, "Trust me, I don't wanna talk to you anymore than you wanna listen, so just hear me out and then you can do whatever the hell you want."

The crowd finally fell completely silent, leaving nothing but the soft wails of the wind for Elijah to contend with.

"Now then," Elijah said, pulling himself up a little straighter. "We've all been bustin' our asses ever since we got entered into this little race. And I know I ain't the only one who's suspectin' that somethin' ain't right. After all, nobody said anything 'bout the dead gettin' killed."

Elijah paused there and noted the riders who were nodding in solemn agreement. At least they hadn't all kept their heads in the sand about everything going on around them.

"The four of us," Elijah went on, indicating himself, Stephen, Theocritus, and Caprice, "ended up goin' on a little trip after those hell horses got released by our Angel friend. We wanted to find out why we were suddenly dealin' with things that can kill the dead."

"Wait, so you just set off to go poking around Heaven's business?" someone asked doubtfully. "Are you four insane?"

"We might be crazy, but we're apparently the only ones who uncovered some real two-faced shit goin' on behind everyone's backs, so shut up," Elijah said flatly. "For instance, did any of you know that the Angel went and had those hell horses made, even though the plan was set for us to catch ponies that couldn't hurt us?"

The riders looked surprised, and a few of them started murmuring to one another. Clearly, they hadn't known that.

"All right, here's another question," Elijah went on. "Did anybody know that we ain't actually guaranteed dead yet?"

That got people talking. The group became shocked and agitated, and the murmuring turned into angry outbursts.

"Then what the hell are we even doing here?!" one rider demanded, infuriated. She snarled like a wild thing as she spat, "If I'm not dead, then I don't want any part of this!"

There were wrathful shouts of agreement, and Elijah sat back in his saddle placidly, simply allowing the group to get angrier and angrier. Their fury was exactly what he needed.

"But they promised us salvation if we win this competition!" a man cried. "What if opting out means going to Hell?"

"If we lose, we'll probably go to Hell anyway!" someone else argued. "And they still haven't told us what it even means to be a goddamn Horseman of the Apocalypse, anyway!"

"It's just another way of saying we'll be slaves!" a woman screamed. "Fuck this! They can take their race and shove it!"

Chaos ensued as the riders' anger reached a fever pitch. Elijah, Caprice, Stephen, and Theocritus watched in silence as the crowd voiced their displeasure. Caprice finally looked at Elijah and said, "I think you've got them now."

Elijah scoffed and then stood up in the stirrups and yelled over the infuriated voices, "Now listen! We don't have to put up with this shit any longer!"

It took some time, but the riders gradually quieted down and focused on Elijah again, though their faces showed they were hardly any calmer. Once he had their attention again, Elijah said, "We may have a shot at turning all this back on the folks keeping us here. We could throw this plan of theirs right in their faces and force 'em to at least start playin' straight with us. But we've gotta work together."

The crowd began frowning at one another and at Elijah. They weren't convinced, but they were definitely listening. For the moment, that was all Elijah wanted.

"We're also gonna need help," Elijah continued. "Which is why I went and found some."

Just then, the door of a windmill just behind Elijah swung open forcefully, slamming against the outside wall of the windmill itself. The riders looked over in surprise, and watched as Nigel Cairnahm stepped out into the wheat field that was Doorfields. The Ervonian looked the crowd over with an unreadable expression and slid his hands into his coat pockets as he said, "Sorry about the wait."

The group stared at Nigel, but it was what accompanied him that had them drawing back and away. Because behind Nigel, on the other side of the windmill's doorway, was a massive crowd of frenzied demon horses that raged and screamed like possessed things.

"I heard you wanted to give Heaven a little Hell," Nigel said with the faint shadow of a dark smile.

# Chapter 34

Elijah's request to Veona and Nigel had been such a huge shot in the dark that Elijah honestly hadn't expected them to agree to it right away. He thought it would require at least a modest amount of convincing, but the Ervonians surprised him by immediately accepting the challenge.

Elijah and the other riders needed something they count on to wreak havoc and possibly even harm otherworldly beings in some form or fashion. The only things Elijah knew for a fact could negatively affect the world as he now knew it were the very things he'd been tasked with chasing and capturing.

"Problem is," Elijah had warned Veona and Nigel back in Ervonia, "I don't know where they're bein' kept. And I sure as hell don't know how you're gonna be able to find 'em."

"It will be difficult, but not impossible, I think," Nigel said thoughtfully. He looked at Veona. "We will need your sight, and my ability to walk Death's domain."

"Snapped together like puzzle pieces," Veona replied with a grin. She slid over to stand behind Nigel, and put her hands over his eyes. "We'll look together," she assured Elijah. "With my eyes and his steps."

"Whatever you gotta do," Elijah said, giving both Nigel and Veona an odd look.

The Ervonians hadn't offered any further details on how they would manage to find the demonic horses, and Elijah hadn't asked. But seeing Nigel standing in Doorfields with a seething crowd of monsters behind him made Elijah decide he would definitely have to ask later. Assuming he and the others weren't obliterated for their hand in the impending rebellion.

It was difficult to see exactly how many hell horses Nigel had brought along with him. While the creatures were stamping, rearing, and bucking, none of them made any attempt to cross over into Doorfields quite yet. They seemed to be waiting for Nigel's permission, which was impressive in and of itself.

"Who the hell are you and what the hell are you doing with those?!" a rider shouted to Nigel. "Are you nuts?!"

"Possibly," Nigel replied with a casual shrug. "I've never made an effort to find out."

"This here's Nigel Cairnahm," Elijah informed the group of riders. "He's from Ervonia and he's agreed to help us." He looked over at Nigel. "And from the look of things, he's already started helpin'."

"To answer a couple of questions that I'm certain you have springing to mind as we speak," Nigel said, "the things you see behind me have all been taken from your respective corrals. You may be wondering if this affects your score at all. To that, I say I've got good news and bad news. The good news is no, it doesn't affect any score. The bad news is you never had a score to begin with. At least, not a score having anything to do with how many creatures you captured."

"What?!" several riders cried in shock and anger.

"I told you it was bad news," Nigel said. The crowd once again became loud and restless. Nigel observed in silence for a moment and then turned to face the monsters behind him. He said something in Ervonian and stepped to the side, allowing the horses to come charging through. Many riders began to retreat in terror, but Nigel looked at the group and held up his hand.

"Stay where you are," Nigel ordered. "I didn't break the Laws of Contending for you to flee before we even get started."

The crowd obeyed, though a good majority of them were still tense and fearful. They watched with wide eyes as a seemingly endless stream of hellish horses ran out of the windmill. It wasn't only the horses, either. The ponies of light that had been collected in the first part of the game were there as well. None of the beasts seemed interested in any of the riders. Once the horses and ponies passed through the windmill entrance, they ran off to their left, where they began to crowd together in one huge grouping. More and more of them continued to enter Doorfields, and soon the herd was so large that even the hills beyond were covered with a sea of demonic horses and ponies.

"This is how much shit we've been puttin' up with ever since we got here," Elijah said to the riders over the thunder of the stampede.

"And for what? They're not even scorin' us the way they said they would! This whole goddamn thing has been a farce to keep us busy."

"It has us wondering if we're really here because of Heaven at all," Caprice chimed in. "They certainly haven't given us any proof!"

"And if Heaven's full of liars and cheaters, why the hell would we want to go there in the first place?" Stephen added. "What makes them any better than the sinners they declare deserving of damnation?"

"The Christians have long claimed that their God is honest and good while my Gods are flawed and unworthy of worship," Theocritus said. "But if this is their God's idea of love and charity, to rip us from our lives and manipulate us into something of which we know nothing, then I will offer no fealty to Him."

As the four spoke, the other riders began to shout and cheer their agreements. A mad desire for justice was setting in, and it was beginning to affect the riders' steeds as well. They pranced, kicked, reared, and roared their hunger for action.

"But we can't change anything unless we do it together!" Caprice yelled. When she spoke again, she lowered her voice, which in turn had the riders quieting down so they could hear her. "Individually, we're nothing more than little drops of rain against them. That's why they made sure to turn us against one another, because as long as we're fighting each other, there's no way we'll unite and turn on them."

"We must stand as one and remind them of our power that they were so careful to try and keep in check," Theocritus agreed. He looked over the crowd of riders before him with wise, war-hardened eyes, and said, "I have seen the power of men and women working as one. I know well the devastation it brings."

"So if you want to bring that devastation to Heaven, we've all got to agree that we're going to stick to one plan," Stephen said. He pointed at the crowd. "Are you going to agree, or are you going to continue to wander around with no idea what's going to come next?"

"*Agree!*" was the thunderous reply. Elijah smirked and pulled himself up a bit straighter in the saddle.

"Then listen up," he commanded. "'Cause we're only gonna go over this once, and once we get movin', it'll be far too late to turn back."

It was amazing what unanimous anger stemming from a betrayal could do to bring people together. Elijah had been impressed the day he was hauled for the gallows by an entire town, but that was nothing compared to watching a group of people band together to challenge Heaven. Any grudges or bad blood between the gathered riders were simply brushed away in the interest of one common goal: revenge.

Once everything was planned out and agreed upon, the riders set out for the Hub with Elijah, Caprice, Stephen, and Theocritus in the lead. Nigel would stay in Doorfields with the monstrous horses and ponies until he was needed. When asked how he would know when that was, Nigel said, "The same way you will."

That was a strange response, but Elijah didn't question him. Mostly because he knew the answer would be a confusing one.

A quiet fury set in amongst the group of riders as they rode back to the Hub. No one spoke, each preferring to let the cloud of hatred in their minds build in silence. None of them knew exactly what they were about to face, but as far as they were concerned, the stand they were about to make wasn't just necessary for them. It was necessary for all of humanity.

The riders and their mounts thundered into the Hub and gathered in a neat battle formation that Theocritus had organized. If they were going to go to war, they were going to do it properly. There were plenty of riders accustomed to going into battle, so it was easy enough for those who hadn't to take their cues from someone nearby. The end result was a silent crowd of dead riders facing the spot the Angel had twice addressed them. There was no doubt the Angel would notice them there. The only question was how long he would make them wait.

Elijah, Caprice, Stephen, and Theocritus sat on their horses and motorcycle in front of the rest of the riders. All four of them were completely willing to shoulder being held responsible for the uprising, and they thought it only fair they should be first in the line of fire.

"Well," Elijah said to the other three, "this might well be the end of the road for us."

"Or the beginning of another one," Caprice declared. Elijah snorted. Goddamn optimist.

"At any rate, it's been quite a ride," Stephen said with a grin. "Looking back, I can't say I regret anything."

"Nor can I," Theocritus agreed. "Of all the people I could face damnation alongside, you three are not the worst."

"Now that just warms your heart, doesn't it?" Stephen remarked to the laughing Caprice.

"Enjoy it while it lasts, 'cause I think Hell's going to be warming up the rest of us pretty soon," Elijah said. He nodded to the distortion of light that was appearing in front of them. The Angel was making his way through.

A vortex opened in front of the congregation of riders, and the Angel stepped out and stared at them. His armor had gone from glowing white to glowing red, making him look even more fearsome and dangerous. Some riders shrank back a little in their saddles like children who knew they were about to be scolded, but no one tried to leave.

"Well?" the Angel demanded, causing a few riders and animals to jump. "You have abandoned your task and assembled purposefully in this place. It is clear you desired my audience. Do not waste it."

"Yeah, about that task," Elijah said with narrowed eyes. "We're here to tell you that we ain't gonna play your games anymore."

The Angel looked at Elijah, any expression he might have had hidden beneath his helmet.

"We're sick of all the lies," Caprice informed the Angel. "You've been manipulating us from the start, and after a lifetime of being manipulated by people, we were expecting to get a break from that once we died."

"But we aren't going to get one here, because we aren't really dead at all, are we?" Stephen challenged. "Did you just forget to tell us that little detail, or was that part of the plan too?"

"You may want to choose your answer carefully," Theocritus warned the Angel. "For it is not only the four of us who are unhappy with what we have learned." He gestured to the crowd behind him. "There are others who are equally displeased."

The Angel continued to stand in silence, but what happened next proved he was listening and understanding. One by one, more vortexes began to appear beside and behind the Angel, and out of each one came more angels. The riders became anxious, but they all stood their ground. They had expected the Angel to bring in reinforcements. They just hadn't expected him to bring in quite so many.

"Return to your competition," the Angel commanded.

"No!" the entire group of riders replied fiercely. The Angel seemed somewhat taken aback by that response. Elijah had to figure the Angel wasn't accustomed to mortals refusing to cooperate.

"You made a big mistake pickin' us for this little game of yours," Elijah said loudly. He leaned forward in his saddle and snarled at the Angel as he went on. "See, we've been dealin' with nightmares and horrors our whole lives. You should know. You probably helped put us in a world that was just filled with 'em."

"Not only did we have to live *with* all those nightmares and horrors," Stephen said, "we sometimes had to *become* everything we hated and feared just to survive out there. We've done shit that would have gotten you tossed from Heaven just for thinking about."

"And for some reason," Caprice said disapprovingly, "you thought that it would be a good idea to take a group of people this bitter and this fierce, and try to blackmail them into going along with whatever the hell it is you need us for."

"Perhaps it was our weariness of the world and our cynicism towards others that led you to believe we would serve you well," Theocritus pondered aloud. "You likely expected none of us would ever form bonds of friendship so long as there was a competition going on. After all, many of us have not had a reason to trust another in a very long time."

"Well, guess what," Elijah snapped. "You're about to really learn just who it is you've been foolin' with."

There was a loud ripping sound as the space next to Elijah was torn apart by unseen hands. Once the opening was formed, Nigel stepped through and looked right at the Angel, who pulled back in shock.

"Negotiator," the Angel said in disbelief. "You—"

"Have broken some very sacred vows," Nigel interjected nonchalantly. "Yes, I know. But seeing as how it's apparent you've done the same, I'm suffering very little guilt over it. And anyway, it's really not me you should be worried about."

Nigel stepped to the side to give the Angel and his comrades a good view of the infuriated horses and ponies on the other side of the opening. The hell horses and ponies of light slammed against one another in a frenzy, trying to get a good view of the angels in the Hub, but none of the monsters passed through yet. They had to await orders.

"You see them?" Elijah asked the Angel over the sound of the shrieking demons. "They're every single thing we've ever done wrong in our lives, right? But you gotta look deeper than that. These things are the result of people who had to try and get by in a world that put them through so much shit that death was somethin' to look forward to. And it turns out that those awful, nasty things are just as angry as we are about this shit, and just as eager for a little justice."

The monsters became even wilder, and began throwing themselves at the passage between dimensions, though they simply bounced back off an invisible barrier set by Nigel. He'd known the beasts' patience wouldn't be reliable.

"Maybe next time you'll think twice about foolin' with a buncha people raised by sin and nightmares," Elijah said to the host of angels.

That was when Nigel unleashed the foaming and screaming horses and ponies of hell. The things instantly raced straight for the angels and attacked them. Swords and spears of light appeared in the angels' hands, and they met the demons head-on, cutting through the onslaught with terrifying efficiency. But although the angels were fierce and capable, they were up against millions and millions of enraged monsters who were getting smarter about how they attacked.

The riders watched, cheering the hell beasts on with war cries and raised fists. Elijah, Caprice, Stephen, Theocritus, and Nigel were the only ones who remained somber, watching the scene play out with a dark quiet. It wouldn't end there, and they all knew it.

The proof came when the Angel who had been directing the riders for so long suddenly slammed his spear into the ground and bellowed, *"Bring out the Ends!"*

# Chapter 35

There was a loud, deep tone accompanied by what sounded like two giant rocks being ground together. Behind the warring angels and monsters, a giant ramp was lowered out of nowhere, opening into a realm beyond the Hub. The riders began to draw back apprehensively, not sure what they were witnessing. Once the ramp had dropped all the way to the ground, four giant horses that stood about fifteen feet tall entered the Hub.

The first horse was a brilliant pearl white, with a long mane and tail that billowed gracefully as the creature moved. It was lovely enough at first glance, but then it bared its teeth and revealed sharp fangs dripping with blood.

Next came a horse that glowed fiery red. Its mane and tail were made of actual flames, and it snorted thick smoke. It snapped once at the white horse's flank, and the white horse wheeled around with a scream and savagely sank its fangs into the red horse's throat. The red horse reared and pulled away, not appearing to care about the flesh that was torn from its neck by the white horse's fangs.

With the first two horses out of the way, a horse with a black coat thundered down the ramp. The black horse was hardly more than skin and bones, and it coughed as it smacked its dry lips hungrily. It certainly didn't act as sickly as it looked, however. It snarled and bucked with a lot more energy than anyone would have expected.

The last horse to emerge was the most frightening to look at. It was a sickly pale green, and when it moved, it went from having flesh and hair to being nothing more than bones with green muscles stretched over them, and then back to being covered in skin again.

The four giant horses lined up to stand side-by-side and bared their teeth at the riders, rearing and shrieking furiously. Elijah's mind raced back to when the Angel had been explaining how the game would be played, and he realized what these creatures had to be.

They were the Four Ends, and they were ready to make good on their names.

Nigel's lip curled in disgust, and he turned to Elijah, Caprice, Stephen, and Theocritus.

"This is what it's all come down to," Nigel informed the four. "Everything you've lived through, both in your life and here in this world of Death, has all been for this moment. It's time to put your sins to good use."

The four riders looked away from Nigel and back to the four massive horses still bellowing wordless challenges, and instead of fear, a cold determination set in. For some reason, Elijah felt more certain than ever before that they were going to make it out on top.

Assuming they didn't get themselves horribly killed.

"Four Ends for four riders," Caprice said somberly. She looked between Elijah, Stephen, and Theocritus. "We're going to have to take them one-on-one. There's no way those things are going to let us team up and bring down one at a time." She turned and pointed at the white End. "I'll take that one."

"And I will take the red one," Theocritus said decisively.

"Hope you can handle the green one, mate," Stephen said to Elijah. "Because the black one's all mine."

"I think that green one and I were made for each other anyway," Elijah said with a shrug. Their choices in Ends were lining up pretty nicely with what Elijah had seen in the reflection of the glass back in San Antonio. It was strange, but Elijah felt it was only right.

"Let's just try and keep them separate," Stephen advised. "The last thing we need is these bastards teaming up and taking us out all at once."

"Better get to work, then," Elijah said. He shifted in his saddle and glared towards the Ends. The pale green End was glaring right back at him, teeth bared and dripping with foam. "But we keep the others outta this unless they got no choice," Elijah added. "We started this. We'll finish it."

"Sounds fair to me," Stephen agreed, sliding on his sunglasses.

Theocritus turned back to the crowd of other riders and loudly commanded, "Hold fast! And should we fall, permit the monsters to leave only over your hard won corpses!"

The crowd fiercely cheered their acknowledgement, and Elijah, Caprice, Stephen, and Theocritus charged straight for the Ends. Elijah locked eyes with the green End, and the giant horse snarled and squared its stance, waiting for Elijah and Delilah to come right to it.

As they raced for the Ends, Elijah suddenly noticed he, Caprice, Stephen, and Theocritus were being joined by a flood of the demonic horses and ponies they'd captured over the course of the game. At first Elijah was worried he and the other three riders were going to have to tangle with Ends *and* a bunch of pissed-off sins at the same time, but then he realized the horses and ponies weren't chasing him and his partners. The monsters were escorting them.

*"It's time to put your sins to good use,"* Nigel had said. He apparently hadn't been kidding.

Encouraged by the backup, the four riders pulled out their Heaven's ropes and whipped them right for the heads of the Ends. The massive creatures balked and ducked the ropes, hurrying to fan out and get the riders separated, then stopped and faced their respective opponents again. The pale green End shrieked a beckoning challenge to Elijah, and Elijah smirked and urged Delilah to go meet it. Once she was close, Delilah neighed fiercely and reared up to kick her front hooves at the End, which shockingly made the giant back up a few steps.

"Come on, you ugly bastard," Elijah dared the End, swinging his rope over his head. "At least try to scare me."

The End snorted green smoke and then barreled forward, snapping its jaws in an attempt to pluck Elijah right out of the saddle. Elijah let out a yell as he dropped down to hang off Delilah's side, letting the mustang choose which way she was going to spring in order to get out of the way. Delilah went left, and Elijah seriously thought he was going to slide down and end up hanging upside-down from Delilah's belly, but mercifully, it didn't happen.

Elijah climbed back up onto Delilah's back in a proper sitting position, and guided her to turn back and run for the End again. Since the monster was so large, it took more time for it to change direction, and Elijah was going to take advantage of that.

As Delilah ran around towards the End's flank, Elijah looked over at his formerly captured hell horses and glowing ponies, which were still keeping pace with Delilah. The creatures were all watching Elijah intently, and it suddenly hit him; they weren't just running with him. They were waiting for direction.

"What, you want in too?" Elijah hollered at the horses and ponies. They screamed and howled in reply, and Elijah snorted. Well, if they were that eager to help, he wasn't going to leave them bored.

Elijah laid Delilah's reins on one side of her neck to turn her towards the herd of his captured sins, and started directing them towards the End. "Get on, then!" he yelled at the monsters. "Get—"

Before Elijah could finish, he was suddenly getting snatched out of the saddle by giant teeth and thrown through the air like a rag doll. That was bad. He actually had enough time while airborne to look and see if any parts of him had been snapped off. They hadn't, but his right side from his shoulder down to his hip was impressively mangled. Elijah wondered if that would heal or if he would be like that forever if he managed to survive.

Elijah hit the ground, and he discovered that a hard knock on the head didn't dull any senses for a dead person. He could see and hear everything happening around him quite clearly. God, everything hurt, though. And that was bad, because the pale End was already turning and snarling at Elijah as it charged for him.

But that wasn't the only thing happening. Elijah's group of horses and ponies were congregating around him in a protective circle, shrieking and kicking warnings at the approaching End. Elijah was being defended, but he wasn't sure how much good that defense would be against the infuriated End. So he began struggling to his feet, noting how his wounds were sizzling and crackling as they knit themselves together. It hurt like hell, but Elijah was fairly certain it was nothing compared to the pain the End was about to put him through.

By the time Elijah was standing, the End was almost on top of him and his protection detail, but a familiar shrieking neigh caught Elijah's attention. It was Delilah, who was barreling straight towards Elijah with her eyes wide and her ears pinned back. Elijah had never been more relieved to see that horse in either lifetime.

Elijah knew Delilah wasn't planning on stopping for him, and he knew what she expected him to do. So Elijah started running in the same direction Delilah was headed, and grabbed onto her mane and saddle to swing himself up onto her back once she overtook him. While Elijah and Delilah ran, the demon horses and ponies lunged forward at the End to distract it. Surprisingly, they did a pretty damn fine job. The End stumbled over creatures that threw themselves underneath its feet, while other horses and ponies kicked and snapped at whatever flesh they could reach. Frustrated, the End screamed as it tried to regain its balance and shake off its attackers. It was only after the horses and ponies were satisfied they'd provided a good head start for Elijah that they turned and ran to catch back up with him and Delilah.

Elijah watched the scene over his shoulder for a moment before turning his attention back to Delilah, giving her a friendly slap on her neck. "Good girl!" he praised as Delilah continued to run. The mustang kicked out one of her hind legs in victory, and Elijah couldn't help but grin a little.

Once there was some distance between them and the End, Elijah turned Delilah back to face the monster once again with his fighting herd still in tow. The End was finally getting its bearings, but once it was steady on its feet again, rather than charging for Elijah and Delilah, it stood there and glared, looking Elijah directly in the eye.

Elijah brought Delilah to a halt, and he could hear the horses and ponies come to a stop around him as well. At first Elijah wondered why the End was just standing there, but the longer he stared into the monster's eyes, the more he understood.

"You respect me a little more now, don'tcha?" Elijah sneered. The End snorted and stamped a hoof on the ground, and Elijah gave it a twisted grin. Delilah began walking towards the End, and Elijah pulled his Heaven's rope off his belt, where it had magically reappeared after he was thrown into the air. The End tossed its head and stamped the ground again, but it didn't take a single step in any direction just yet.

"I get what this is now," Elijah said to the End darkly. "They made you real big and bad, but bein' big ain't all it takes, is it? You thought it'd be easier than this."

The End snarled fiercely, but its eyes were walled like those of a terrified wild mustang. Delilah kept going forward, and Elijah began swinging his rope. He wasn't about to take his eyes off the End and give it an advantage, but he could clearly hear the sounds of the other three riders fighting and challenging their own Ends. The commotion of horses and ponies mingled with the screams of the Ends told Elijah that the others had at least figured out how to use their sins to their advantage as well. But all of that wasn't quite good enough. They needed to find a way to end the battle for good.

Even though they were fighting separately, the four riders were still in it together. Elijah wasn't going to let it all be for nothing. He had to find the weak spot for those Ends and tell the others.

The pale green End in front of Elijah reared as Delilah drew even closer, and out of sheer impulse, Elijah cast his rope out towards the creature. The lasso looped around the End's right front leg, and the End screamed like it was being dipped in acid. Elijah grabbed the rope with both hands and wrapped it around the horn of Delilah's saddle before yelling to Delilah, "Get on!"

Delilah took off like a shot to her right, yanking the rope, and the End's leg, in front of the End's body. The giant monster fell forward and went crashing to the ground, shrieking and kicking its legs frantically.

Elijah didn't waste a second. As soon as the End was on the ground, he turned and looked to the other three riders. He needed to make sure they were going to hear what he was about to tell them. And from the looks of them, the tip couldn't be coming at a better time.

Caprice had been knocked off Shu, and was in the process of climbing back into the saddle with her hat missing and her movements suggesting she was in a lot of pain. As Caprice mounted, Elijah could see she was bleeding through her clothing from around her heart.

Stephen's left arm looked as though it had nearly been torn off, and was hanging uselessly at Stephen's side as he worked to guide Cleopatra with just one hand. The good news was that the arm seemed to be mending itself even as Elijah looked at it, just as Elijah's injuries had been healing themselves.

Theocritus looked unhurt, but he was soothing a wounded Benedicta from his place on her back, and was glaring fiercely at the red End. Luckily, it looked like the horses could heal as quickly as their riders, because the gash in Benedicta's neck was slowly closing itself up.

"Hey!" Elijah called to the other three riders. They looked over at him in surprise, and Elijah hollered, "The legs! Go for the legs and get the fuckers on the ground!"

The other three riders called back their acknowledgements, and Elijah turned his attention back to his own business. He needed to step things up before the End could get back to its feet. Once Elijah had glanced at the End to make sure it hadn't managed to get up in the few seconds he'd looked away, Elijah looked to his herd of horses and ponies, which had been eagerly awaiting his order, and yelled, "What're you waitin' for? Go get that son of a bitch!"

The sins reared and screamed in a rather frightening chorus, and every single creature Elijah had captured during the race for the Apocalypse charged straight for the pale green End. Elijah pulled on his Heaven's rope, which freed itself from the End's leg and came sailing back to him just in time for the horses and ponies to overtake their target.

The herd swarmed the End, throwing themselves against its fallen body, and snapping and kicking wherever they could. They even piled on top of one another so they could reach more places to damage. The pale End screamed and kicked madly as the smaller creatures tore into its flesh and gnawed on its exposed bones. After a hard struggle, the End managed to get to its feet, but the onslaught didn't stop. The horses and ponies continued to viciously attack the End's legs, covered in thick, green blood that poured from the End's wounds.

The End was trapped and continued to be overwhelmed, and Elijah actually reined Delilah in so he could take in the sight for a moment. He looked over to check on the progress of Caprice, Stephen, and Theocritus, and liked what he saw.

All three of the Ends were swarmed in seas of angry sins embodied by horses and ponies. The other riders were glaring up at their respective End with the cold, determined looks of people who knew they'd already won, but had no plans of cutting short the duration of pain. For the first time in his life or death, Elijah felt a surge of pride in the accomplishment of the others around them. They'd made it through Hell, and they were coming out on top.

"You see?!" Elijah yelled to the cornered and frantic Ends. "Do you get what you're up against, now?! You shoulda just let us die and go to Hell! Maybe then you wouldn't be goin' through Hell yourselves!"

"No, that's just it," Caprice called to Elijah as she clamped a hand over her still-bleeding chest. "They *are* our Hell." Then she bared her teeth at the white End and added, "And we'll use our Hells like a weapon to show that we're far worse!"

"An eye for an eye!" Stephen agreed fiercely.

"What humanity does here, let no Angel forget!" Theocritus bellowed. He raised his Heaven's rope and said, "As one!"

All four riders sent the ends of their ropes flying for their respective Ends once again, this time sending the ropes over the Ends' heads and latching onto their throats. Each of the monsters gave one final horrific screech, and their forms began to shift. And the Ends weren't the only ones who began to change.

The demonic horses and ponies that belonged to Elijah, Caprice, Stephen, and Theocritus all began to shift and glow. Soon the Ends, horses, and ponies were nothing more than blinding beams of light, and with a sudden flash, those beams of light shot right into the chests of the four riders. Elijah felt a slam of power, and he could feel himself being knocked right off Delilah's back.

The world went dark and quiet. And for just a little while, Elijah finally knew what peace felt like.

# Chapter 36

Elijah's eyes snapped open, and he found himself staring up from the ground at Delilah and multiple concerned-looking riders.

"The hell happened?" he blurted out.

"We're not really sure," a rider said. It was Senet. She offered her hand to Elijah to help him up, and he took it a bit clumsily. Once he was sitting upright, he started looking around with bleary eyes.

"Where's—" Elijah began, but then he spotted his three partners nearby, each being helped up off the ground just as he had been. The angels were all gone, as were the Ends, the demonic horses, and the glowing ponies. The Hub was once again peaceful and quiet.

Nigel was the one pulling Caprice up to her feet, and he looked between her, Elijah, Stephen, and Theocritus, and said, "I hope you realize just how interesting that was."

Before anyone could tell Nigel to shut up, movement at the portal that led to the home of the Embodied caught everyone's attention. Elijah had to look twice, because he could have sworn the portal to that realm had been further away from everything in the Hub before. But then his brain did a quick recap of everything that had just happened, and Elijah decided that transporting portals were near the bottom on the list of Shit to Find Confusing.

The liquid in the portal shifted even more, and moving with slow and easy grace, Death, then Birth, then Time, and finally Fate filed into the Hub and approached the group. The majority of the riders drew away from the figures in awe and fear, but no one moved to actually flee. It was just as well, really, because the Embodied didn't seem to notice anyone except Elijah, Caprice, Stephen, Theocritus...and Nigel.

"Why am I actually surprised to find you here?" Death asked the Ervonian as he and the other Embodied came closer. "You would think I'd have learned by now."

"It's the old age," Nigel replied airily. "Don't feel bad. I'm getting up there, myself."

"No matter how 'up there' you become, I will still be far older," Death remarked. The riders glanced at one another, and Elijah wondered if they should be worried for Nigel. After all, the Ervonian had just done some serious meddling in what could have been considered a divine plan. Nigel didn't appear to be bothered, but Elijah considered it safe to say at that point that Nigel didn't have a generous sense of self-preservation.

"It is fitting that he is present anyway, husband," Birth laughed to Death. She draped her arms over Death's shoulders with a contented smile and continued, "Fitting that our incarnate selves would see this to the end." She turned to grin at Nigel. "I see Veona's eyes looking through yours."

"As she writes on my face with a pen back in the living world, I have no doubt," Nigel muttered to himself. Caprice snorted, and Elijah rolled his eyes. He was rather confused and a little worried about what was going on, and he knew the other riders were as well, but with Death, Birth, and Nigel all acting so nonchalant, it was hard to stay tense.

Fate stepped in front of the other Embodied then, her eyes still closed, but her smile directed straight at Elijah and his three partners. "Come forward, Keepers of the Four Ends," she beckoned, holding out her star-crusted hands. Elijah, Stephen, Caprice, and Theocritus looked at one another, and then dutifully walked over towards Fate. Their horses and motorcycle were right behind them, following on their own.

"Long and hard you four have fought to arrive at this moment," Fate said warmly as the riders approached. "A moment in which you finally find reward for your efforts and aches. A moment of triumph and vindication."

Elijah and the others stopped just in front of Fate, and Elijah honestly didn't know what to say or think. This certainly didn't appear to be the moment right before they were cast into Hell for their rebellion.

"There is more to luck than people think," Fate went on. "What appears to be a lottery may be a puzzle. Those who look deeper and fight to better worlds around them, regardless of how the dice may fall, will find themselves victorious in many fashions."

"W-Wait a minute," Caprice stammered, her eyes wide. "Are you saying we did it? We actually won?"

Fate's smile broadened and she turned to Birth, who danced forward with a laugh to stand in front of Caprice.

"My daughter," Birth said warmly, brushing her hands over Caprice's cheeks. "Once your conquests brought only shame and personal pestilence."

Birth reached up and plucked a hat out of thin air. It was a lot like the one Caprice had worn before, but it sparkled with glowing white gems which were set in it as if it was a crown. Very gently, Birth placed the hat on Caprice's head and said, "Now you will be Mother of Conquest and Bringer of Pestilence to those who would shame and defile."

As Birth spoke and the hat was lowered onto Caprice's head, Caprice began to transform. Rather than a petite woman with fair skin and blonde hair, she became the white figurine with flashing lights for eyes Elijah had seen in the restaurant window. Caprice didn't seem to notice much other than the fact she had begun to glow white, because she simply looked down at her hands with an air of subdued surprise.

Then Fate walked serenely over to Theocritus and faced him with her closed eyes and peaceful smile.

"My son," Fate said warmly, reaching out to lay her hands on Theocritus's shoulders. "Formerly only a war lord in title, for what sort of lord serves selfish men with small-minded aims?"

Then Fate reached up much like Birth had, except she produced a large sword, which flared into a brilliant blood red as it was moved.

"Become Father of War, the force which governs the rise and fall of civilizations," Fate said, offering the sword hilt-first to Theocritus. "Be the hammer that drops with my dice." The soldier took the sword, and he began to shift from looking like a man of flesh and blood to a crimson red being made of smooth stone. Just like Elijah had seen in the window, the polished surface which was Theocritus's skin cracked as he moved and revealed red light within, but then filled itself in again almost instantly.

Stephen was next, being approached by Time. "My son," Time said in his calm and even voice. "Long did you lead others to starvation. Luring them into sickness, and steeping in the regret that followed."

Time lifted his hands and pulled a balancing scale out of the air above Stephen's head, then offered it to him. "Become Father of Famine. Measure by my inevitability, and be free of guilt and shame."

When Stephen took the scale, his midsection, eyes, and mouth all began to shrink away, leaving the harrowing, gaping holes which had been burned into Elijah's brain after seeing it in the window's reflection. Flies swarmed the edges of the holes, but moved out of the way obediently when Stephen swept a hand in front of him to get them out of the way.

And then Death was walking over to Elijah, staring down at him with that faceless mirror of a head. Elijah looked right back at Death, gazing past the nonstop display of people's dying moments in the reflective glass.

"My son," Death said gravely. "A longtime dealer and seeker of Death. One always aching to know Death better than the rest."

Death lifted his hands, and Elijah heard faint whispers behind him. He looked back and found wisps of wraiths and hideous creatures fading in and out of view behind him in a constant swirl. The longer Elijah looked, the more he realized a good chunk of the ghostly crowd consisted of the hell horses and ponies he and the others had captured.

"Now become Death for your realm," Death went on, prompting Elijah to look back at him. "Not me, but of me; the face I never had."

Elijah turned back to face Death again, and he could feel somewhere in his gut that his appearance had shifted so that he was the rotted, walking nightmare he had seen gazing back at him from the window back on Earth. One look down towards his then-skeletal hands confirmed it.

With all of that said and done, the Embodied stepped back and bowed to the Four Riders. Elijah and the other three looked around, and they discovered the other riders and Nigel were bowing as well.

"Wait, so what does this mean?" Elijah asked, still a bit dumbfounded. "What are we supposed to do?"

"You find new life!" Birth laughed. "Reborn! With new purpose and new being!"

"You will walk realms of your home and realms here beyond," Time added. "You will become links between those unseen and those who cannot see."

"So we get to go home?" Caprice asked hopefully.

"Yes," Fate replied kindly. "And you will not be limited to one time, one space, or one dimension within. You and your noble steeds may travel—and will travel—as you choose. But know you will be called upon, and you must answer."

"What about them?" Stephen asked, indicating the group of riders behind them. "Where will they go?"

"They will awake back in their bodies and back in their lives, remembering all this as nothing but a dream," Death assured.

"Thank God," one rider piped up. Several people laughed, including Birth.

"What about those of us who don't care to go home?" Elijah asked flatly. "We have to go too?"

Fate hummed a musical note and moved to stand in front of Elijah. She smiled down at him and folded her hands carefully in front of her.

"You always wished you could change your world," Fate reminded Elijah. "Don't you want to go back and change it?"

Elijah watched Fate for a moment and then finally smirked a bit.

"You drive a real hard bargain, Lady," he informed her.

"I always have," Fate agreed with a laugh. "And I always will." She reached into the pouch hanging at her waist and pulled out a large black and gold die.

"Now," Fate said with a wide and playful smile, "shall we roll?"

# Epilogue

"Any last words?" the hangman asked Elijah from his place at the lever. Since it was a lever to a pretty sad excuse for a gallows, Elijah didn't find the man all that threatening. Honestly, Elijah was more irritated with him than anything. Couldn't a guy get a second to think quietly before being hanged?

"Yeah, I do," Elijah said to the hangman flatly. "Remember what I said a minute ago, 'cause I meant it." He looked towards the crowd. "Once this sewin' thread you call rope snaps and I get up, you better get runnin'. 'Cause we're gonna have real problems." Elijah looked back to the hangman and made a face. "Seriously, you even really need to pull that? I feel like this damn thing's gonna drop out from under me if I just breathe wrong."

The executioner's reply was to throw the lever that opened the trapdoor beneath Elijah's feet. Elijah dropped, and the rope shockingly did hold up. Elijah had a split second to be impressed, and he took it, ignoring the deafening crack in his ears of bones being snapped. He even managed to have the final thought, *Lady Luck, I better get the chance to sit down with Death after this, 'cause he's gotta be more pleasant than you've been.*

Elijah was given another split second after his neck was broken, but that split second was far more productive and fulfilling than any of the thirty-three years Elijah had spent living as a breathing man. And once that strange little split second was over, Elijah's soul went rushing back into his body, and Elijah heard Fate's words whisper once again in his mind.

*"Now...shall we roll?"*

A brilliant white light flashed in the middle of the crowd which had gathered to watch Elijah's execution, and a glowing white female figure atop a large, mechanical, white horse appeared out of thin air. Luminous blue eyes looked around sharply at the crowd from beneath the woman's large, glittering hat, and the entire group simply stared at her, entranced. She was terrifying, but she was also hypnotically lovely. Then without a word, the woman pulled out a shimmering whip and sent the end of it snapping at the rope that was tied around

Elijah's neck. The rope didn't hold that time, and Elijah went crashing to the ground.

People screamed and fled in terror as their survival instincts suddenly kicked in, but the woman and her horse didn't pay any attention to a single one of them. The pair simply watched Elijah push himself to his feet and brush himself off like his head wasn't resting sideways on his broken neck.

"You know, John and I were cooking dinner," the glowing woman said, sounding extremely put out. "Couldn't you get one of the guys to come save the day?"

"And miss hearin' your melodious voice whine and complain about it?" Elijah asked. He took hold of his head with his hands and viciously snapped his neck back into place. As he did, his skin and eyes began to rot away, and a pale green light began to seep out of his bones and eye sockets. "Now, DeGaglia, where's the fun in that?" Elijah asked.

Even with her mostly featureless face, Elijah could tell that Caprice was rolling her eyes. Elijah wasn't sure what she was pouting about. He'd done the decent thing and waited for her to go and see her husband before asking her to help him retrieve his mortal self. Elijah would need it later, so he'd have to get it eventually. And Caprice should have felt damn honored Elijah picked her to help. At least, that was how Elijah felt about it.

There was a thunder of hooves, and a skeletal horse which glowed the same green color as Elijah came streaking around a corner, whinnying her hello. Elijah went to fetch his hat from where the idiot executioner had tossed it, and then headed over toward the horse.

"There's my girl," he greeted Delilah. The mustang tossed her head with a clack of bones, and Elijah climbed up onto her back. Elijah was barely seated when Delilah cheerfully trotted over to Shu and gently bumped her nose against his. Shu gave a metallic whicker, but then his demeanor suddenly flipped, and he turned his head to direct a demonic metal scream at a living bystander who'd pulled a gun.

Caprice looked over at the man with the gun, and snapped the weapon from his hand with her whip, slicing open his hand in the process. "*Leave*," she commanded in a powerful and echoing voice.

The man had already started screaming, so he went ahead and completed the cowardly image by running like hell.

Elijah watched the man go, and then turned to Caprice and bluntly asked, "You ever show up at your house lookin' like that to see if your husband would survive the shock?"

"Oh my God," Caprice sighed in exasperation. The pearly white surface on her face melted away, and Caprice used her normal human face to give Elijah a pinched look. "Is this *really* all I came here for? To amuse you? I was about to get a foot rub while everything cooked."

"Well, shit, better not keep you from that," Elijah said. He signaled for Delilah to get moving and called to Caprice, "I like apple pie. Y'know, for the next time I come for a visit. You were goddamn stingy last time."

"Oh, I will see you in hell, Elijah!" Caprice shot back, though she was laughing as she said it.

"We tried that, remember?" Elijah retorted, turning in his saddle to look back at Caprice. "It didn't stick!"

# Fate's Interlude

# Conquest

It was a quiet night in Washington, D.C., and it greatly disturbed Yaron.

"It does not make sense to me," the guardian angel muttered. He shifted his towering frame restlessly as his multitude of eyes surveyed the office belonging to his human charge. The mortal man sitting nearby continued reading and signing documents, completely unaware of his divine protectors. "Four Earthly months she has loitered here continuously in plain sight," Yaron went on to the other angel in the room, "and now she conceals herself from our eyes."

"Her kind will always be mysterious to us," Nitza reminded Yaron calmly. The smaller, softer-spoken angel with three human faces gently laid her hands on the shoulders of the mortal man at the desk. In doing so, she passed on a sense of peace to ease his work-related stress. "The Father told us we should not expect to understand their ways and manner."

"We are charged with keeping and protecting the Father's flock," Yaron said in a flat tone. "I would be a poor guardian and warrior to disregard concern."

"The Horsemen are no threat," Nitza insisted.

"That is not what I have heard," Yaron said darkly. Two of Nitza's faces frowned at that, and she moved closer to Yaron, watching him carefully.

"What is it you've heard?" Nitza asked. She didn't care for the act of spreading stories and immersing oneself in the words of others. She would find a hole in whatever Yaron told her, and use it to convince him it was nothing more than festering anxiety.

Nitza's heart was always in the right place, but Yaron was in no mood for comfort. Something was wrong. He could *feel* something was wrong.

When the White Horsewoman called Conquest first made an appearance within the city, Yaron and Nitza hadn't thought much of it. With the End of Days inevitably approaching, every angel knew they would occasionally encounter the Apocalyptic Four roaming the Earth. And since the United States was currently one of the most powerful

246

countries on the living Earth, it made sense Conquest would visit to spur legislation toward whatever cause she had in mind. What was strange was the fact that, for the past four months, Conquest hadn't left. She and her horse simply remained in the Capital, haunting the steps of various U.S. politicians day after day.

But then suddenly Conquest wasn't around anymore. No one saw her depart or had any clue where she might have been headed. She and her horse had simply vanished without a trace.

Why had she been there so long in the first place, if only to depart without leaving any sort of effect?

All of these wonderings would seem like nothing more than paranoia to Nitza, and Yaron knew it. As a result, the only answer he gave to her question was, "Disconcerting things." Nitza frowned and opened one of her mouths to say something, but she was interrupted by the sound of someone approaching the office. Both Nitza and Yaron turned to look, and drew back at what they saw.

A male figure that glowed with pale, sickly green light stepped through the closed office door as if it wasn't even there. He wore dark, tattered clothing made for riding in the hot sun, complete with the sort of hat the angels had seen human cowboys wearing to shade themselves. Not that the man had any skin to protect. Whatever flesh he'd had was gone, leaving only bones and green light.

In one hand, the man held a coil of rope, which shimmered the same green color as he. His other hand grasped a set of reins attached to something out in the hall, blocked from view by the office door.

Once inside the office, the man turned his skull toward the angels and stared at them with deep, empty eye sockets.

Neither angel had to wonder who or what the man was. They already knew, and it was enough to fill them with hopeless dread.

He was the Horseman of Death. The Undoer of Protection. Yaron had been told he could cancel out the angelic guardianship of mortals. If this Horseman painted a target for harvest, not even a league of angels could stop him.

Yaron had no intention of becoming another chapter in that story. He moved his hand to the hilt of his sword, but the rider they called Death pointed at Yaron with his coiled rope.

"Now I would just hang on right there, if I was you," said Death. "I got a lotta shit to do, and I ain't in the mood to kick your ass."

"What are you doing here?" Yaron asked, his voice like thunder. It would have made even most other angels cower, but Death wasn't affected in the slightest. He simply hooked his rope onto his belt and gently tugged on the reins still in his other hand. Doing so prompted a skeletal horse the same color as Death to poke its head through the door inquisitively. After only a brief look around, however, the pale green horse pulled back out into the hall, disinterested.

"If I tell you it's none of your goddamn business, will you just get outta my way?" Death asked. When neither angel moved, Death said, "Didn't think so. That never works. All right then; guess I'll be sweet."

Death reached into one of his trouser pockets and pulled out a small purse of black and gold cloth. He tossed it to Nitza, who caught it in surprise and went to open it.

"This here's for your trouble," Death said, pointing at the purse. "You don't gotta like it, but I expect it'll cover ya."

Inside the purse, Nitza found a multitude of brilliant gold coins stamped with an insignia both she and Yaron knew well.

"The Mark of the Father," Nitza breathed reverently. She looked at Death warily and asked, "You came with His blessing?"

"Blessin' is kind of a strong word," Death replied, scratching his bony jaw. "Begrudgin' tolerance is probably more accurate."

Nitza and Yaron were silent for a moment. No one could even touch an object with the Mark of the Father unless they had permission from the Creator Himself. There was no way the Horseman could carry a forgery. If Death had those coins, it meant he was doing the will of the Creator. And angels who stood in the way of His will faced unquestioning damnation.

Yaron looked over at the man still blissfully unaware at his desk. He and Nitza had been with the man since his birth. They had sheltered him from harm, soothed childhood fears, and supported him through temptation. Under their care, he had grown and matured into a man who did his best to contribute to the Earth however he could.

How could the Creator ask them to abandon their child so cruelly?

Finally, Yaron hung his head in defeat and told Death, "You will not face opposition from us." Nitza's posture sagged as grief began to consume her, but Death wasn't affected by either angel's emotional plight.

"Glad t'hear it," the Horseman said, tipping his hat. He turned to leave the way he came and said, "Now if you'll excuse me..."

"Wait," Nitza said woefully. Death stopped and looked back, and Nitza asked, "What are you planning to do?"

"Me?" Death asked in surprise. "I'm just pavin' the way for the lady. She'll be doin' all the real work."

There was a sudden flash as an explosion of white heat ripped through the building. Yaron and Nitza watched in horror as their human charge went flying with the rubble, and turned to look for the source of the blast. Among the flames and smoke was none other than the Horsewoman of Conquest, watching the scene from atop her massive white horse of steel. Her eyes flashed sharp blue beneath her glittering white hat, and her voice rang in the angel's ears like bells:

*"I'll take it from here."*

www.ingramcontent.com/pod-product-compliance
Lightning Source LLC
Chambersburg PA
CBHW050505260626
47157CB00004B/1199